LOVE
me now

NATIONAL BESTSELLING AUTHOR

CELESTE O. NORFLEET

LOVE me now

ARABESQUE®

LOVE ME NOW

ISBN-13: 978-0-373-83170-8

www.kimanipress.com

Printed in U.S.A.

To Fate & Fortune

Dear Reader,

This is the story you've been waiting for, Trey's story. The ultimate elusive bachelor, Trey Evans has been dodging and hiding from Louise "Mamma Lou" Gates since he was first introduced in my 2004 Arabesque release, *Irresistible You.* Since then he's been in several novels, but has always managed to somehow slip through Mamma Lou's matchmaking fingers, until now. In *Love Me Now* his time's run out. He collides with children's fashion designer Kenya Whitaker and finds that he's in for the time of his life. She's smart, focused and determined to get exactly what she wants—and she wants sexy Trey Evans in the worst way.

This is the seventh book in the MAMMA LOU MATCHMAKER series, following *Priceless Gift, One Sure Thing, Irresistible You, The Fine Art of Love, Following Love* and *When Love Calls.* It's fun, it's fast and it's hot. I know you'll enjoy reading Trey and Kenya's romance as much as I enjoyed writing it. If you've missed reading any of the previous matchmaker series books, check out my backlist on my Web site. Also, don't forget to pick up my upcoming Kimani Romance and Kimani TRU books and look for a new Arabesque title next year.

Please feel free to write me and let me know what you think. I always enjoy hearing from readers. Please send your comments to conorfleet@aol.com or Celeste O. Norfleet, P.O. Box 7346, Woodbridge, VA 22195-7346. Don't forget to check out my Web site at www.celesteonorfleet.com.

Best wishes,

Celeste O. Norfleet

Prologue

"Speech, speech, speech," Lynette, Kenya, Asia and Sidney, the Whitaker women, chanted as they clapped and cheered. It was the end of a lovely spring afternoon. Outside in the yard, beneath the spreading oak tree, they sat around a picnic table surrounded by the perfect setting. Their traditional Saturday Memorial weekend picnic had been perfect. The weather, the food and even the conversation had been pleasant, minus the occasional arguments, of course. Theirs was a family of high energy, emotion and love. It showed in everything they did.

James Whitaker sat at the head of the table looking at the faces of his family surrounding him, all smiling and happy. How could he possibly tell them what he'd done? He couldn't. Their disappointment wasn't something he could handle. He'd finally done something right; now it was all for nothing. He was back at square one again.

Fifty million dollars had a way of redeeming a man. He had been their hero, their savior, and he wasn't ready to go back to the way things were. He had to try. He stood, half smiling, and nodded thankfully.

His girls were his real treasures, his sweet spot. His wife of over thirty years was his rock. Three daughters, each talented and vastly different, were his heart. They each possessed something of which he wished he had more—strength, courage and resourcefulness.

Kenya, the oldest, was his strength. She was beautiful, intelligent and dependable. She always found a way to get around any obstacle. Asia was his dreamer. She was beautiful, getting the best features of both parents. She had dreams larger than life, and a will and courage to make them happen. Sidney was his baby, the youngest. She was impulsive and spirited. Nothing and no one ever held her back. Her resourcefulness was her greatest asset. He loved them all and disappointing them was going to break his heart.

"Come on, speech, speech," they chanted again.

"Okay, okay, enough already. I'm really not worthy of such gratitude. I haven't done anything."

"Of course you have, dear," Lynette said. "You made all this possible—our new home, the wealth, Kenya's design boutique, Asia's acting career and her new apartment in New York—"

"Yeah, speaking of which," Sidney interrupted, "when exactly am I getting my apartment?"

"Would you let Mom finish, Sidney," Kenya said.

"Fine, whatever, it's just that everybody else got a place to live except me."

"You have a place to live, Sidney," Asia said. "Here."

"Yeah, but it's not my own apartment."

Lynette smiled. "And now our vacation of a lifetime. You did it all, honey. I know I've been hard on you in the past about your gambling, but I have to admit, you were right all along. Patience and perseverance finally paid off. You did it, dear. You hit the big one." They all cheered and applauded.

James smiled weakly. Hearing his wife say such things was tearing him apart inside. Yes, he was finally able to give his family things that he couldn't afford before. Thank God the house and the trip were already paid for, at least.

"I still can't believe you're going," Kenya said, smiling at her mother sitting across from her. "A second honeymoon in Africa for a month, that's so romantic. You're gonna have the best time ever. You're right. It is a vacation of a lifetime."

"Remind me again, why can't I go, too?" Sidney joked.

"Because it's the honeymoon they never had, Sidney, that's why," Kenya said firmly.

"I wasn't asking you, Kenya. Besides, I was only joking. You always take things so seriously."

"Yeah, right," Kenya said, knowing better. She knew her younger sister too well. *Spoiled* was an understatement. Sidney got whatever she wanted, when she wanted it. She always wanted to be the center of attention no matter what. Most of all, she lived for drama.

"Seriously, you need to lighten up, Kenya. I was only joking with Mom and Dad."

"Yeah, right," Asia added sarcastically.

"Nobody's talking to you, Asia. Shouldn't you be heading back to New York, anyway? What time does your train leave?"

"Come on, can we please end the afternoon without another argument?" Kenya said.

"There's no way I'd horn in on Mom and Dad's honeymoon. They know that. I'm not that insensitive. Jeez, give me a break," Sidney said.

"If I remember correctly, you're the one with separation issues," Asia said.

"For the last time, Asia, he came on to me, not the other way around. Not that it matters, 'cause he wasn't worth it, anyway," Sidney insisted.

"That's not what he said," Asia countered.

"That's what happened," Sidney reiterated.

"Not again," Kenya moaned, expecting the usual.

"Girls, girls, enough already," Lynette interjected.

The sisters glared at each other. The usual argument was just seconds away. "All right, you two, enough of that. Your mother's right. This is supposed to be a celebration, not another one of your fights."

"She started it," Sidney complained childishly.

"Never mind who started it. Your mother and I are flying out this evening, and we'd like this afternoon to be calm and drama free," James said.

Lynette nodded then touched her husband's hand. "Thank you, dear." James, still standing, smiled down at her tenderly.

Asia and Sidney nodded, relenting easily.

"I'm just so happy you're finally going," Kenya said, knowing her mother's love of travel and of everything African.

"Me, too," Asia said.

"Me, three," Sidney added.

"I still can't believe it," Lynette said. "It's a trip I've always dreamed about. Never in my wildest dreams did I imagine it would actually happen."

"Thanks to Dad," Kenya said proudly. James smiled weakly.

"Now you, miss lady, don't forget the ground rules." Lynette directed her attention to Sidney.

"Yeah, yeah, I know. No parties, no men and no fun."

"Not exactly, but close enough," Lynette agreed.

"Mom, give me a break. I'm an adult, remember?"

"Then act like it sometimes," Kenya muttered quietly.

"Exactly," Asia added.

"Fine, why don't you just lock me up in a chastity belt and be done with it. I'm surprised you're actually gonna leave me here alone."

"You won't be alone. Kenya will be stopping by."

"See, that's wrong. You let Kenya and Asia do whatever they wanted when they were my age."

"Where did you get that idea?" Asia asked.

"They were stricter on me because I was the oldest," Kenya said calmly.

"All I have is one more semester to go and I'm out of college and on my own. I'll get my apartment and work with Dad at the company," Sidney said happily. James tensed instantly.

"What about grad school?" Kenya asked.

"That's your thing, not mine," Sidney said. "All I want is the condo in the city that Dad promised."

"Keep your grades up and stay focused and we'll see," Lynette said. "In the meantime take care of the house. That reminds me, James. We did take care of all the bills, right?" James nodded silently.

"I'm twenty-one years old, Mom," Sidney stated. "You know, I could do that for you. I swear, sometimes you still treat me like I'm thirteen years old."

"That's because sometimes you still act like you're thirteen years old," Asia sniped.

"Get over it, Asia. He didn't want you anyway."

"That's enough, girls," Lynette said just before the battle between her daughters was about to resume again.

"Talk to her. She's the one acting all hung up. And for the thousandth time I said that I was sorry, but for what I have no idea. 'Cause nothing happened," Sidney insisted.

"You shouldn't have been in the situation."

"Nothing happened. And besides, how was I supposed to know that you were serious about him?"

"I had a ring on my finger, Sidney. Big hint," Asia said.

"That's enough, both of you," Lynette stated.

"He didn't want you, Asia, that's why he was trying to push up on me. Big hint," Sidney shot back.

"If you weren't trying to seduce him every time my back was turned—"

"Oh, please, I warned you before he stepped up to me at the club. I was hanging with my friends and he just came up to me. So what was he doing out clubbing, anyway?"

"He was a grown man. I didn't think that I needed to keep tabs on him."

"Well, I guess you did," Sidney said hotly.

"Yes, I did, because of my baby sister," Asia added.

"You trusted him?" Sidney asked.

"No, Sidney, I trusted you."

"He wasn't worth it, anyway, Asia. He was drunk and stepping up to every woman in the club. I don't know why you were checking him, anyway. All he had going for him was his big—"

"Sidney," Kenya said firmly, "that's enough. Asia, you, too." As usual, Kenya had the last word.

"I was just gonna say, big bank account," Sidney muttered. "And you need to chill on that, too, Kenya. At least we get out and actually date from time to time."

"This has nothing to do with my social life," Kenya said.

"What social life?" Asia said. Sidney snickered.

"Face it, ever since…when—" Sidney hesitated, then looked at Asia for conformation "—twelve months ago with Craig, you've had a serious man drought."

"Believe it or not, I don't tell you everything about my social life."

"That's 'cause you don't have one," Sidney muttered. Asia laughed and Kenya glared at them both. "I'm just saying," she added.

"I've had enough of this, I'm gonna go pack my things," Asia said as she headed toward the back door.

"Fine, whatever," Sidney said, sulking as usual. "I'm going to the store." She stood and headed toward her car parked in the driveway.

"Kenya—" Lynette said, seeing both daughters walk away.

"I'll talk to them," Kenya said, assuming her usual role as the eldest daughter.

"Wait, we need to talk first," James said quietly.

"Sure, about the trip?" Lynette asked.

"No, something else has come up. It's about the business."

"I'll go talk to Asia and Sidney," Kenya said, seeing the deep furrows in her father's forehead.

"No, actually this affects you as well, and I need to tell you both before I lose my nerve. I don't really want Asia and Sidney to hear this just yet, so I guess I'd better tell you now."

"What is it, dear?" Lynette asked as she started gathering the empty picnic plates. She had a nervous habit of busying herself when she sensed trouble. Kenya helped.

"Do you want the bad news or the really bad news?"

Both women stopped and looked. Kenya's father had a way of getting attention. At this point he had all he needed. He pulled out a bottle of Pepto-Bismol and tipped it to his lips. After a longer-than-usual swig, he wiped his mouth with his hand and screwed the top back on. His hands shook nervously.

"Dad, what is it? What's wrong?" Kenya asked.

"James?" Lynette asked in a soft voice.

James looked at his wife and his oldest daughter. Lynette was his world. Crushing her dream would devastate her, but he knew she wouldn't say a word. Kenya, his oldest, was his heart. She was smart and levelheaded. Maybe she would think of a way to get him out of all this. He grabbed the bottle of Pepto-Bismol and tipped it to his lips again.

Chapter 1

"I'm desperate, you're my only hope. They're killing me over here. They don't listen to what I say, and they've completely trashed the place." Trey Evans looked around miserably at his once immaculate house. He didn't even recognize it. It had only been five hours but already his house was a complete mess. Trey thrived on order and control, and losing both at the same time was a nightmare for him. "I need you here now, please," he pleaded.

She didn't even try to veil the I-told-you-so amusement in her voice. "I thought you told me you planned for this. You said that you had everything under control. You had a backup plan in place just in case, remember? And, if I'm not mistaken, you also said that you didn't need my help."

"I did have a backup plan. I called an agency a few days ago. I interviewed three women yesterday afternoon."

"And?" she prompted.

"And unfortunately I got the distinct impression that they were more interested in taking care of me than the twins. I think they considered the interview more of an invitation to fill the position by my side permanently." She laughed out loud. "This isn't funny. Kelly, I need you over here now," he insisted more firmly.

"Trey, I told you the last three times you called, I can't do it. It's impossible."

"Nothing's impossible."

"This is," Kelly Rhames, his assistant, said, seeing the flight attendant opening the breezeway to the waiting plane. "Trey, I'm boarding a flight in exactly one minute. I can't just tell everyone to stop, hold everything, while I pop over to your house."

"I'll get you a private jet to take you wherever you want to go," he promised desperately.

"I can't," she said.

"Sure you can," he cooed, turning on the charm.

"Trey, this was your idea, remember, a three-week cruise in the Mediterranean. We've been looking forward to this for weeks. I'm not going to pass it up."

"I'm not asking you to pass it up. I wouldn't ask such a thing, you know me better than that. But I had no idea this was going to happen."

"You can run a multimillion-dollar company, and move millions around like Monopoly money, but when it comes to two toddlers, you panic."

"I'm not panicking."

"Yes, you are. You got yourself into this," Kelly said, more than a little amused by the situation.

"I know, I know. I thought it was going to be easy."

"You are kidding, right?" she asked rhetorically.

"You wouldn't believe what I've been going through this morning. There are toys everywhere. They don't listen to me and every surface in the house has messy, sticky fingerprints. And I have no idea how they got Cheerios in the DVD player." Kelly chuckled. "It's not funny. I need help," Trey said.

"You certainly do, but not from me."

"Okay fine, then find someone for me."

"You just can't order up a human being, particularly one with the credentials you need," his assistant said. "Besides, it's a holiday weekend, everybody's—"

"Kelly, I don't care what you have to do, or how much it costs, I need somebody over here now. I can't do this alone."

"Sorry, Trey, you're on your own."

"Am I gonna have to make this a direct order and put your job on the line?" he threatened sternly. "I'm serious." The conversation was over as far as he was concerned. End of discussion. He didn't want to hear excuses or promises or anything else. He was used to an immediate response, and he didn't like waiting for anything or anybody. All he wanted was results. And that's always what he got. Except…

Kelly chuckled, knowing, of course, that Trey was kidding. "You know that won't work with me or anyone else that knows you well. You may be the Iceman to the rest of the world, but not to those who really know you."

"Fine, Ms. Rhames," he began, "I'm making this a direct order. Your job is on the line here. I don't care what you have to do, no excuses, just do it."

Of course she ignored the empty threat. She'd been his personal assistant for too long to take him seriously. She turned, hearing the first boarding announcement, and saw her husband motion to her. "Trey, relax, you'll do fine. Few bachelors get the opportunity to test the waters like this. Just calm down and enjoy the ride. I gotta go. Take care. And before you ask, I'm not calling you and don't call me. See you when I get back." She hung up.

Trey was stunned. He stood there a few seconds with the phone still at his ear. He couldn't believe this. Saying no to him wasn't exactly a brilliant career strategy. Few people had even dared try something so risky. Kelly did it repeatedly.

But to her credit, she kept him in check. She reminded him of his principles, and was his very own Jiminy Cricket at times. How their relationship came to be what it was was beyond him. One day she just stood up for herself and talked back, even scolded him. Since then, she was in charge and it seemed he worked for her.

The phone rang. He answered. "All right, fine, I'll see what I can do, but no promises." She hung up again.

He smiled then nodded his head assuredly. If anyone would come through for him she would. He tossed his cell phone onto the sofa. Frustration shadowed his face as he looked down at the seemingly innocent twins grabbing on to his legs. If anything, he'd learned that the sweet sparkle in their eyes belied the mischievousness of their actions.

"What did you do? Better yet, what are you about to do?" he asked suspiciously. The question was rhetorical, of course. At sixteen months the twins spoke just enough to communicate their needs. They also seemed to have a language that only they understood. He was outnumbered, two to one. They had the advantage and they knew it.

"Whatever it is, don't even think about it," he warned. With playful expressions, they smiled back at him. They giggled then dashed off in two different directions. "Oh, no, you don't, not this time. I got you." He quickly scooped up his cousins and held them securely under his arms. They giggled and squirmed, trying to free themselves, but his grip was tight.

"What was I thinking?" he muttered, bemoaning his current situation. His head was pounding. He was jet-lagged, overworked and just plain exhausted. Maybe hanging out with his friends all night, then flying in at dawn, wasn't one of his better ideas. Of course, volunteering to watch the twins for a week was another huge blunder. He still had no idea what made him do it. Yes, he did.

"What, you think I can't do it?" Trey had bragged a month earlier after the monthly poker game with his family and friends. He looked around the table. It was obvious that no one took him seriously.

"Give up," Raymond teased, "you're not gonna win."

"Let's just say you'll never have to prove us wrong. The likelihood of your babysitting skills actually being tested is remote at best," Tony said as he fanned out the cards in his hand.

"What do you mean remote?" Trey asked. Faced with a challenge, he never backed down.

"Well," J.T. began, "that would mean Madison, Tony, Mom, Dad, Kennedy, your mother, Mamma Lou, Juliet, Regina, Hope, Faith, Alyssa, Raymond, Randolph, Juwan, Colonel Wheeler, Dennis and about two hundred and fifty other people on the list were unavailable. But don't worry, you're babysitting just after a dog catcher in Arizona named Pete." They all laughed.

"Wait, wait," Trey complained, "how in the world is Raymond so high up on the list? He doesn't have kid skills, either."

"I do have a medical degree," Raymond informed him.

"Plastic surgeons aren't real doctors. They hand out cosmetics at counters," Trey said. Tony laughed. Raymond nearly fell over laughing. Juwan just shook his head as Randolph cleared his throat and looked away.

"I can't believe this, my own cousin's gonna hang me out like that, huh?"

"Come on, Trey, you're only concerned with business," J.T.

said. They all nodded. "Taking care of toddlers—twins—is a full-time job. That means no distractions."

Trey eyed them indignantly. The fact that they had absolutely no faith in his babysitting skills was insulting. Never one to back down, he stepped up to the challenge.

It was the last hand, the most important one of the night. It was never for cash. Everyone anted up, tossing in a task they either needed done, or immensely disliked—painting the garage, cleaning windows, detailing cars, cleaning out the attic or, in this case, babysitting. Everyone folded except Trey and Tony. Tony won. When Madison found out days later, she was livid with both of them.

"Trey, are you sure you're ready for this?" Tony asked several weeks later.

"I still can't believe you wagered babysitting the twins in a poker game," Madison said sternly to her husband. "What exactly were you thinking?"

"I had a full house," Tony said. Madison looked at him menacingly. "Okay, okay, it was all in fun, Madi," Tony promised. "Who would've thought that we'd actually need a babysitter on such short notice." Madison shook her head. "Look, don't worry about it. You go, I'll stay here."

"No, we'll both stay," Madison said. Trey was her first cousin. She loved him dearly, but he was in no way responsible enough to care for her twins.

The actual trip wasn't scheduled for another two months. But when Madison found out that her sister Kennedy was pregnant, plus had a virus and had to go on immediate bed rest, she knew she needed to be there. Unfortunately, the twins weren't ready for the long trip yet.

"No—Madi, Tony, why should you?" Trey protested. "With Kennedy pregnant and on bed rest, you need to be there. They need you. With the museum show opening, Aunt

Taylor is gonna need all the help she can get. They're looking forward to you being there, both of you. Go, take a break, enjoy. I'll take good care of the twins while you're away."

Madison looked worried. "I wish Hope could come down or Faith didn't have that nurse's seminar. And Juliet—"

"Juliet is eight months pregnant and counting. There's no way she can run behind the twins. Hope is pregnant and in the middle of a major fund-raiser at the Ray of Hope Foundation. Alyssa is still getting her grandmother settled at the Spirit Center in San Francisco. See, everyone's either away or unable to come. I'm here, ready and willing," Trey said.

"Trey, you have absolutely no idea what you're getting into," Madison added.

"Are you saying that I can't do it?" Trey challenged.

"This isn't a dare or a competition, Trey. The twins will wear you down. They're toddlers. There's no way you can handle them alone," Tony said. "What about hiring Mrs. Thatcher for the week."

Trey shook his head. "I can't believe you have so little faith in me."

"It has nothing to do with having faith in you," Madison said. "It has everything to do with not being used to having kids around the house. You're the only bachelor I know who keeps his home immaculate without a housekeeper. Kids are messy. Twins are doubly messy. Mrs. Thatcher is a godsend. We've used her on several occasions. I just hope she's available. Or we can even call Mamma Lou."

Trey instantly froze. The mere mention of the name gave him the shivers. "No need to call Mamma Lou," Trey said quickly, adding firmly, "I can do this, alone."

Tony smiled knowingly then shook his head. He remembered that reaction well. His grandmother was notorious. Bachelors feared her like the plague.

"What about work?" Madison interjected.

"True," Tony added, "you're not the kind of guy to just stay home and play Mr. Mom for a week."

"What, I can't take a few days off? I own the company, remember? I can pretty much do what I want. So, with that said, have a little faith. I can do this. It'll be my pleasure."

"Okay, fine," Tony relented. They looked at Madison.

"Okay, okay, but I'm giving Kelly Mrs. Thatcher's phone number, just in case."

The expression on their faces was all the motivation he needed. They had relented and finally changed their minds. He smiled victoriously. He had successfully convinced them that he could do it. Now the question was, could he?

A day later, he got Kelly to pick up a few things. He personally went to toy and furniture stores and spared no expense. He intended to do this right. Nearly cleaning them out, he purchased everything he ever imagined the twins might need or want.

When Madison and Tony saw the room he prepared, they were stunned. They made a few changes, but ultimately, he was on top of this game, as usual. He expected the week-long stay to be a breeze. He was wrong.

The twins squirmed and squealed in his arms. He sighed heavily. "It must have been low blood sugar or a temporary lapse of sanity," he muttered as he deposited them in a playpen set up in the dining room. Moments later he turned to the mess in the kitchen. "How could two little kids make such a huge mess?" he asked the empty kitchen.

When Tony and Madison dropped them off before dawn, they were peacefully asleep in their baby beds. He expected them to remain that way, at least for a while. But as soon as the door closed they woke up, and he'd been running around ever since—five hours, twenty-three minutes and a few odd seconds.

The cereal-covered kitchen floor crunched underfoot. Trey lifted his bare feet and grimaced. It had taken him half the morning just to get them dressed and fed. Most of the food was still on him, on them and all over the kitchen. He peeled the French toast he'd cooked off the floor and refrigerator then grabbed a broom.

It took thirty-three minutes to clean the kitchen although it usually only took fifteen. He looked at his watch. Tokyo would be opening in a few hours. He needed to review Friday's closing numbers to get a jumpstart on the market. It was a holiday here in the States but not in the rest of the world. Business was business and he never lost sight of that.

He went into the dining room and peered into the playpen. The twins were innocently playing with their toys. They looked up at him, then at each other. Trey squinted warily, sensing a possible coup in progress. He knelt down to eye level as they stood holding on to the mesh-padded sides. They smiled, and he couldn't help but chuckle.

His cousin, Madison, and her husband, Tony, had created two adorable children. With large brown eyes, fat cheeks and perfect pouty mouths, they looked more like cherubs than toddlers.

"I get the feeling you two know exactly what you're doing." They giggled. He couldn't help but laugh, too. "All right, you two, so here's the deal—play nice and let your cousin Trey watch the business report. Afterward, I'll let you have ice cream and pizza for lunch, okay?"

They laughed again then babbled something only the two of them understood. One reached out and grabbed his ear and the other grabbed his nose. Trey chuckled as he hugged them close. "Okay, I'll take that as a goodwill handshake."

He sat them back down in the playpen then went into the living room. He picked up the remote control and turned on the television. A large high-definition flat screen brightened as a cartoon character happily jumped from letter to letter. He reached down and removed the DVD and placed it on the side table. He removed his syrup-stained T-shirt, sat down and then turned to the business channel. Finally, peace and quiet. He was back in control.

He attached his Bluetooth earpiece, grabbed his glasses, opened his briefcase and pulled out his laptop.

Tokyo would be opening in a few hours and then London. He focused on Treasury numbers and market volume and activity. He believed that trading would be heavy when the market opened. He e-mailed his instructions to his associates overseas. They sent confirmations almost immediately, with hard copy to be special-delivered to him within the hour.

Everything would be handled exactly as he instructed. Confident in his decisions, he took off the syrup-stained T-shirt, sat back and waited for the market to open. He may not have been in the office, but for all practical purposes, the office was wherever he was. He watched intently as numbers flashed. Ten minutes later his eyelids drooped. He jerked awake, then a few minutes after that he dozed off.

A crash woke him up, then the house phone rang, his cell phone rang and the doorbell chimed. He looked at his watch—he'd been asleep for only twenty minutes. He grabbed the remote to silence the television. Pushing the wrong button, the sound level blared instead. He quickly turned it off, grabbed his cell beside him and then ran to the playpen. "Hello," Trey answered hastily, with his Bluetooth still in his ear.

"Hey, Trey, you all right? What's going on?" Tony asked. Trey didn't answer right away. "Trey, you there? Everything okay?"

Trey cleared his husky throat and half chuckled as the doorbell chimed again. He looked down at the empty playpen.

"Yeah, yeah, of course everything's okay. What, did you think I couldn't handle it? I got this." He saw that a toy, some books and a stack of CDs had been pulled to the floor. He picked them up and tossed them in the playpen. "I told you, man, don't worry," he said calmly as he looked around in a panic and quickly scanned the area. There was no sign of the twins. He hurried to the kitchen following a trail of CDs.

"They're my twins, Trey, and sometimes even I can't handle them," Tony confessed. "You sound rushed, panicked."

"I'm fine, we were just playing hide-and-seek."

"What...hide-and-seek?" Tony exclaimed.

"I'm joking, I'm joking, man, chill," Trey said, charging into the kitchen. The twins were sitting on the floor. They immediately looked up innocently. One had a CD in his mouth and the other was fanning a dish towel around.

"Trey, its Madi. What's going on? Is everything okay there?" Madison said, having obviously taken the phone from her husband. "What's this about hide-and-seek?"

"Calm down, Madi, I was just joking with Tony. The twins are fine, they're right here. Hold on, I'll let you talk to them." He turned off the Bluetooth and put the cell phone to Jonathan's ear. He said hi, then a few other words, then laughed. "That was Jonathan."

"I know my son's voice, Trey. Put Johanna on."

Trey gave Johanna the phone. She grabbed and held it like she knew what she was doing. She smiled happily and talked, answering yes and no mostly. When she started laughing Trey reached for the phone. She held tight. He gently pried the cell away from her. She started whimpering. Trey picked her up. She grabbed at the cell again as he maneuvered away from her reach.

"She really likes this cell phone," Trey said.

"Johanna loves any phone," Madison said. "There's a toy

cell phone in one of the bags we brought over this morning. Trey, remember, if you need help, I can always call someone. I think Mamma Lou is probably headed to D.C."

"No, absolutely not. I'm fine."

"Trey," Madison said.

"Madi, not to worry. As a matter of fact we were just about to have a morning snack. The three of us are in the kitchen even as we speak." The doorbell rang again. He'd forgotten all about it. If that was the nanny Kelly hired, he didn't want her to leave. Holding Johanna securely, he quickly grabbed up Jonathan. With a twin under each arm, he juggled his cell and hurried to the door.

"Trey, are you sure everything's okay?" Madison asked.

"Of course, Madi," he said easily as he opened the door wide and motioned for the woman to enter. "So how's the flight so far?" he asked, motioning again for her to enter. She just stood there looking as if she were in shock. Madison continued talking. Trey beckoned again; she still didn't budge. She just stood there staring, looking confused. This was his nanny?

Kenya Whitaker stood impatiently, waiting for someone to answer the door. Fury clouded her good sense as she rang the bell a sixth time. She'd been ringing the bell for almost five minutes now. She knew someone was home because she heard the television blast, and the crash of something falling from inside.

"Trey Evans." She steamed silently.

How could anybody be so cruel as to take advantage of someone like her father? Granted, he wasn't the most straight-and-narrow person in the world, but he had a good heart. In the end that's all that really mattered. But the flip side of that was unscrupulous businessmen who preyed on his naiveté.

Men like Trey Evans, who assumed that since they were rich, they ruled the world and everybody in it.

She'd seen it before, those in power taking advantage of those without. It was the shark syndrome, the big fish eating the small ones. They set their own rules and when there was blood in the water they closed in. They had no shame, no sense of morality and no scruples. All they cared about was their own success, even at the expense of someone else.

She looked up at the stylish Woodley Park residence. The large, stately town house was on a modest tree-lined street that cut between the National Zoo, Rock Creek Park and Washington's National Cathedral. It had a gated front yard and was at least three stories high. An eclectic mixture of old and new, like the rest of the row houses, it looked like it had been renovated, restored to look like it was from the nineteenth century. It was typical of what she expected of the area. Apparently, Trey Evans was good at what he did, but then most con men and criminals were. Unfortunately her father found this out the hard way.

Of course she blamed herself. If she'd been more attentive to what was going on, and not so single-mindedly focused on her own goals, maybe she could have stopped this before it got to this point.

Her father's lottery winnings and all her parents' dreams right along with them had been stolen. Five million dollars had just vanished into thin air. It was impossible. How do you wrap your brain around something like that? She still couldn't believe it when her father announced that it was all gone. The image still hung in her mind.

"The bad news is that—" James paused, sighed, then swigged more Pepto-Bismol "—I'm broke."

"Ha-ha, very funny, Dad," Kenya said, smiling. Her dad

was the worst comedian in the world. If there was a punch line to anything, you could bet he'd mess it up.

"Honey—" Lynette began softly.

"It's no joke," he said, looking into his wife's eyes. "The money's gone. Bad advice, bad investments, it's just gone. I messed up, but it wasn't my fault. I guess I trusted the wrong man. He took everything. All of it, it's gone."

"James—"

"Wait, Dad, what do you mean, he took everything? Who? People can't just rip off that much money, just like that, right?"

"Yes, but I made bad investments and I borrowed against the business."

"Bad investments, Dad? You borrowed against your business? All of it?" Kenya asked.

He nodded. "To expand my stake in a real estate investment firm. I had to. It was more than I expected. I figured it would appreciate so I bought thirty-five percent more."

"Wait, I still can't understand why you invested in a real estate firm. You were a Realtor for thirty years. You know how risky that can be even in a good economy. Never mind. None of that matters now. You invested in real estate, so what happened to the money?" Kenya asked.

"Because of the economy, the value of the fund kept going down. Eventually everything just fell apart. It was a gamble and I lost."

"Oh, my heavens," Lynette finally whispered.

"Wait, what's a real estate investment fund?" Kenya asked.

"Truthfully, I don't really know," James said.

"James, you gambled our lottery winnings without knowing what you were doing?"

"No, no, of course not. The fund advisors were supposed to invest the money aggressively, but wisely, too. I don't know what happened. It was supposed to shield us from regulations and taxes. They used speculative strategies and tax loopholes."

"This doesn't make any sense," Kenya said.

"Is any of this even legal?" Lynette asked.

"Yes, yes, of course," he stammered hesitantly.

"Dad, there must be some way to straighten this out, get the money back. We can sue the investment firm."

James shook his head slowly. "Everything just tanked. Instead of making profits, we kept losing money. There were fees and capital requirements, then nothing. The fund was almost worthless so I invested the rest in this speculative real estate venture. It was supposed to triple our investment."

"You mean your real estate business, right?" Lynette asked.

"What about the business?" Kenya asked. "That's still okay, right?"

"No," James said slowly, "the venture capital fund owns it now."

"Who owns it?" Kenya asked.

"Honey, don't worry. The house is ours, nobody can take that away. The trip is paid for in full. We have everything we need. It's just the other things." He looked at Kenya. "I'm so sorry, baby, your dreams—"

"Dad, don't worry about it. I have money from before, plus I still have some of the money you gave me last year. It's all in a money market account, I can get it out. You and Mom can take it."

"No, Kenya," Lynette said, "we'll make do. We always have. I still have other investments. We'll be okay," Lynette said.

"We'll need to pay attorney fees," Kenya said.

"Attorney fees? What attorney fees?" James asked.

"We'll need an attorney to sue the guy who manages the fund and get everything back," Kenya said.

"No, we can't," James said emphatically.

"Of course we can. But the question is where to start. I guess we have to dig out all the transaction records and investment paperwork first. Your lawyers are gonna want to see it as soon as possible. We also need to contact your accountant. He's gonna have to dig through what actually happened," Kenya said in a determined voice.

"No, we can't."

"Dad, we need to get on this as soon as possible. The longer we wait the worse it might be."

"No, we'll do nothing, at least not until your mother and I get back from the trip," James said.

"What? Dad, you have to be kidding me. You lose that much money and you don't want to do anything about it for a month? That's crazy. We have to do something now. We'll get your attorney—"

"I got rid of him. He was giving me bad advice."

"Okay then, we'll get another attorney. Your accounting firm can find us—"

"I'm not with them any longer," he said. "We had a financial disagreement."

"Fine, we'll go after the guy directly. We can get the money back. I can confront this person first thing tomorrow morning. Who is he?"

"Kenya, give your father and me a minute alone."

"Mom, you're supposed to leave in two hours. What am I supposed to do, twiddle my thumbs for a month? We have to do something, take action. We can't just let it go."

"There's nothing you can do right now," James said.

"Dad—"

"Kenya, please—"

"Fine, but this isn't over. Nobody just steals from us and gets away with it," she vowed. "Wait, one more question. Who runs the fund?"

"Trey Evans," he said.

Two days later...

Her parents had arrived safely in South Africa and started the adventure they'd always dreamed of having. They'd made her promise not to tell her sisters. They were going to take care of everything as soon as they got back. Kenya had other plans. As soon as they left, she went to work. It didn't take her long to find out who was responsible.

Meticulously methodical, she learned everything there was to know about Trey Evans and his company. TE Acquisitions & Associates was mega-successful thanks mainly to Evans. There was quite a bit written about the company but not as much about the man. Apparently his personal life was low-key. She learned what she could then speculated about the rest.

She had no intention of letting this go. When her parents got back in a month, she intended to have every cent right back where it was supposed to be.

She rang the bell again. She knew exactly what she was gonna say. First she'd introduce herself to make him nervous. Knowing that a Whitaker was in his face should definitely make him panicky. Then she'd point her finger in his chest, then accuse him of lying, cheating and stealing. She'd call him a back-stabbing snake who takes advantage of others. She'd list everything he'd done to her father. Then, when he was begging for mercy, she'd threaten to call the police and the SEC if he didn't return her father's money and everything that belonged to him.

She smiled, knowing that in a few minutes she'd get exactly what she'd come for.

She rang the doorbell again, this time longer and more determinedly. There was still no answer. Obviously Trey Evans didn't have the guts to face her. "Coward," she muttered then turned and stepped down to leave. As soon as she got two steps away, she heard the front door suddenly swing open. She turned quickly, stunned, as her mouth gaped open. She blinked several times, refocusing her eyes. Was she really seeing what she thought she was seeing? She was.

So this was the mighty Trey Evans, with twins?

Chapter 2

At first glance, the man standing in the open doorway took her breath away. It was one thing to research and see photos, but it was another to be standing face-to-face with him. Suddenly overwhelmed, she took a step back. He wasn't at all what she expected. She wasn't sure what she imagined. Maybe horns, pointed ears, a snakelike tail and a distinct odor of charred brimstone. Instead she got this—half-naked man standing in the doorway holding a cell phone and a squirming child under each arm.

Kids, kids…nothing in her research showed that he had a family and children. But he obviously did, and here they were. She wondered what else her research hadn't revealed about Trey Evans.

She had barely wrapped her brain around the whole holding-babies concept when she started taking notice of what was actually right in front of her. It was the second glance that damn near leveled her. Trey Evans was standing there, half-naked. Breathing took on a whole new meaning.

He was barefoot and wore only loose-fitting sweatpants, no shirt. He was eye candy, pure and simple. His arms were muscled columns, deliciously strong and firm. His chest, at eye level, drew her immediate attention. Masterfully rippled, firm with abs so well-defined, they seemed almost unreal. She followed each superbly defined indentation, lower and lower, seeing the delicate trail of wispy hairs dip until they vanished.

Now it was the waistband of the bright white sweatpants that captivated her. They hung low just below his washboard-flat stomach and north of a visible protrusion. The man was pure sex appeal. She dropped her head then suddenly braced herself. She almost stopped breathing as her heart pounded and her knees weakened. There was no way a man should have a body like that. He was just plain mocha-delicious. The possibility of going lower made her shudder inwardly as her skin goose-pimpled. Kenya smiled to herself when a less-than-innocent thought strayed into her mind. Just imagine—

Whoa. What are you doing? Are you out of your mind? You're not supposed to be ogling this man. He's the enemy, a contemptuous, egomaniacal jerk, she chastised herself harshly. *Stop staring, close your mouth and do what you came to do.*

She jerked her head up quickly, looking straight at him. Fiery green eyes sparked with gold flecks stared back at her. They were cold and penetrating, tinged with she wasn't sure what… Anger, fury, lust? *You gotta be kidding me.* She glared back at him, refusing to be intimidated. "Trey Evans?" Kenya finally said indignantly. Still on the phone, Trey nodded and stepped back. "Good, you and I have some business to discuss."

He nodded again then motioned for her to enter. She stood there. No way. She had no intention of stepping foot inside his house. She was going to take care of all this right here on the doorstep. Going inside meant stepping onto his home court and giving him the upper hand, and there was no way she was doing that.

Barely covering the mouthpiece while juggling his armload, he frowned then whispered, "Come in." She glanced beyond him into what looked like the foyer area. "Come in," he repeated with the same action.

He shifted one tot, an adorable little girl, to his hip. She immediately began grabbing his nose and pulling at the earpiece. He maneuvered away. The juggling and jostling made the other child laugh and squirm. Amused, Kenya tried hard not to laugh. She needed to keep a straight face, show no sign of weakness. But the image of Trey was too funny.

"Madi, sweetie, hold on a minute, there's someone at the door," he said, then pulled the earpiece out and pressed the mute button. "Would you please take care of this," he demanded. "You need to settle them down and make them listen to me." He offered her the little girl.

Kenya stepped back and looked at him as if he were crazy. "They're toddlers, they don't listen to anybody."

"Well, you need to control them, then."

"Me?" she said.

"Yes, you. Who else? Why do you think I'm paying you?"

"First of all, you're not paying me and secondly—"

"Look," he interrupted rudely, "do your job, handle this. One week, no drama. I don't want a date, a relationship, a future or anything else, got it? So whatever preconceived notions you have about you and I being together, drop it. You're here to do a job, so do it."

Kenya, stunned, stood with her mouth wide open.

He leaned down and set the squirming babies loose. They stood a moment, holding on to his legs and looking up at her. Then, as if on silent cue, each took off running.

Trey replaced the Bluetooth in his ear as he turned to watch where they were going. One stopped at the toy by the playpen and the other kept going. He looked back at her before pressing a button on the earpiece. "You want to get in here and get them?" he whispered. Without waiting for her reply, he turned and walked away, leaving her standing there on the front step in the open doorway.

Kenya couldn't believe what she was seeing, what she had heard. The door was left open. She could either walk away or go inside. There was no way she was going to walk away. Looking around ominously, she walked inside slowly, and then closed the door behind her. Trapdoors, swinging axes, rolling boulders…she was ready for anything. Whatever game he was playing, she needed to be ready to take him on.

The inside of the house was massive, much larger than it seemed from the outside. Following him, she walked to the huge living room area. Trey was standing with his back to her. He was still on the phone joking and talking calmly. He picked up some papers and began talking about Africa and something he had going on there. She instantly thought about her parents. But he didn't seem to be referring to them. She backed up and went back to the foyer, in the direction the toddlers had gone.

Hardwood floors, gigantic windows and high ceilings flowed throughout the space. She walked into the dining room. It was a nice size, larger than she expected. Everything was perfectly in place except for a half-collapsed playpen beside the dining room table. A wall of windows and French doors lined the opposite side of the room. She walked over and peeked out through the sheers. There was a large patio with a pool and spa that were surrounded by a safety gate.

She turned and continued into a bright and sunny breakfast room. Beyond that was the large modern kitchen. Center island, chrome appliances, marble tile floors and countertops surrounded her. It was phenomenal, straight out of a designer showroom. Perfectly clean and perfectly neat, the place shined like new money. She was sure no one had ever cooked in there.

As soon as she walked in, the toddlers looked up. One was banging on the cabinet door and the other was pulling on a dish towel that was beneath a plastic bowl. It was obvious what was about to happen as the bowl inched closer and closer to the edge. "Okay, new plan," she said, hurrying to grab the bowl. She moved it quickly, then stooped down and held the towel. "Hey, you, what are you doing with that?" She reached to the counter beside the bowl and grabbed a jack-in-the-box. "How about a trade?"

The toddler surrendered the towel then grabbed her and held on tight. Kenya, caught off guard, laughed then lost her balance and collapsed to the floor. She got a huge hug. Soon the other child walked over and gave her a hug also. Still holding the jack-in-the-box, she sat each child down on her lap then began turning the knob. Moments later, sitting in the middle of the kitchen, they were giggling and playing. Slightly sidetracked, Kenya was totally immersed in the joy of being with them.

Trey picked up the remote and turned on the internal security cameras. The television screen divided into nine sections. He centered on the kitchen camera, seeing his new nanny sitting on the floor with Jonathan and Johanna. He smiled; it was a nice scene. She turned the knob on the jack-in-the-box and when the clown popped up Jonathan and Johanna squealed, giggled and fell out laughing. It seemed the simplest action delighted them. Apparently his new nanny knew exactly how to entertain.

"So what are you having for lunch?" Madison asked.

"Cold pizza, fried chicken, champagne and caviar," he joked offhandedly.

"That's not funny, Trey. Don't forget I left you the cooler, food instructions, plus food for today. All you have to do is warm it up."

"What cooler, what food instructions?" Trey asked. He seriously had no idea what she was talking about.

"Trey, Tony put a cooler on the counter this morning. He also put stuff in the refrigerator."

Trey scanned the camera around the kitchen and spotted a large silver ice chest on the counter by the refrigerator. How did he miss seeing that? "Madi, I'm joking. Of course I know about the silver cooler. It's still sitting right on the counter."

"What did you have for breakfast?"

"We decided to make French toast for breakfast."

"Oh, good, the twins love French toast."

"That's probably why most of it was stuck to the kitchen ceiling."

"Very funny," she said.

"Who's joking? Listen, I need to get back to the little guys before they finalize the takeover. I have a feeling they're plotting to overthrow me." Madison chuckled. "Have a good time over there and don't worry about us. We're just fine. Tell everybody I send my love."

After getting a few last-minute instructions from both Madison and Tony, Trey ended the call and removed the Bluetooth. But instead of going to speak with his new employee, he stared at the kitchen scene a few minutes more. He wanted to observe her interacting with the twins.

They continued playing with the jack-in-the-box. Then, Johanna got up to walk away. The nanny held on to her hand. Johanna pulled, but was held in place.

Trey stepped closer, interested, anticipating the nanny's next move. Both Jonathan and Johanna were on the verge of the terrible twos. He watched as the nanny averted Johanna's temper and attention by letting her turn the knob on the toy. She squealed with delight when the clown popped out. Afterward Jonathan had a turn. Trey smiled and nodded. "Nicely done."

They played a few more minutes then she set the toy aside. She began singing the alphabet song. The twins, using her hands, clapped along. Afterward, they sang "Twinkle, Twinkle Little Star" and the "Itsy Bitsy Spider" song. Johanna and Jonathan held on and clapped her hands as she did the hand movements. When two choruses of each song ended, they sat quietly talking.

Curious, Trey moved closer to the screen. Although he couldn't hear what she was saying, it must have been sufficient enough to prompt Johanna to reach out and hug her again. "Impressive," he said. Moments later, she said something to Jonathan, prompting him to hug her, too. "Very impressive," he added. That was enough for him. The twins were notorious for their tempers. If they didn't take to you right away, you'd know it. He was proof of that.

Both were intensely independent. Johanna was extremely selective and Jonathan was fiercely protective. It had taken weeks for Trey to get on Johanna's good side. Every time he picked her up, she'd scream. But he was persistent, and she finally accepted him.

So, he assessed, if her references checked out, he'd offer her the position. But in actuality, he had little choice. It wasn't like he had a dozen more nannies lined up outside his door. She was the one. The twins accepted her, so that was that.

Yes, she would be perfect, he decided. Granted, she seemed completely inept earlier, but obviously she'd got herself together. Also, she was a bit younger than he expected, but maybe that wasn't such a bad thing. He panned in closer to get a better look at her profile.

She was definitely attractive, just his type. But then, some would infer that most women were. He knew he had a reputation. But he was at least honest about it. He loved women and women loved him. He was always up-front and honest with them. He made sure they always knew that he wasn't interested in marriage or a long-term relationship.

Of course, some of the women didn't believe him. They foolishly assumed they could change him, make him fall in love with them. They were wrong. They wound up getting hurt and blaming him. Not his fault. As far he was concerned, he'd warned them. They didn't listen.

An attraction had to be immediate for him to even bother. After that it only took a few hours, usually one date, to know if they were compatible. Anything more was a waste of time, his and theirs. Why fault him for knowing his mind? But some did. Rumor had it that he'd even been mentioned on one of those "ihatehim.com" Web sites.

He focused on the nanny again. She had a nice body, he noticed…or rather his body noticed. It had been a long time since his body reacted so strongly so quickly. While she was checking him out in the doorway, he was checking her out, too. Now, he watched her lips move. They were full and luscious, and he wondered what kissing her would be like. He smiled, considering the possibility of making love to the nanny.

It was obviously too clichéd. He'd always followed his own rules and did exactly as he pleased, within reason. So the whole idea of being with the nanny seemed too predictable. He decided to pass. She turned around. Her eyes brightened. Trey felt a lustful twinge. Or maybe he'd reconsider.

But all that had to be put on the back burner. Now, he needed to focus on the care of Jonathan and Johanna. The twins seemed to like her. That was a definite plus. So the only thing left to do was complete negotiations.

Satisfied, he turned off the television. All his worries had been taken care of thanks to Kelly. He knew she wouldn't let him down. She was truly amazing. He had no idea how she was able to get someone so quickly, but he was delighted that she had. Her connections never ceased to amaze him. Whatever he needed, whenever he needed it, she was able to deliver. He made a mental note to give her a nice bonus when she got back.

Just as he turned to go to the kitchen, his cell rang. He answered. There was a problem at the office. An important client was having a problem and needed him. He talked through the situation with his associates, but it still required his personal attention. He had to go in. He made arrangements to meet the client later that afternoon. But first, he had to get the twins situated.

Like a man in total control of the situation, Trey strolled into the kitchen with assured ease. As soon as he entered he stopped and smiled. The nanny was still sitting in the middle of the floor with a twin on each knee.

It was a touching scene. She was a natural. The twins had laid their heads on her shoulder. Perfect. She was exactly what he needed. They were quietly sitting there. What more could he ask?

He stood in the doorway as she hummed and rocked softly. Unnoticed, he spared a moment to really observe her. She was definitely attractive, but also understated. Her hair, thick and full, was pulled back in a ponytail making her look like she was a teenager, but he could see she wasn't. She had soft brown skin the color of cinnamon. She sat perfectly erect and had a dignified quality that he found appealing.

They obviously hadn't said much to each other so he could only go by what he saw. He remembered her eyes sparked when she looked at him. There was a fire in her. He liked that in particular. Okay, still, he needed to get a few things straight with his new nanny. "All right, let's get a few things straight. I have to go into the office this afternoon and I need—" he began.

"Shh, quiet," she whispered over her shoulder. "They're asleep."

Trey walked over and looked down. Both kids had fallen asleep on her lap. He picked Jonathan up, and then held out his hand to help the woman stand. Each with a baby in their arms, they went into the dining room. Trey prepared to lay Jonathan down in the toy-crowded playpen.

"Wait, don't you have a crib or something for them?" she whispered.

Trey nodded then led her upstairs to his bedroom. Two large toddler beds had been set up side by side in a large alcove sitting room. He laid Jonathan down, then took Johanna and laid her in her bed. Kenya removed their sneakers, socks and jeans, and then covered them with a sheet. She looked around. There was a toddler seesaw, a larger slide and several other large toys in the bedroom. The whole room looked like a play yard.

"What?" Trey whispered, seeing her questioning expression.

"Don't you have a baby monitor?"

Trey pointed across the room to his bed. There were a few dozen gadgets and more toys lying there. Kenya picked up the monitor and turned it on. She handed it to him. He placed the unit on the table by the beds. Trey looked at her for approval. She nodded. He grabbed a shirt and put it on and they crept out quietly.

"Good job. Okay, as I was saying, I need to go into the office this afternoon," Trey began again.

"Wait," Kenya said, hurrying to catch up with his long strides.

"We need to get a few things straight if I'm going to hire you."

"Hire me?" she questioned, still following him.

"Yes, you've got the job. Now first of all, the twins, Jonathan and Johanna, are sixteen months old. You need to be in control every second because they're fast—"

"No, wait, there's been a mistake," Kenya interrupted.

"You'll need to keep them quiet, particularly when I'm working. I'll be here at home most of the time this week," Trey continued as he headed downstairs back to the kitchen. She followed. He opened the refrigerator door and grabbed two bottles of water, handing her one. "I'll obviously need you here the rest of the afternoon. You can go later to get whatever personal things you'll need to move in."

"Personal things to move in? You mean here, live here? No, you've got it wrong," Kenya stammered.

"Yeah, clothes, shoes, whatever. Pack for the week."

"Pack for a week?" she repeated.

"Yes, I presume Kelly told you that your services will be required this afternoon, plus the rest of the week, of course. I'm sure Kelly already has your references, but I'll also need a copy."

"References?"

"References, yes, what's the problem? You're repeating everything I say. Are you not grasping this arrangement?"

"Are you crazy?" she asked.

"Excuse me?" he asked, completely stunned by the turn of events.

"You heard me. Are you crazy? First of all, you left your toddlers in the kitchen alone. Do you have any idea what could have happened to them? You've got things hanging down off the counters, chairs that could topple over, a broom just leaning against the wall, not to mention nothing in here is childproof. So the question remains, are you or is the woman who left you with these babies crazy, because you're a complete incompetent. I should seriously call child services."

"Listen, Ms.—" Trey began.

"No, you listen. I didn't come here for this and what possible excuse could you have?"

"Okay, I fell asleep. They got out of the playpen and then—"

"You what? You can't just decide to take a nap when you have toddlers in the house. You don't have a clue, do you? And you don't just walk off and leave toddlers in the kitchen, alone with a complete stranger. Do you have any idea what could have happened while you were on the phone chatting with your girlfriend?"

Trey looked at the chastising nanny, then nodded. "You're absolutely right. I'm a complete incompetent when it comes to child care. That's why you're here."

"No, that's not why I'm here."

"Here's the deal, I need a nanny for the week. The twins already accepted you, that's half the battle, believe me. So I'd like to hire you."

"You want to hire me as a nanny?" she asked.

"Yes, of course."

"No thanks. I didn't come here to be a nanny. I came here to—"

"I don't see the problem. You're already here."

"The problem is that I'm not a nanny-for-hire." She handed him back the bottle of water.

"Look, I get that you're not Mary Poppins, fine. That doesn't negate the fact that I'm strapped. I obviously need your help. You're qualified, you're a woman and you have the job—take it."

"I don't want the job, and being a woman has nothing to do with taking care of children."

"Tell me something I don't know," he muttered. "But be that as it may, I still need help."

"You need help, all right," she affirmed, "but you have the wrong person."

"Look, you're here now. I'll draw up a temporary contract this afternoon." He walked over to the cooler, which was still on the counter. There was a piece of paper with instructions on top. "Here, these are instructions." The doorbell rang. He looked at his watch. "It's naptime now. Afterward they'll need lunch. I'm sure whatever you need is in the cooler. If you need to contact me, I'll be in my office. The numbers are on speed dial." He handed her the monitor's receiver then walked out. She followed.

"Wait," she called after him. "I didn't come here for this."

Trey continued walking. "I'm expecting a delivery from the office. I need you today and the rest of the week. We can discuss your pay when I get back." The doorbell rang again.

"Wait. You're not listening."

"I presume a flat fee for the week would be acceptable," he said.

"No," she said.

"Fine, we can negotiate later."

"Would you please just shut up and listen," she said, raising her voice. He finally stopped. "I didn't come here to be your nanny. I need to talk to you about my father."

"We can talk about your father later."

"No, we need to talk about him now," she insisted. They both heard one of the twins starting to whimper. They looked at the receiver then at each other. Trey already had his hand on the doorknob.

"Do you mind?" he said.

"Yes, I do mind. I didn't come here to play nanny."

"Okay, fine, whatever it is you need to talk about we will, later."

"Fine, but this isn't over," she said, turning to go back upstairs.

Expecting the hard-copy confirmations from the office, Trey opened the front door and froze.

Chapter 3

Louise Gates and Colonel Wheeler stood smiling. Trey was uncharacteristically speechless. "Well, good morning, Trey," Louise said joyfully.

"Mamma Lou," Trey stammered.

"We weren't sure you were home. It took you a while to answer the door."

"Mamma Lou," Trey repeated as his eyes glazed over.

With two massive teddy bears in his arms, Colonel Wheeler stood just behind her. "Colonel Wheeler, Mamma Lou."

"Yes, dear," she said, "you said that already."

"What are you doing here? I thought you were back on Crescent Island."

"Not just yet. We had a few things to take care of first," she said. Trey, usually the epitome of calm, just stood there with his mouth open. "This is for you. A nice young lady left it and I promised to hand-deliver it to you."

"Thanks," Trey said, taking the envelope.

"Well, dear, aren't you going to invite us in?" Louise asked.

"Uh, yeah, sure, come on in, sorry. It's just that I'm surprised to see you. You've never been here before. I thought you were home. Come in. Colonel Wheeler, how are you, sir? Let me help you with those," Trey babbled, grabbing a bear as he watched Louise leisurely walk into the house.

"Fine, fine, just fine," Otis Wheeler said, smiling as he relinquished one of the huge teddy bears to Trey. Colonel Wheeler shook his head and chuckled. The panicked fear in Trey's eyes was priceless.

The effect Louise Gates had on the young men around her was astonishing. As soon as she showed her face they all shut down mentally. Successful businessmen and intellectual powerhouses, they hemmed and hawed, stammered and stuttered and practically ran for their lives. He'd seen it over and over again.

"I received a concerned phone call this morning. Apparently, I hear that my great-grandchildren are a bit too much for you. I was asked to stop by since they knew we were still in the area."

Trey made a mental note to have a nice long talk with his cousin and her husband. "Not to worry, Mamma Lou. I've got everything under control. The twins just went down for a nap." He ushered them into the living room.

"Oh, what a shame," she said, "I was looking forward to seeing them. Well, I won't disturb them now. I'll stop by again later."

"Later?" Trey repeated.

"I guess Kelly must have just overreacted a bit."

"Kelly? She called you? When?"

"About thirty minutes ago," Louise said as she sat down next to Otis. "She's on a plane over the Atlantic. The reception was terrible, but she said something about you needing help with the twins. I promised I'd stop by. But it looks like you have everything under control."

"Thirty minutes ago," Trey said. How was that possible? Unless the woman upstairs wasn't who he thought she was. "Mamma Lou, Colonel Wheeler, I'll be right back," Trey said.

"And who is this lovely lady, Trey?" Louise asked as Kenya walked into the living room.

Trey turned to see the nanny staring at him. "If you'll excuse us a moment, we'll be right back." Trey walked over to Kenya and then guided her back to the foyer.

"You're not a nanny and Kelly didn't call you. One question, who are you and what are you doing in my house?" The deep bristle in his voice imparted the seriousness of his irritation.

"That's two questions," she joked, falling back on her usual coping mechanism. Trey wasn't amused. He glared at her. His green eyes darkened, then focused like daggers. "Look, I just came here to talk to you about my father. You insisted I come into your house."

"Trey?" Louise called out. "Is everything all right?"

"Yes, I'll be right there, Mamma Lou," Trey said over his shoulder. "Come on," he said, and marched them through the dining room to the kitchen.

"Look, I get that you're in the middle of something right now," Kenya said. "So fine, I'll stop back later."

"No," Trey said, suddenly blocking her retreat. "Damn, okay, this is how this is going to work. You're gonna go back in there, smile pretty and agree with everything I say. No questions asked."

"Uh, excuse me, I don't think so. I'm leaving."

"I do, and you're not leaving, at least not now," he said, sharply, quickly. "You will nod and smile and do whatever else I say, understand?"

"No," she said plainly.

"No," he repeated, amazed at her reply.

"No. Exactly who do you think you are?" she asked in all seriousness. Trey looked at her, stunned by her impertinence. People didn't usually say no to him, particularly women. "Contrary to what you assume, I'm not one of your little playthings, someone you can order around and manipulate. I'm a grown woman. I don't work for you, nor need anything from you. That includes a date, a relationship or anything else. The only reason I'm even still here is because of the two babies upstairs. They're innocent, and there's no way in good conscience I would leave them alone here with you. But now that your grandmother is here—"

"Lady, I've had women try to sneak into my house before, but you take the cake."

"You think I snuck into your house to get with you? You arrogant son of a..." She paused for control. "You are truly unbelievable. And if I remember correctly, you insisted I come in."

"Because I thought you were the nanny my assistant hired."

"I came here for my father. I told you that, repeatedly," she said, raising her voice slightly.

"Trey?" Louise called out.

"Shh. Okay, listen, whatever it is with your father, I'll take care of it. Right now, I need you to do this favor."

"What favor?"

"I need you to pretend we're together, a couple."

"What? No way," she said.

"Look, whatever you want for your father, a job, investment analysis, tickets to the opera, whatever, I'll take care of it. Just do this."

"How do you know I don't already have a man in my life? I might be married or engaged for all you know."

"You're not and you don't," he said assuredly, and then leveled his gaze at her. "Believe me, I know. Besides, this is only for right now, it needn't go beyond the next few minutes. As soon as she leaves, you can drop the act."

Kenya paused a moment, considering her response. She could lie and call him on it or she could take advantage of the situation, exactly like he took advantage of her father. The terms right now implied that he was desperate. The advantage had shifted in her favor. "Put it in writing, a favor for a favor," she said plainly.

"We don't have time."

"Put it in writing," she repeated. The stern seriousness of her tone belied the gleeful exhilaration she felt inside.

Trey looked directly into her soft brown eyes. He knew that look. It was the same look he had when he'd found an opponent's weakness. It was the same look he had right before he took advantage of it. He smiled approvingly. The instant physical attraction he'd felt had changed to admiration. He liked her style. That's exactly something he'd request under the circumstances. She grabbed the piece of paper with the instructions from the counter and scribbled something on it. "Sign it."

Trey grimaced, yet he still took the pen and signed. A twinge of apprehension shot through him—signing without reading was unprecedented for him. Even when his attorneys combed through contracts, he needed to thoroughly read the documents himself. But there was no time. Whatever she wrote he presumed it was appropriate given the situation.

He handed the paper back to her. She took it. A twinge of something shot through her as their hands touched. She wasn't sure if it was excitement or fear. All she knew was that she might have just made a deal with the devil. She looked at the signature and nodded slowly.

"Okay, deal, a favor for a favor," she said, then offered her hand. Instead of shaking he grabbed her hand and nearly dragged her back into the living room.

"Louise Gates, Otis Wheeler, I'd like you to meet a very good friend of mine. This is—" he paused, realizing his dilemma.

"Hi, Mrs. Gates, Mr. Wheeler, I'm Kenya Whitaker. How do you do."

"Hello, dear, call me Mamma Lou. Everyone does."

"And I'm Colonel Wheeler, Kenya. What a very pretty name," he said as he shook her hand.

"Thank you, sir, Mamma Lou."

"So, Kenya, tell us, how long have you known Trey?" Louise asked, spying Trey's guarded expression.

"Four months," Trey blurted.

"Not long," Kenya answered at the same time, then looked at Trey. Kenya smiled nervously. "I guess it has been that long. Funny, it seems like we only just met."

"Four months, huh. Do you work together?" Louise asked.

"No," Trey said, and then looked at Kenya.

"No, I'm a designer."

"A designer," Louise said, impressed. "How nice. What kind, fashion, interior, computer, industrial—"

"Fashion. I design children's clothing. I'm currently in the process of opening my own boutique in town."

"Children's clothes, how wonderful," Louise said. "So, I assume you've met my great-grandchildren, then?"

"Yes, of course, Jonathan and Johanna are adorable," she said easily, hoping they were the great-grandchildren to which she referred.

"They are indeed," Colonel Wheeler said, nodding.

"Shame they're asleep now," Trey said.

"Would you still like to pop up and see them? They're asleep but it would be a shame if you didn't get a chance to at least see them," Kenya said then looked directly at Trey. He glared at her as she smiled innocently.

"I'd love to," Louise said. She walked over and tucked her arm in with Kenya's. They walked toward the stairs. Trey groaned inwardly as he picked up the two teddy bears. He and Colonel Wheeler followed.

On the way to Trey's bedroom, Louise and Kenya talked nonstop. Trey strained to hear what they were saying, but was sidetracked when Colonel Wheeler asked about business. Trey answered and talked naturally, but still strained to hear the women's conversation. The last thing he needed was more surprises.

Through the bedroom, to the alcove, the twins were still happily asleep. Louise and Colonel Wheeler hovered over them, smiling as Trey and Kenya stood by the open door. "What was all that about?" Trey asked, trying to keep his voice low.

"All what about?" Kenya asked quietly.

"You, inviting them up here, then you and Mamma Lou with your heads together, chatting like you're best friends."

"Oh, that," Kenya sassed playfully.

"What'd you talk about?"

"Nothing much, just girl talk, you know."

"No, I don't know. Do me a favor…"

"Another favor, what, so soon?" she asked, smiling confidently.

A muscle in Trey's neck twitched. "Do me a favor, no more girl talk, understand? Stop it," he snarled.

"How am I supposed to stop it? I'm just honoring my end of the deal. We're supposed to be together, right? She wanted to know about you. So I told her."

"About me? What did you tell her?" Trey queried.

Kenya just smiled, delighted to so firmly have the upper hand. "Ask her," she responded.

"Just stop it," he said slow and easy, enunciating each word in warning.

"Or what?" She stepped up to him and countered his challenge. Enjoying her position, she looked directly into his heavenly green eyes. It was obvious that he was angry. But at the moment, there wasn't a single thing he could do about it. She firmly held the upper hand. Trey glared at her. She stiffened her chin with added defiance.

Then to her surprise, his expression changed. Instead of replying, he smiled knowingly. She looked into those eyes, searching for some sense of what he was thinking. There was nothing. He was totally unreadable. Seconds later she relented. "Okay, fine, I guess I just got carried away."

Trey glanced past her and saw that Mamma Lou had turned to leave. He quickly grabbed Kenya, switched their positions and kissed her, pinning her against the door frame. To both their surprise she readily melted into his arms. It lasted only seconds, but Kenya was certain he had rattled her brains.

His strong arms encircled her, pulling her close. Her mouth was open to him and he entered, penetrating deep. His tongue thrust repeatedly, sending tingles along every nerve ending in her body. She felt, and readily accepted, his weight pressed against her. He was hard. She pushed away from the frame, desperate to get closer to him, to feel more of him. The kiss deepened as they entered a solitary world, where only the two of them existed. It was easy, natural, as if they'd been kissing forever.

"All right, you two, none of that in front of the youngsters," Louise said as she and Colonel Wheeler walked back over to the doorway.

Trey took a slow step back with his gaze pinpointed at Kenya. "Sorry," he said, smiling at her, "I guess I got carried away."

With her words thrown back at her, Kenya seethed. The upper hand she assumed she had was nothing more than an illusion. How do you win with someone like Trey? He was motivated and focused, everything she thought she was. But compared to him, she was a smitten schoolgirl pining away for the popular guy.

"That's right, save it for later," Colonel Wheeler added, with a wink to Trey.

Louise sighed and looked back. "They're such angels," she said as she walked out of the bedroom to the hall.

"Not quite," Trey admitted, picking up the receiver.

"Gave you a bit of a rough time, did they?" Colonel Wheeler said humorously.

"I expect that's one reason why you have Kenya over here so early. Thank you, dear, I know you were very instrumental in the care of my great-grandchildren."

"Actually, I didn't really do anything. Trey handled everything perfectly. He's a natural."

"Is that right," Louise said, smiling at Trey. She tucked her arm in his as they followed Colonel Wheeler and Kenya down the stairs. "She's a keeper, I like her a lot," she whispered to Trey.

"Mamma Lou, no matchmaking, please," Trey pleaded earnestly.

"Trey, dear, how can I possibly match you with someone when you've obviously already found the perfect woman for you?"

Trey looked at Louise then to Kenya. He shook his head. "Mamma Lou—"

"I saw it in your eyes when she stepped into the living room. Then I saw it again when you kissed her. The two of you have something special. There's a fire there."

The fire she saw had nothing to do with romance. But telling that to Louise Gates was like signing his own bachelorhood death sentence. He wasn't about to do that. So he just nodded. The last thing he wanted was to get into a detailed conversation about his nonrelationship with Kenya. Moments later, Trey and Louise stood at the front door. Colonel Wheeler and Kenya were already outside talking at the car.

"It's a shame the twins were asleep," Trey said, changing the subject.

"No problem, we can see them this evening."

"This evening?" Trey questioned.

"Yes, that way we can get to know your lovely young lady. She is sweet, and so intelligent. We talked about her new design boutique. You must be very proud of her."

"Yes, I am," he said, looking at Kenya as she laughed, apparently joking with Colonel Wheeler. Her face lit up and her smile was radiant. Her eyes twinkled and her face shone. "Uh, actually, Mamma Lou, I'm pretty sure I have a previous engagement this evening."

"I know. Kenya mentioned that she'd be working late this evening. She said something about expecting a large shipment. I assume you'll be helping her at the boutique."

"Yes, of course," Trey said cautiously.

"Well, then, Otis and I will stop by the boutique and see the twins there. We'll babysit while you two take care of the delivery."

"The twins, at the boutique," Trey said.

"Of course, Trey, you're not going to leave the twins here alone, are you?" she asked, chuckling.

"No, no, of course not. We'll be there," he promised as Kenya walked over.

"Good, then I'll see you two this evening." She reached up and kissed his cheek. "Goodbye, dear, we'll see you later." She walked over to the car. Colonel Wheeler held the door as she got in. They waved as they drove off.

"What was that?" she asked without turning to him.

"What?" he asked innocently.

"As if you didn't know—the kiss. That wasn't part of the deal."

"All-inclusive," he said, looking away.

"You're exactly as they say."

"Is that a compliment, Kenya?"

"If you consider manipulative and egocentric complimentary then, yeah, enjoy," she said.

"All that," he said, smiling mischievously.

"Yeah, all that," she answered sharply.

"Well, I guess I should thank you. Nicely done, you handled yourself admirably," Trey said approvingly as he turned to her.

"Don't congratulate me," Kenya said.

"Why not? You did a very convincing job."

"I lied to a sweet old lady."

"You honored your end of a deal."

"That's right." She finally turned to him. "It was all business, right? Everything is about business for you."

"Not everything," Trey said seductively.

"Oh, please, don't even try it," Kenya said, spinning around and walking away. "Consider that your one and only."

"My one-and-only what?" he asked, with mock innocence.

She turned around. "You know exactly what I'm talking about—kiss, your one-and-only kiss with me."

He smiled. "Is that a challenge?"

"You should be ashamed of yourself. How could you just lie to her like that? She's your grandmother, what's the big deal if you're seeing someone or not. What, is she going to give you a billion dollars if you get married?"

"Call it self-preservation," he said, smiling wryly.

"Whatever you call it, it was still a lie."

"Hey, you were right there with me the whole time. You could have said something. You could have broken our deal."

"And break a grandmother's heart, no, I'm not that cruel. She obviously loves you, although I have no idea why."

"Because I'm charming," he said seriously.

"Don't flatter yourself, that's not what I'd call it."

"What would you call it?" he asked softly.

She turned again. He was too close as his question reverberated in her mind. *Sexy, heavenly, charismatic, desirable, seductive.* Kenya stepped back. This was getting too intense. Obviously, Trey played by a set of rules she knew nothing about.

"What did your grandmother mean by seeing the two of us later?"

"At your boutique. Apparently you invited her."

"I invited her?" Kenya asked, stunned. "No, no, I didn't invite her. Well, not exactly, anyway. I told her to stop by. But I meant later, after the boutique was open, not now."

"Mamma Lou hears what she wants to hear."

"Apparently she's not the only one," she said. His sexy smile had Kenya's stomach doing flips.

"I have to go," she said quietly. "I'm already an hour late. I presume you can handle the twins on your own now," she said as she went back into the house.

"Of course," Trey replied.

"Just keep your eye on them and you'll do fine." She looked around quickly then headed to the dining room to retrieve her purse.

"So what are we going to do about this evening?" he asked, following too close.

"What about this evening?" she asked, turning.

"Mamma Lou expects to see us," he said, moving closer. "Together."

Kenya opened her mouth to speak but nothing came out. He was too close and her heart was about to jump out of her chest. Her stomach quivered and her legs were weak.

He had found her weakness. He was challenging her and she was losing.

"Don't worry, I'll make up some excuse," he said, knowing that he'd gotten to her.

"Why did you really do it?"

"Do what?"

"Kiss me," she said softly.

"Is that a request?"

Kenya's stomach jumped. Every fiber of her being screamed yes as she shook her head no. Trey smiled. He had, of course, expected the question. "You asked for it."

"I did not." She saw victory in his eyes. "You know what, you're a real jerk. No, I take that back. You're not a jerk. You're a spiteful, depraved degenerate," Kenya said.

Trey smiled. "A bit personal, don't you think. It was only one kiss, unless of course..." He moved closer.

"Don't even think about it," she warned feebly as she placed her hand on his chest. The feel of his solid body pressing on her hand made her tingle. An instant recollection of him standing in the doorway shirtless flashed in her mind.

"Well, then by all means, tell me what you really think of me."

"Oh, baby, you don't want to know what I really think of you."

Trey looked down at her hand still on his chest and smiled broader. "Now you're just being a tease."

She quickly removed her hand. "Must you manipulate everybody and every situation?" she asked heatedly as she moved around him toward the front door.

He stepped between her and the door. She held her ground. Their bodies were nearly touching. "First of all, character assassinations aside, you don't know me and certainly not the whole story. Mamma Lou has been after me for years, and I have no intention of getting caught by her or anyone else, now or ever."

"What do you mean, after you?"

"Trust me, I know what I'm doing."

"Trust you, that's a joke."

"You mean being that I'm a degenerate and all," Trey said softly.

"Yes, exactly," she said, feeling the closeness of his body again.

They stared at each other a few moments. A slow easy smile pulled at Trey's lips. He focused on her eyes. They were exceptional—dark, almost black, with specks of golden ice. Then his eyes drifted to her lips…soft, sweet and pouty, perfect for kissing.

"Don't even try it," she warned, backing up. Her heart thundered in her chest yet she kept her calm. But she knew if he kissed her, she'd probably jump him right there on the floor.

"Try what?" he asked innocently.

"Kissing me again."

He leaned in slowly. "I wouldn't dream of it. Although, sweetheart, when or if I decide to *try* kissing you again, there'll be no question about you wanting it."

"Please, save it for one of your little playthings. As far as I'm concerned you're definitely not my type."

"Sweetheart, I'm everybody's type," he said.

"Don't flatter yourself." He leaned in; she didn't budge. "I have to go," she said, nearly breathless.

"Consider this your free pass."

Kenya quickly stepped around him and left. She did what was referred to as a speedy retreat. She got in her car and drove off as quickly as possible.

Trey stood in the doorway, smiling. He had enjoyed that tremendously. The first battle was always the sweetest. He'd successfully taken her out of whatever game she came to play on him. Over the years he'd seen them all. He expected she was no different. They all wanted one thing—him. But the whole helping-her-father thing did intrigue him. That was a first. She actually seemed passionate about it.

He opened his cell and pressed a button that connected him to his office. "Get me everything you have on Kenya Whitaker." He hung up and smiled. It had been a long time since he had a worthy opponent. This should be very entertaining.

In the sixth century B.C., Sun Tzu outlined the definitive treatise on warfare, military strategies and combat tactics. Using mathematics and science, he outlined an approach to warfare with keen precision. His ideas had become Trey's formula for success. He had studied and honed his skill using them to his advantage. He'd mastered the rules of engagement and used them in dealing with all aspects of his life, both business and personal.

Every opponent had a weakness, one that they hid well. His task was to find and exploit that weakness and to use it to his advantage. He didn't enjoy the easy, quick victories as much, but rather the know-it-alls that assumed they could take him on. Even the seasoned players who played the game to perfection and still lost amused him.

He'd lost count of all the times he went up against someone and quickly discovered their weakness. It was his job and he loved it.

But once in a while he would come up against someone whom he couldn't figure. Kenya Whitaker was that person. She wanted him, but instead of revealing her motives, she retreated. He kind of liked that. Seldom did he have the opportunity to chase. Women usually chased him. He smiled. The challenge of the pursuit would make victory sweet. The phone rang. He picked up. "Yes?"

"Good day, my name is Mrs. Thatcher. I'm calling for Mr. Trey Evans."

The call instantly stilled him. His personal phone numbers

were unlisted. That meant if you didn't get it from him or someone very close to him, you didn't get it. So hearing an unrecognizable voice was a rarity.

"Speaking."

"Mr. Evans, my name is Mrs. Thatcher. Mrs. Gates filled me in on your particular circumstances. I understand you are caring for Johanna and Jonathan Gates and are in need of my services for a very short duration."

"That's correct. I'll need to see your references."

"My references are being e-mailed and faxed to you."

Trey walked to his home office. The fax machine had already delivered the references along with a "you owe me big-time" note from Tony. "Mrs. Thatcher, I understand you already know Jonathan and Johanna."

"Yes, lovely children. A handful, but most twins usually are, particularly at this age."

"Okay, I have your references here. When can we meet?"

"I was told you needed someone immediately. I'm available at your convenience."

"Excellent. Why don't we meet at my office in two hours?" Trey gave her the address then hung up. Finally, everything was back to how it should be. He touched his lips and smiled. All and all, it had been a very interesting morning.

Chapter 4

Kenya headed to her parents' home after leaving Trey's place. She needed to regroup. Trey had definitely rattled her. All her research was for nothing. Everything she learned was useless. When confronted by him, to her dismay, she crumbled like a stale cookie. She intended to intimidate him; instead she kissed him. Granted, he kissed her first, but still, she willingly cooperated. What was wrong with her? What was she thinking? He'd obviously done it to confuse her, and it had worked.

Always in control, always focused, she never let anyone get to her, not anymore. Losing control was a sign of weakness. She vowed she'd never do that again. In business, as in life, there were winners and losers. Her father had taught her that and she learned her lesson well.

She'd come up against powerful men before. Each time she had successfully held her own. They tried to use and manipulate her, but instead she used them to get exactly what she wanted. But this time, with Trey, it was different. She'd been steamrolled.

He was no ordinary opponent. But this wasn't over. She needed to come up with a different approach if she intended to help her father. Realizing she'd been overwhelmed, she contemplated her next move.

Moments later she pulled into the brand-new community. New homes sparkled and shone like polished diamonds. Mostly flat and surrounded by miniature trees, the community boasted upscale living for anyone who could afford it.

The newly developed area was very different from the old stately townhomes she had just left. She pulled up in front of her parents' home. As lovely as it was, it lacked the impressive stature of Trey Evans's house, but she was grateful for that.

She looked up at the imposing structure. The newly purchased home in Arlington certainly wasn't where she grew up. Sometimes she missed the small tree-lined street and close-knit neighborhood. There, everyone was a family. When one was in need, everyone pitched in to help. Here, at this new place, no one knew who their neighbors were and, shamefully, no one really cared.

Her parents had sold the smaller home and moved into a more impressive one, which was more suitable to their newfound wealth. Kenya smiled. The words *newfound wealth* stuck in her mind. At the moment, it was all an illusion, the money, the design boutique, her dreams, everything.

She opened the front door and went inside. "Hello," she called out. "Sidney?" There was no answer. Apparently her sister was out, which was fine with her. She needed a few minutes alone with peace and quiet. She dropped her things on the living room sofa, and then headed for the kitchen. The closer she got, the more intense the smell seemed. It was a foul stench, like something was burning. In the kitchen she looked around then spotted the source. The coffee machine had been left on. She turned it off and yanked the cord. A spark made her jump.

"Sidney," she called out in vain. She grabbed the handle but flinched, releasing it instantly. It was scalding. The electric base was charred black. She picked up a dish towel, grabbed the pot handle again and then hurried over to the sink. Black residue from what was once coffee was chipped and charred on the bottom of the pot. She turned on the water to cool it, but instead it made a popping sound then instantly shattered. "Sidney," she said, seething quietly.

"What?"

Kenya turned around to see her sister standing in the doorway in a T-shirt, baggy boxers and slippers, yawning. "Sidney, I almost burned my hand. You left the coffeepot on again."

"Would you please chill out," she mumbled sleepily.

"One of these days you're gonna burn the house down around you. Then what are you gonna do? Believe it or not, the simple everyday chores, such as turning a coffee machine off, are just as important as partying all night," Kenya said, and then began cleaning up the mess in the sink by gathering broken glass with a dishtowel.

"For your information, I was up late last night studying, not partying. As usual, you don't know all the facts and as usual, you are overreacting," Sidney said in the monotone voice she often used when her older sister annoyed her. She walked over and peeked into the sink. "Wait, I didn't do that," she said, pointing to the broken glass everywhere.

"No, it broke when I turned on the cold water," Kenya said, continuing to gather glass with the towel.

"So why'd you turn on the cold water?"

"Because the carafe was scalding hot," she snapped.

"So you just should have let it cool. Everybody knows that. Now look what you did. You have to buy Mom another carafe."

Kenya looked at her younger sister. She was so much like their father. Nothing was ever her fault. She always had an excuse for everything. The fact that she created the problem was completely lost on her. But she was right about one thing—of course she knew that turning cold water on hot glass would shatter it. "Sidney, if you hadn't left the machine on all night, then the pot wouldn't be broken."

"I didn't pour cold water into a hot carafe and shatter it. You did that."

"Never mind," Kenya finally said, knowing she'd never get her to understand. Sometimes her sister's easygoing, lackadaisical attitude annoyed her. It was matched only by their father's. As scary as it seemed, sometimes Kenya envied them.

"Need help?" Sidney asked.

"No, I got it," Kenya snapped, making her second trip to the trash can.

"Have you heard from Mom or Dad today?" Sidney asked as she grabbed the trash can and wedged it under the rim of the countertop. She angled it, making it much easier to just scoop the broken glass directly into the trash can.

Kenya removed the last of the glass then washed down the sink. Sidney dropped the towel in the trash and put the can back.

"Aren't you going to wash that?" Kenya asked.

"It's got tiny shards of glass embedded in it. I don't know about you, but I don't want to take a chance on getting my hands all cut up over a two-dollar dish towel."

"Don't you have a class this morning?" Kenya replied.

"Yes, mother," Sidney said sarcastically, "but it was canceled. Did you just come over to check up on me, or is there another reason why you're here so early?"

"No, I just needed to…" Kenya began, but stopped. She

leaned back against the counter, watching her sister examine the coffee machine. There was no way she was going to tell her that she had been flustered by a man. She was the oldest sister, the one in charge. She was perfect, always responsible and accountable. To appear otherwise would be out of character. "Make sure you were okay."

"That sounds a lot like checking up on me."

"Do you need anything?" Kenya asked, walking out of the kitchen. Sidney followed.

"What's wrong with you?" Sidney asked. "You're all jittery and nervous."

"I'm not nervous. I just wanted to check on my younger sister. Is that so bad?" Sidney looked at her suspiciously. "Never mind, don't answer. What's the rest of your day look like?"

"I have to study for my class tomorrow and then prepare for my internship the rest of the day."

"How's that going?" Kenya asked.

Sidney smiled. "It's an internship. I'm working for free. How do you think it's going? But it does have its perks, so I'm dealing with it." Sidney sat on the arm of the sofa as Kenya grabbed her purse. Kenya looked at her, then at the sofa, then back at her. "Fine, fine," Sidney said and stood up.

The rule had always been not to sit on the arm of the sofa. Kenya was not about to let it slide just because her mother was away. "Okay, if you need me, call me. I'll be at the boutique all day. But I need to make a few stops first. Do you want to grab breakfast?" she asked. Sidney looked down at herself then at Kenya. "Never mind," Kenya said, knowing it would take her sister at least two hours to get dressed. "I'll see you later."

Kenya left, then climbed back in the car and drove off. What was wrong with her? She'd nearly burned her hand on a carafe she knew was hot, put cold water in a hot glass container and hadn't even thought to move the trash can to the sink. Was her brain on permanent lockdown?

No, she'd gotten distracted, something she seldom did. She prided herself on always being focused on a goal. Kenya chastised herself for her behavior. What was she doing, flirting, kissing? Getting sidetracked by some Wall Street Romeo? Not again. Frustrated, she slammed her palm on the steering wheel. The sting made her flinch. She looked at her slightly inflamed palm. It was red but not burned. She sighed heavily.

Come on, girl, get it together. Snap out of it, he was just a man, an ordinary man. No big deal.

Wrong, he was a big deal, and she knew it.

Wealthy or attractive men never affected her like this. They'd come and gone in and out of her life before. She'd been in like, in love and in downright lust. Wait. Maybe that was it—lust. She realized that explained everything. She had researched Trey and his string of women. They chased and he led them on. All that testosterone had obviously subconsciously intrigued her. That's why she kissed him back. After all, she was only human. Then, of course, seeing him half-naked didn't hurt. His body was damn near perfect.

His body. "Mmph," she hummed, expelling a slow, satisfying moan then licking her lips. The thought made her smile. *Being with him must be...* "Mmph, mmph, mmph," she moaned again as she shook her head. She wouldn't even know what to do with a body like that. No, she took it back. She knew exactly what she'd do, over and over and over again. Now that naughty thought made her really smile.

The next few miles found serious focus eluding her as Trey Evans strolled in and out of her thoughts repeatedly. No matter how hard she tried to reshift her focus, her thoughts always came back to him. She was totally and completely preoccupied. "Stop it, stop it, stop it," she scolded and commanded herself. "Why do you keep thinking about that man?" she muttered.

Then it hit her. Of course, she realized. It all made sense. He was the main reason for her aggravation, she reasoned. He was the cause of her father's pain and she wanted to get back at him. That's why she kept thinking about him. Yes, of course.

No, that wasn't it. And lying to herself wouldn't change anything, and she knew it. It was his smile, his chest, his incredible eyes—they all stayed with her. She still couldn't believe he'd kissed her. Worse yet, she'd kissed him back.

She parked, got out and then spent the next hour in the fabric store picking out swatches and material, and trying desperately to distract herself. She shopped, bargained, plotted and planned, but he was there the whole time, never very far away.

The problem was that everything she thought she knew about him was completely wrong. He was an immovable force with a very definite way of getting a point across. Kenya touched her lips as she stood in the checkout line. She didn't still feel his mouth on her, but the memory was certainly clear enough to make her shudder.

She looked around to the other customers in line and those who still mingled about. Thankfully they were too busy dealing with their own dramas to even notice her. She quickly checked out and hurried back to her car.

What was it about him? Maybe it was the first sight of him standing in the doorway, or maybe it was because she hadn't been with anyone in a while. But whatever it was, he was definitely getting to her. No, past tense—he'd gotten to her. Every time he had looked at her with those green eyes, she flushed. The sexy way he smiled, his mesmerizing gaze and his kiss... He was sexy. No, he was sexual. No wonder he had the reputation he did. She could just imagine... "Whoa," she said aloud. What was she doing? She was doing it again. "Stop it."

Well, the one good thing about the morning was that all of a sudden, she had gotten a burst of energy. She'd been dragging around the past two days; now she felt like she could run ten miles without stopping. Apparently the situation had energized her.

After going from store to store, she finally completed her errands. She drove back to the boutique, loaded up the purchases, then headed to the front door. Juggling her packages, she dropped a bolt of fabric as soon she inserted her key into the lock. As she picked up the fabric the front door swung open.

"And where the heck have you been all morning?" Shelly Turner asked as she opened the door before Kenya could touch the knob. Kenya juggled the packages again as she walked in. Shelly closed and locked the door behind her.

"Sorry, the errands took longer than I expected. I got everything on the list. I even found the perfect ribbons and notions. Did the electrician get here yet?" Kenya asked as they walked straight through to the workroom.

"Yep, here and gone. Here's the estimate." Shelly handed Kenya the paper from her desk.

Kenya read the detailed estimate. She looked up at Shelly. "What's this, a joke? Where's the real one?"

"That, my dear, is the real one. Apparently what we thought was a short is actually a serious wiring problem. He said that the place has to basically be rewired. Also, according to him we have at least seven code violations and two serious fire code problems." The lights flickered and dimmed, almost to make her point. They both looked up. "I checked the account. We don't have that kind of money. We need at least twenty-five hundred, fifty dollars immediately. And that's just to get the job started."

"Two thousand, five hundred fifty dollars," Kenya repeated as she sat on the nearest stool.

"I figured I can scrape together a thousand dollars, maybe another five hundred if I pawn my grandmother's ring. That's fifteen hundred. Can you come up with the rest?"

"My checking and savings accounts are already tapped out," Kenya said as she slumped over the cutting table. "I could break in to my money market."

"No, absolutely not, remember we said that our money market accounts were for dire emergencies only. They're a last resort. We're not that strapped yet. We just have to be creative," Shelly said. Kenya started chuckling. "What?"

"Nothing."

"No, what? Tell me. I could use a good laugh after dealing with that electrician all morning."

"I was just at this guy's house this morning. He's probably worth a couple trillion dollars. He wanted me to be his kids' nanny and then to play nice when his grandmother stopped by. Why don't I just ask him for the money?"

"Fine, perfect, promise him anything, be the nanny, do his laundry, whatever, just get the money."

"I was joking, Shelly," she said sarcastically. The last thing she wanted to do was to go back to Trey and ask him to repeat his offer.

"I'm not. Look, do you want this to happen or not?"

"Of course I want this to happen. We've dreamed about this since our first day at Parsons. We were going to open our own design studio and boutique, our label, our designs, our garments. We're almost there."

"Exactly, so what if we have to get a couple of part-time jobs to tide us over. We've done it before. There's nothing wrong with expanding our horizons from time to time."

"We also need to focus on our work—our clothing line for next season is only half-done. There's no way we have enough designs to fill the boutique yet," Kenya said.

"Okay, fine, no nanny, no part-time jobs, then what? We need money fast. If the electricity goes out on us one more time..." She looked around the workroom. "I guess we could sell our sewing machines."

Kenya slumped over farther. "Okay, first of all you're not gonna pawn your grandmother's ring and we're not gonna sell our sewing machines. You love them, I love them. They're the centerpiece of the boutique. They're what gave us our start. We'll find another way. If you can get a thousand, I'll come up with the rest somehow. When did he say he can get the work started?"

"As soon as we give him the down payment," Shelly said as she sat down at her drawing table.

"Okay," Kenya said, then stood up and started gathering and emptying the packages she'd brought in. The more she thought about everything that was going on, the more furious she became. Everything that could go wrong had—her father, his business, the money, and now her business was in jeopardy.

All this was because of Trey Evans, a greedy, spiteful, conniving bully. She picked up a few rolls of ribbon and shoved them down. Then she grabbed several bolts of fabric and slammed them on the cutting table. The loud noise made Shelly pop her head up from her sewing.

"Whoa, whoa, whoa, calm down," Shelly said.

"Sorry, I was just thinking, that man is infuriating. I need to find a way to get back to him," she grumbled.

"Fine, we can always get another electrician."

"No, no, not him, I'm talking about Trey Evans," she huffed.

"Trey Evans," Shelly said, then paused. "Oh, right."

"The one and only Iceman," Kenya said, tossing more supplies onto the table. "I met him this morning. Believe me, the name is well-suited."

"You went to see him," she surmised easily enough. "I thought you were gonna wait on that."

"I couldn't."

"Oh, so that's where you went this morning, the trillion-dollar nanny guy. Wait, why did he want you to be a nanny?"

"Don't ask, it's ridiculous," Kenya said.

Shelly shrugged. "So did you at least get a chance to talk to him about your dad?"

"No, his kids were there."

"He has kids?" Shelly asked.

"Twins, toddlers, they're so adorable. But he's a walking, talking control-freak. I don't know what their mother was thinking about having kids with him and then leaving them with him. He doesn't have a clue."

"Ah, so that's why he wanted you to be his nanny."

"Can you see that happening?" Kenya asked facetiously.

"Yeah, actually I can, you'd be a great nanny. You practically raised your sisters and you love kids."

"That's not the point, Shelly."

"I guess you couldn't reason with him about your father, huh?"

"I never even got a chance. The man is unbelievable. He's like a block of ice. He exhuded power and control from every pore. It's like the world centers around him. Talk about arrogant."

"Intimidating?" Shelly asked.

"More like power-hungry fanatic. I can't imagine actually doing business with him. The whole time he was so single-mindedly focused on one goal, getting a nanny. I could barely get a word in edgewise. Talk about self-centered. Can you believe him?"

"Actually it sounds very familiar."

"If you're implying that I'm anything like him, I have never—"

Shelly laughed. "No, no, I'm just saying. When you set your mind to do something, few things get in your way, and you know that. So don't even try to be frontin'."

"Well, still, he's just unbelievable."

"A mistake going there this morning, huh," Shelly surmised.

"Yeah, a big mistake," Kenya said.

"Again, I thought you were supposed to wait until your folks got back."

"I thought I could reason with him. I see why they call him Iceman, he's impossible. He messes with your mind and gets you all confused."

"Well, yeah, he's a mega-successful businessman, right? That's what they do."

"I know but not like this. This guy is like a tidal wave. He's intense."

"Did he threaten you or something?"

"No, of course not, nothing like that. What I mean is he's smart, diabolical-smart." Shelly started laughing. "It's not funny, Shelly," Kenya told her.

"I know, I know. My bad. It's just that you make him sound like he's some kind of comic book villain with a stovepipe hat, handlebar mustache and black cape."

"I know it sounds crazy but that's how it was. I mean, he gets inside your head and reads your mind or something. I think it's his eyes. Green with golden specks, they're mesmerizing, maybe even hypnotizing."

"Girl, what did that man do to you?"

"Nothing," she said far too defensively, and then calmed down. "I mean, nothing. It's just that when he looks at you, I swear, you forget everything. It's like his eyes penetrate you, going right through to your soul."

"Really," Shelly said, growing more interested.

"He opened the door half-naked and I swear I couldn't

breathe. I just stood there looking at the man's chest like I'd never seen one before. I must have looked like a complete idiot."

"Um, half-naked sounds kinda sexy-hot to me."

"Oh, yeah, he's that, too."

"Sexy?" Shelly asked. Kenya nodded and signed heavily. "Damn, girl. Whatever happened this morning, he really got you all upset, didn't he?"

"No, not upset. Well, more like off balance, I guess."

"No, don't even try it. He got to you. Look at you, you're all flustered and flushed. Are you attracted to him?" Shelly questioned.

"If by attracted you mean, do I want to crush him and wipe that smirk off his face, then the answer is yes."

"The lady doth protest too much, methinks."

"No way," Kenya denied, "and don't quote *Macbeth* to me."

"It's Shakespeare's *Hamlet,* act three, scene two."

"Whatever. The thing is, how do I get to somebody like that? There's no way I can afford to take him head-on. So I've been considering what to do."

"What you do is, wait for your folks to get back."

"No, I have to do something now. I just can't sit around and do nothing. The way I figure, he's a man, so he has one weakness. I just need to use it against him. It's called leverage."

"How do you mean leverage?"

"Trey Evans loves women and he loves a challenge. So I'm gonna be exactly what he loves. That way I can find out how to get to him."

"Why don't I like where this is going?" Shelly asked.

"This isn't going anywhere," Kenya assured her.

"Yes, it is. This is another one of your classic obsessions."

"My what?"

"You heard me. I swear, you'll do anything not to have a life."

"Excuse me! Hello! I have a life, look around."

"A social life, Kenya. You're in here almost fifteen hours a day. That's wrong."

"So are you," she insisted.

"Yeah, but I have a life, friends, hobbies."

"It's a new business and we have to put in the extra time."

"Sure, but not to the exclusion of everything else," Shelly said. "When's the last time you went to the movies, grabbed a show or even went for a walk in the park?" Shelly asked. Kenya opened then closed her mouth. "Uh-huh, see, you can't even answer that question. Now look what you're doing to avoid getting a life. When was your last date, ten months ago? Come on, girl, get out there. Have some fun.

"Don't get me wrong, I realize that this thing with your dad is major, and I'm behind you one hundred and ten percent. I just don't want to see you getting yourself hurt again."

"I have no intention of getting hurt."

"Nobody ever does."

"Shelly, I know what you're saying and I get it. But I have to get back out there in my own time. So if keeping myself occupied, plus helping my family, is the way to do it, then so be it. I'm in the driver's seat now, I choose when, who and how."

"Okay," Shelly said.

"Now, the key is getting back into his house. I'm sure he has a home office. I'm sure there's something in there I can use as leverage against him."

"You intend to go through the man's house?"

"Why not?" Kenya said.

"Do the words *breaking and entering* mean anything to you?"

"I'm not going to break in. I'll be invited."

"Yep, I definitely don't like where this is going."

"Look, I have to dig up whatever information I can get on him. He's not going to just say 'Here, take your father's company back.' I have to make him. That means leverage."

"You mean blackmail, right?" Shelly said. Kenya didn't respond. "Okay, say you get your leverage, then what?" she asked.

"Then I get the company back."

"And that's the end of it?"

"No, then I'll go to the Securities and Exchange Commission and file a complaint. Even if he buys his way out or if the complaint doesn't stick, he's bound to lose business once word gets out that he's under investigation from the SEC."

Shelly shook her head. "You've got it all planned out, a double cross."

"That's right," Kenya said proudly. "I'll do exactly what he did to my father. I'll get him to trust me, and then I'll take everything away from him."

"Just like that?" Shelly inquired.

"Yep, just like that," Kenya said. "He won't know which way is up once I'm through messing with his head."

Shelly broke up laughing. Kenya looked at her, then realized what she'd said. "You know what I mean."

Still chuckling, Shelly nodded. "Yeah, and I seriously hope you're joking about all this."

"A little revenge never hurt anyone. Let's face it, my dad is never gonna get what he's due."

"So the best thing is to wait until your folks get back, and then they can take him to court. It'll take a while but you'll get something."

"In the meantime, he gets away with it—no, I don't think so. What if he does this to someone else?"

"So you're just gonna walk up to him and say, 'Hi, I need you to trust me so that I can ruin your life.'"

"No, I'll tell him that I want to learn about the market or something. You know, stroke his ego. I'm sure his is huge."

Shelly smiled and started chuckling. "Would you please get your head out of the gutter?" Kenya protested.

"Sorry, so what you're actually saying is that you intend to trick him and use him to get what you want. That sounds mighty familiar."

Kenya bristled. She knew Shelly was talking about Craig and how he had used her. "I intend to get my father's money back. If he thinks that he's getting something in return then that's his problem."

"Spoken like a true player. Don't you think he's gonna know that you're your father's daughter?"

"There're a million Whitakers out here."

"Oh, so he's a millionaire businessman idiot now, who doesn't have sense enough to figure out that you're James Whitaker's daughter? Come on, Kenya."

Kenya paused. Shelly was right. Trey probably had a full dossier on her the second she left his house. "You're right, so I'll just tell him the truth. He won't expect it."

Shelly shook her head. "Girl, you'd better be careful with that revenge thing. My grandmother always said messing with people's heads was like dancing on thin ice over deep water. What will you do when this master plan of yours cracks and you fall?"

"I'll swim," Kenya said assuredly.

"Tread, is more like it," Shelly said.

"Whatever. Enough of that. I'm gonna do it and that's it. Okay, now about this estimate."

"Oh, please don't tell me that you've got a master plan for that, too."

Kenya ignored her remark as she picked up the estimate and looked at it again. "I'll get started on my half."

"And I'll do my half and in five years' time…" Shelly began as she always did.

"We'll look back on this and laugh," they said in unison. Kenya smiled and shook her head. She was forever pragmatic and Shelly was the perpetual optimist.

"Shall I break out in a chorus or two?" Shelly asked.

"No, please don't," Kenya said.

"Are you sure? Let's see, I could sing 'My Favorite Things' or 'Tomorrow,' or an all-time favorite, 'Over the Rainbow.'"

"None of the above," Kenya said firmly. Shelly's voice was nice, but once she got started singing happy songs, as she called them, they'd be stuck in her head all day.

"Just asking," Shelly joked. "For real, everything will work out, you'll see. Your mom and dad will be fine. We'll find the money to get the place rewired, and open in two months just like we planned."

"It's not just Trey or the electrical thing. It's me. My mind has been a blank for the last two days. You've been picking up the slack for me. Maybe I'm just losing my grip. I hate to bring all this drama in here."

"Girl, please, that's what friends are for and that's what partners do. When one is low the other takes the lead and vice versa. How many nights have you stayed up with me and my drama? So chill, you're not losing your grip. I got this for now, okay?" Shelly said. Kenya nodded. "Now here's some good news. I found a trim manufacturer in Baltimore that's going out of business."

"That's good news?" Kenya said.

"One man's loss is another's gain. I'm headed up there now with the last of the petty cash. I hate being a vulture and picking from a carcass, but—"

"I know, but if we don't take advantage, someone else will."

"Exactly. I'll probably be there the rest of the day, so I'll see you later this evening. How late are you staying?"

"Late," she said. "I'm gonna get some work done."

"Okay, see you later," Shelly said, then left.

Kenya started thinking. Was it possible? Could she really find a way to blackmail Trey? Shelly was right, revenge was tricky. It could backfire on her. But she had to take a chance. Maybe she could start by doing the nanny thing.

She was certainly qualified. Not to be a nanny, of course, but at least to babysit. She was even certified. She had common sense and the experience of having helped raise two younger sisters. Plus she babysat for half the old neighborhood. Babysitting was the only way she could think of to get back into his house. Once there she'd figure something else out.

Chapter 5

Three floors in the Mallet Building, one of the most prestigious addresses in D.C., belonged to TE Acquisitions & Associates. But what most didn't know was so did the entire building. Trey Evans, owner and CEO, made a habit of being in control of everything. Buying the building was a necessity for him. And since he had a tendency to get what he wanted, with few exceptions, he did just that.

TE was an elite investment and asset management firm. They primarily dealt with high-risk venture capital, but also had financial advisory and personal wealth management divisions. They represented individuals, professionals, entrepreneurs and companies. They handled estate planning, retirement services, securities and other services.

The offices were impressive with the three main divisions each occupying a floor. Each operated independently with Trey at the center of the well-structured organization. Everyone eventually reported to him. Trey's offices were of course the most impressive and had a large conference room area.

Sunlight streamed in and saturated the open office space through glass-panel doors. Trey stood looking out the window. His view was breathtaking. All of Washington, D.C., lay in front of him. He sighed heavily. His job tested his resolve daily. He bought and sold, moving millions of dollars around without a second thought. The investors' faces disappeared in a morass of conquests and defeats. The latter only seldom occurred. Once, he'd allowed himself to be distracted by emotion and nearly lost everything he'd worked so hard to attain. That would never happen again. He'd learned his lesson well.

Now he masterfully manipulated lives and careers like a marionette puppeteer. He planned, maneuvered and orchestrated. He pulled the strings and irrevocably changed people's lives. He took advantage of weakness with gutsy moves that oftentimes devoured his opposition.

Some men did it for the money, others—like his father—for the power. He played the game for the challenge. It was the game Trey loved and he played it well. He was a winner and he intended to stay a winner. That meant staying focused and never wavering from the target. But he had wavered, at least momentarily, first with the would-be nanny and then with Mamma Lou. One, he could quite easily avoid, but it was the other that had left him distracted.

He had an itch and there was only one thing to do.

The woman behind the fiery eyes still haunted him. He had impulsively kissed her. But he didn't do anything on impulse. Every move he made was planned, well thought-out and deliberate. And yet, he had kissed her. Why? He knew why.

"Here's the breakdown of depreciation, industry analysis and comprehensive data on the secondary market. It's been six months, time's up. Okay, Trey, so with all that in mind, what do you want to do with this acquisition?"

"Which acquisition?" Trey asked, turning and looking at his senior managing executive, Joshua Garfield. He had no idea what he was talking about.

"I just told you. Let me guess, you haven't heard a single word, have you?" Joshua asked.

"Every other word actually," Trey confessed, walking back to sit behind his desk. He pulled out his red folder. Inside were his hard-copy files of every open project TE Acquisitions & Associates was currently working on.

"That can only mean one thing. There's a game on. Who is it, what company are we looking at?" Joshua asked, pumped for action. This was the part of business they both loved. Completely simpatico, Trey and Joshua were the perfect team. In all respects they were as close as brothers, although few actually knew the truth. They were half brothers with the same father. Together they planned, strategized, adjusted, forecasted and, finally, carried out their takeover. God help their target.

"I'm still considering the options. I'll let you know. Let's get Caine out of the way first," Trey said, not completely lying. There was indeed someone he had his eye on, and as he said, he was still considering his options.

"Good enough. Okay, I'll drop the attorney legalese, here's the Cliff's Notes version. One more time for those in the back of the room," Joshua said, smiling, reminding Trey of something their grad school economics professor always said. He pushed the prospectus across the desk to Trey.

"James Whitaker," Joshua began reading, "previous owner of Whitaker Real Estate Investment Company. It's a small real estate investment firm and brokerage service. Basically it's a small operation, one location, high-grade computer setup, but nothing major. They primarily invested in real estate in depressed and undervalued areas. He invested heavily and when the market collapsed he lost everything."

Trey nodded and smiled. "He was clever, I'll give him that. I still can't believe he had the nerve to make a move like that. He didn't even tell his partner."

"It was bold," Joshua said. "I still think he knew exactly what he intended to do when he signed with us to be a client. He might have been a real estate broker, but he was no fool."

"Interesting maneuver, nonetheless," Trey said. "He might have actually poked me in the side if he'd been a bit more patient and low-key. But the main thing is that he found a weakness. One I never saw and one I never want to see again."

"We're already covered. The crack has been sealed."

"Permanently?" Trey asked. Joshua nodded. "Good."

"He must have done a lot of research on you and the company to get so close," Joshua said. Trey nodded. "So what do you want to do with it?"

Trey sighed. "How viable is the company?"

"Not too bad. Cost and asset ratios are acceptable with obvious limits, naturally. All in all it's not a bad little company. Actually the idea is a pretty good one. But, of course, that's not our main business."

"Exactly, the only thing we make is money," Trey said. Joshua nodded.

"So, options," Joshua began. "Sell it, strip it, drop it into a nonsense portfolio package, or..." He paused, and Trey looked up at him with interest. Joshua smiled and continued. "We can do the same thing you did the last time someone tried to take you."

Trey remembered well. It was the court case that had labeled him the Iceman. "Only problem is," Joshua said, "I don't believe he has the capital."

"Nah, tell you what, table it for the time being. Give it another month. I'll deal with it then."

"Okay, you're up to speed," Joshua said, closing his folder.

"What's happening with Cedric Caine?"

"Cal's latest figures are in the folder. They look good, a bit high, but it's to be expected, considering," Joshua said, and then shook his head. "Man, I don't know about your new protégé."

"Cal?" Trey questioned.

"Yeah, I swear I've never seen a man so excited about anything in my life. You'd think it was his whole career that was on the line."

"He'll be okay. He just needs to settle in. It's only been a few months and this is his first big move."

"I hope we're not setting ourselves up with him."

"What do you mean? We'd be one of only a handful of privately held companies in this industry to launch this type of venture. Two financial institutions merging into one, the ramifications are incredible. We have to give it to him. Cal brought us a winner."

"Where does he get all this information on Caine? Look, I know we want to set up our own fund and I agree it's the next logical step. But this is too pat."

"He's good at what he does."

"I hope you're right. Whatever. Speaking of which, Cedric Caine should be here in a few minutes."

Trey nodded. "Good."

"We're in the final stages of preparations. But to tell you the truth, I'll be glad when this deal is done. There's something about a man who's too eager to sell his family's company that worries me."

"It's a sweet deal," Trey said, still impressed that the perfect deal had come along at exactly the right moment.

"Too sweet if you ask me."

"Come on, Joshua, no risk, no gain. It looks like hiring Calvin Potter was a good move after all."

"Yeah, but looks can be deceiving."

Trey laughed, remembering earlier that morning and the would-be nanny. "Tell me about it." Trey glanced over to see Joshua's expression. "Come on. Don't tell me you're still skittish. We checked, double-checked and triple-checked. As far as we know, and a few things we didn't know at the beginning, Caine Enterprises is a viable business."

Joshua nodded his agreement. "Where's he getting his intel on this?"

"Presumably the same place we get ours. He studies the market. He's a go-getter. He saw a good deal so he jumped on it and since Cal is the one who initially put the whole thing together, I think he should be in on the next meet." Joshua nodded. "It's a good deal no matter how we stack it. There's no soft edge."

"I agree, on paper it looks great," Joshua said. He was all for the merger at one point. But soon after he began delving into the company, his gut feeling soured.

"But," Trey prompted curiously, "you think we should consider pulling out?" Joshua nodded slowly. "It's the same thing Regina's been saying. But I'm not convinced. I've been looking for a deal like this for years. It's perfect, exactly what we're looking for," Trey said.

"And it's too perfect. Maybe that's what concerns me about the whole thing. It's too pat, too effortless. Nothing handed to you is ever that easy."

"Our job is to stay one step ahead. We need to know what our competitors know before they know it."

"Exactly, so either he's psychic or he's getting some outside or inside help."

"I'll tell you what, why don't you add a couple more checks to that. Better safe than sorry."

"Agreed," Joshua said.

"Have Cedric chill when he gets here. I'm gonna hit the nursery again."

"Okay, that's it. What's going on with you?"

"What do you mean?"

"I get the twins and the nanny distraction, but this is different, the vague expressions, complete disinterest in business. Cool I get, even detached, but, man, you're damn near mellow. What's with you, or better yet, who is she?"

"She?" Trey asked.

"Don't even think about trying to fool me. You and I go back too far for that. Women come and go. I've only ever seen you this distracted once before."

Trey shook his head. He knew deceiving Joshua would be impossible. They were too much alike. "I'm not distracted, exactly. It's nothing really. It's just that this woman was at the house this morning. At first I thought she was the nanny I asked Kelly to hire for me, but I found out she wasn't."

"Well, who is she, what does she want?"

"Something about her father, I think he needs a job or something."

"Why would she go to you, at your home?"

"I don't know."

"What's her name?"

"Kenya Whitaker," Trey said. "I already asked for a workup on her but I think I'll—" Joshua started laughing. Trey looked at him. "What?"

"Trey, man, you really are out of it today, aren't you?" The expression on his face said it all—he was clueless. "Damn, man, what did she do to you already?"

"What?" Trey asked, knowing he'd missed something.

"Trey, you said her name is Kenya Whitaker, as in James Whitaker, Whitaker Real Estate Investment Company. It's all in the file," he offered, pointing to the paperwork on his desk. "James and Lynette, so that would make your visitor, more likely than not, his—"

"Daughter. Interesting," Trey said, smiling.

"What's interesting is that you didn't make the more than obvious connection sooner."

Joshua opened his own folder and began scanning the information. "Here it is in his personal data, he has three daughters—Kenya, Asia and Sidney."

"What does it say about them, her?"

"Kenya is the oldest, twenty-eight years old, a graduate of Parsons School of Design in New York. Currently residing in D.C., and that's all we have on her."

"That's all?" Trey questioned.

"Trey, James and Lynette are our clients, not his daughters. We did a full workup on him and his wife. We only needed the daughters' information for insurance purposes."

"Kenya is James's daughter. Interesting," Trey repeated, touching his lips.

"Is that all you can say? The man tried to scam you, and then he claimed that you took advantage of him. He threatened to file a lawsuit, claimed he wasn't fully apprised of the ramifications of what he was doing. I was in the law library for two weeks preparing for that."

"But he never filed. And now, months later, his daughter shows up on my doorstep. Yes, I'd call that very interesting."

"Obviously she thinks she can get her father's company back."

"Obviously," Trey said, half chuckling.

"If that's the case then you can blow her off."

Trey smiled. "No, not so fast. It takes a lot of guts to stand on a man's doorstep with the sole intention of demanding retribution. I think I'm going to give her a bit of leeway."

"Oh, man," Joshua said, shaking his head, "I can see it on your face. You're like a cat with a toy mouse ready to play."

"Come on, I seldom get to play with such a worthy and attractive adversary anymore."

"There's a reason for that—you don't play fair."

"Fair, what's fair?"

"Why is she demanding the company back?" Joshua asked. "It makes no sense." Trey shrugged. "Unless, of course, she doesn't have the whole story," he said.

"I'm guessing not," Trey said.

"Trey, play nice, drop it now while you can. You don't need drama and distractions right now," Joshua suggested, knowing that he wouldn't.

"Actually, there is a small snag."

"You mean the fact that she probably most definitely hates you?"

"Okay, maybe a couple of small snags. But the one I'm concerned about is Louise Gates."

"Mamma Lou? What about her?" Joshua asked, looking suddenly stressed.

"She stopped by the house while Kenya was there. Mamma Lou assumed we were together."

"Now let me guess, you let her."

"I didn't see any reason to disappoint her. I figured it was a way to keep her off my back."

"Enter drama and distractions."

"Not at all, I can handle Mamma Lou."

"Famous last words, man. One of these days that old lady is gonna have you cornered. And all the dancing in the world won't get you out of it. She's already gotten, what, how many of your friends and family?" Joshua stood to leave.

"Nah, none of that matters. I'm too fast for her. You see, my theory is if you move fast enough and see her moves in advance, there's no way she can get you."

"Didn't your cousin J.T. say the same thing?"

"Ah yes, but J.T. got distracted. That's not gonna happen with me, I assure you," Trey said smugly as he stood and followed Joshua out the door. "I'll be down in the nursery."

Joshua shook his head and watched Trey go. He headed to his own office just down the corridor. He and Trey had also been friends, although the bond of brotherhood was delayed for years. A product of an illicit affair, Joshua had the same father as Trey, a man they both despised and with whom they never communicated.

They met in prep school and even then Trey was a master planner. Usually quiet and reserved in public, he was often misunderstood. The press branded him the Iceman, cold and unfeeling. Notably, they continued to write that he stabbed at his competition, decimating them into oblivion. But the truth about Trey was known to the small inner circle of family and friends around him. He was nothing like that.

Trey was a fiercely private man. Public interviews were rare, as he was often distrustful of those whom he didn't know. He'd been burned and used once too often. Trey had learned too much of human nature. Those who took, he took first. In business, he never went after a company unless they first made a move on him. The Whitaker incident was a perfect example. To stop Whitaker was to take him down completely. He had no choice.

Had James Whitaker been up-front, he would still have his company and still be enjoying success. Instead, he greedily wanted more. And that was his failure. It was a blow because Trey actually liked the old guy. But greed was often a man's downfall.

Joshua knew that Trey had great insight. When it came to business he saw beyond the surface. Joshua chuckled to himself as he sat down at his desk. Shame that Trey didn't have that same insight now or with Mamma Lou. As of this morning, he was already a goner.

He obviously didn't have a clue. Just like J.T., he'd been distracted since the second he walked into the office. There was no way the old Trey wouldn't have made the connection between the last names. Obviously he had no idea that he was already a goner. The only thing left to do now was start planning the bachelor party, and have his tuxedo cleaned and pressed.

Trey smirked and chuckled as he took the elevator down to the second floor. He was completely assured of his invulnerability. Mamma Lou had no idea with whom she was dealing. Sure, all the other guys had gotten themselves trapped—albeit loving traps—but not him. He had no intention of taking that walk.

A few minutes later Trey walked into the Li'l Tykes nursery, located on the second floor of the office building. He had added the nursery a few years ago when he noticed some of his employees having child-care problems.

He stood at the window and saw Mrs. Thatcher, his new nanny, sitting with the twins and a few other children. The place was full. He walked in. Several workers immediately looked up, smiled and nodded. He returned their gesture then walked over to Mrs. Thatcher and the twins.

"So, how are the three of you getting along?"

"Famously," Mrs. Thatcher said happily. "They are adorable. And just like twins, I believe they have that psychic connection."

"Yeah, tell me about it," Trey said as he sat down at the small table. "Here's the contract as per our discussion. I believe you'll find everything in order. But, by all means, have your attorney look it over."

"I'm sure that won't be necessary. I've been told that you're an honorable man." She pulled a pen from her purse and quickly signed her name, then handed it back to Trey.

"Thanks for the compliment, but to whom do I owe the graciousness of such astute accolades?"

Mrs. Thatcher chuckled. "If you want to know who told me about you, it was a mutual friend." She smiled pleasantly, obviously not willing to say more.

"Discretion, I like that. So where are you from, Mrs. Thatcher?" Trey asked, knowing he would get the information he wanted eventually. All he had to do was keep her talking and off guard. She'd tell him without even realizing it.

"All over, but mostly Manchester," she said.

"New Hampshire?" Trey asked.

"England. We were army brats. I spent most of my time overseas. Then I married and lived in England for some time. After my husband died I moved to the States, although one of my sisters recently moved back to England."

"Hence the accent," he noted.

"I didn't realize it was still discernable."

"Barely," Trey said. "So where are you now—D.C., Virginia, Maryland?"

"Not too far. I'm staying with my other sister."

"Where's that?"

She smiled at his presumed cunning. "Not too far."

Trey nodded casually, having hit a wall with his questioning. "So what does your sister do?" he asked.

"She and her husband own a cleaning service. And that's the end of this line of questioning."

Trey laughed. He'd been found out. "Mrs. Thatcher, you and I are going to get along perfectly."

She smiled and nodded her agreement. "I was told that, as well."

Trey laughed again. "Okay, so how were they?" he asked as he watched the twins play with the few remaining children.

"Angels, of course," she said. "We did have a little discussion about sharing our toys with others, but other than that, we got along famously."

Trey nodded. "Okay, about this evening—" Before he finished his cell rang. "Excuse me." He stood and stepped aside. "Hello?"

"Trey, it's Mamma Lou," the soft, sweet voice announced. A sudden chill shot through him as his heart instantly lurched, and not in a good way.

"Hello, Mamma Lou, what can I do for you?" he choked out, hearing his voice almost crack for the first time since puberty.

"Question, dear—what time will you be stopping by the boutique this evening?"

"What boutique?" he asked.

"Kenya's place, of course. Otis and I are visiting friends and we've decided to stay for dinner. We won't be dropping by until later."

"Mamma Lou, that really isn't necessary. I'll be happy to stop by with the twins. There's no need to drive into the city."

"No, no trouble at all. We're already in the city. I'm looking forward to a nice long visit with my great-grandchildren and, of course, Kenya. She seems like a very nice young lady. I'm looking forward to seeing her again and, of course, seeing her boutique."

"But, Mamma Lou, Kenya's probably going to be busy."

"Then we'd better not stay too long."

"What I mean is that…I'm sure the shop isn't quite ready for visitors."

"Oh, we're not visitors, dear, we're almost family."

"Family?" Trey repeated. "Mamma Lou, I'm sure she'll be too busy with—" he began, then went blank. For the first time in as far back as he could remember words failed him.

"Oh, dear, dinner's on the table, we'll have to chat later. Now you go ahead and take care of those angels. I'll see you at the boutique later this evening."

Before he could come up with an excuse Louise had hung up. There was no way he could get out of it. Louise Gates was meeting him and his girlfriend of four months this evening, and she obviously wasn't taking no for an answer. She was good, very good.

Chapter 6

Kenya was finally able to concentrate on her work. Ideas popped into her head so quickly, she could barely sketch them. Excited, her thoughts flowed like an open dam. She barely kept up. Dresses for little girls, in bright colors with bows and ribbon, pants and tops for little boys, in muted hues with trucks and patches—she envisioned them all. They were fanciful, delightful and perfect.

She successfully traced and basted four designs in muslin. Then she cut, pinned and tailored a garment to a form and then began outlining basic patterns. She'd just finished painstakingly gathering, ironing and forming pleats along the waistband of a dress when her cell phone rang. Startled, she hurried to grab it. "Hello?"

"Hey, girl, what's up?" Asia said happily.

"Hey. Nothing much. What's up with you? How was that audition the other day?"

"Which one, the commercial or the soap?" she asked.

"Either, both," Kenya said excitedly.

"I knocked it out of the park. I got the commercial job. But I'm still waiting to hear back about the soap opera. I have a callback tomorrow."

"Are you serious, you got the commercial and a callback for a soap? Asia, that's fantastic. I'm so proud of you," Kenya squealed.

"Yep, I got it. My agent called me this morning. It's not really acting. It's more modeling with dialogue, but it's something, my foot in another door. Plus I still have the off-Broadway production gig going on."

"Asia, you're seriously gonna be a star."

"And you're gonna design my clothes and clothing line and Sidney's gonna manage us both."

"In that case we're pretty much doomed."

"Be nice," Asia said, as usual taking on the the middle-child role of peacemaker. She was the balance between the two extremes. Where Kenya was levelheaded and focused, and Sidney was spontaneous and unpredictable, Asia was even-tempered and calm. "Now, speaking of Sidney, she called me earlier."

"Don't tell me you two are at it again."

"No, no, nothing like that, we're fine. She was right—he was a jerk. I guess I was too lazy to see it."

"You know what," Kenya began, "I think we seriously underestimate our little sister. She has an astute ability to read people."

"She gets it from Mom. She can be really good at reading people when she puts her mind to it."

"You're right. Anyway, what did Sidney want?"

"She didn't want anything, she was concerned about you. What's going on down there? She said you were all upset about something this morning."

Kenya sighed. Sidney was far too intuitive her for own good. It was something Kenya, to her dismay, had never really mastered. "Nothing," Kenya lied too quickly..

"Wrong answer," Asia said. "Try again. Acting and lying are seriously not your forte."

"Fine, but you have to promise you won't tell Sidney. You know how she can be when she's upset."

"Okay, but now I'm worried."

"Before they left for Africa, Dad told me and Mom that there's a problem with the money."

"What kind of problem?"

Kenya took a deep breath. "It's all gone."

"What?" Asia said.

"Yeah, that's pretty much what I said. As far as I know, the house, the trip to Africa, the cars, your apartment, Sidney's education and my place here are all safe. But everything else is gone."

"How is that possible? Where did it all go?" she asked.

"That's a good question," Kenya said.

"But he's a millionaire, literally."

"Not anymore."

"That can't be right. Wait, so what about Dad's business?" she asked.

"He said that it's gone, too."

"Did he sell it?" Asia asked.

"No, according to him, he was swindled."

"Swindled from him, like from a con man or something?"

"See, that's the part I don't really get. He dropped this bomb on us two hours before they were leaving. I never got a chance to get all the details. I asked him about it when he called to say they arrived safely. He just said not to worry, and that he'd take care of everything when he got back."

"That's a whole month from now. Anything can happen in that amount of time."

"Tell me about it," Kenya readily agreed.

"So wait, how can someone just take somebody else's business like that? It just doesn't make any sense."

"Actually it does. It happens all the time—takeovers, mergers and boardroom coups. You hear about it all the time in the news."

"How is that possible? I thought that he was doing so well."

"I'm still confused about all that. But from what I gather, Dad made some bad investments and dried up all the cash. Apparently he put a lot of the money in real estate funds and they tanked. So he kept sinking more and more money into them and then all of a sudden there was nothing left. He lost everything."

"I can't believe this. Didn't he talk to somebody? Maybe he was given bad advice. Dad knows real estate. He doesn't know investments."

"That means he should have researched the business himself. There's no way he was given bad advice. How could he not know that his investments were tanking? No, something's up. None of this makes any sense."

"Well, can't he get the money back?"

"Asia, when a person's investments tank, there are no second chances, no do-overs. You can't ask for your money back."

"I know that, but what if it was deliberate? And what about his so-called investment advisors? What were they doing all this time? Weren't they supposed to protect him from this?"

"That's what I'm checking in to. Apparently his investment advisor owns the business now."

"What?"

"Yeah, I know. That's definitely suspicious. I think Dad was right. He did get swindled."

"What about his partner, Calvin?"

"I tried calling him yesterday. I even stopped by Dad's office. It's weird, everything is exactly the same. It's like nothing changed. I asked about Calvin. He's MIA. The people at the office said that he quit working there months ago."

"So the company is still open."

"Yes," Kenya said.

"But I thought you said that he lost the business."

"He lost it to someone else. They're keeping it open."

"See, this makes no sense," Asia said firmly.

"I agree, none of this makes any sense."

"Do you think Dad just gambled it away?" Asia asked.

"I hope not. I really hope not," Kenya said. Asia sighed on the other side. There was silence as each considered the reality.

"So wait, Dad told you all this right before they left. Where was I?"

"You and Sidney were arguing, then both of you went into the house and she went to the store."

"That's why everybody looked so shell-shocked when I came back down. I knew there was something going on. Okay, so what happens now?"

"I looked around in Dad's files and came up with a name. It's the guy that owns the company now. I paid him a visit this morning."

"What happened, what did he say?"

"We didn't get to really talk about it. I'm gonna pay him another visit."

"What can I do?"

"Nothing. Dad didn't even want you to know. But I guess I just had to talk to somebody."

"I'm glad you told me."

"Sidney can't know," Kenya warned. "She'd be devastated. Then only heaven knows what she'd do."

"I understand," Asia said. "So, when you try again and don't get anywhere with this person, I guess we're just gonna have to wait until Mom and Dad get back."

"We'll see," Kenya said, knowing that there was no way she was just going to let it drop like that. She intended to get every last penny back before her parents came home.

The sisters went on to discuss possible solutions, then ended the conversation talking about their parents in Africa. "Okay, do me a favor, keep me up on what's going on," Asia said.

"Yeah, definitely," Kenya promised. "Good luck with the commercial and the soap opera callback."

"Thanks. Call me later. See ya."

After hanging up Kenya went back to work. Surprisingly enough, she was more focused than ever. A few hours later she looked up. Shelly was walking back in loaded down with packages.

"Hey, have you been sitting there working like that this whole time?"

"Yeah, I guess so," Kenya responded. "What time is it?"

Shelly looked at her watch. "It's a little after five o'clock. Holy cow, Kenya, look what you did," Shelly said, astonished.

Kenya glanced around. Shelly was right, the workroom was a disaster. There were bits and pieces and scraps of fabric and swatches everywhere. Cut ribbons and threads littered the floor. Bolts of fabric lay half-unrolled, some on tables, chairs and even across a sewing machine. The only thing that wasn't a mess were the six children's designs on the forms against the wall.

"You're right. Oh, man, look at this place."

"Who cares what the place looks like, I'm talking about the garments," she said as she walked over to the forms. "Look at these outfits. They're fantastic."

Kenya walked over to stand beside Shelly. She tilted her head and squinted. She had to admit, the designs were good. Some of the outfits were in the beginning stages, while others were already complete.

"Girl, what came over you? This morning you were saying that you were losing your focus and now this."

"I guess I got it back."

"I'll say. Oh, my goodness. I know exactly what will go perfectly with this one. Hold on," Shelly said, rummaging through one of the shopping bags she'd brought in with her. She pulled out a small baseball cap, grabbed a straight pin and a swatch of fabric. She cut, then pinned, a basketball on the cap, then placed it on top of a form. The outfit was complete.

"Perfect, and what about—" Kenya began.

"Ah, yeah, and we can do this," Shelly finished.

"Oh, cool, now how about this on the tracksuit. We can—"

"Yeah, yeah, definitely, I like it. Maybe we can—"

"Wait, over here on the dress—"

A few minutes later they were both on a sewing machine. They added finishing touches and strokes of bold color. One cut a pattern, while the other designed and embroider-stitched an appliqué. They worked together, then separately, then back together again. Like a well-oiled machine, their technique was masterful. When they had finished, they stepped back to examine their work. "Girl, we are good," Kenya said. Shelly nodded.

They took a moment to review each of the outfits. Caps, socks, purses, belts, dresses, shirts, pants, sweatsuits—everything was perfect. This time they were complete outfits, head to toe.

"I love them," Shelly said.

"Me, too," Kenya added.

"Each piece is exactly perfect."

"Talk about a signature style. Girl, I think we found it. These are fantastic."

"These are more than fantastic, they're us."

Kenya and Shelly squealed happily while jumping and hugging each other. Maybe today wasn't a total loss after all.

"Okay, that's it. I'm through for the night. My eyes are beginning to blur," Shelly said, stretching.

"Why don't you go on home. I'll clean this mess up."

"I think I'm gonna take you up on that. After the long drive to Baltimore, getting stuck in traffic, searching for remnants in a seventy-five-year-old shop, I'm exhausted. I'll see you tomorrow."

"All right, good night."

Kenya walked over to the designs. She readjusted several items then grabbed her sketch pad and made a few notes for the clothes manufacturers. She removed a garment, turned it inside out then sat down at the sewing machine. She'd just tucked it beneath the metal foot when she heard something. She looked up to see Shelly walk back into the workroom. "I thought you were leaving," she said, readjusting the needle and stitching.

"Oh, I left, but then on my way out, we had a customer."

"A customer," Kenya said, looking up from the sewing machine. "That's impossible. We're not open yet."

"You've been holding out on me. Now I know why you were so late and so frazzled this morning."

"What?"

"There is a gorgeous man out front, with two adorable kids."

"What?" Kenya repeated. Her heart thundered. She knew exactly who it was. She got up and peeked out the door. She turned back. There was no one out there. She turned again and saw him standing up by the front counter. He had on a dark chocolate open-neck shirt with perfectly cut jeans and he looked good enough to eat. "Oh, no, I'm not ready for this. Get rid of him."

"No way," Shelly said. "What happened to all your big talk? You wanted to get to him, so here's your opportunity."

"Shelly, come on, get rid of him. I'm not ready. Just tell him that I'm out for the rest of the week."

"Look, go out there and take care of that man."

"Shelly—"

"Don't 'Shelly' me, girl, you are seriously overdue when it comes to getting your groove on."

"This isn't up for debate, and for your information I am just fine when it comes to getting my groove on." Shelly gave her the look. "Okay, fine, maybe not. But this is not the time to have this discussion. Get rid of him."

"Just go out there," Shelly said.

"No. I can't. I'm not ready, I need to think this through," she whispered.

"See, that's what your problem is, you think too much," Shelly said. Kenya peeked out again. This time Shelly pushed her farther out and closed the door. "Shelly, you are so dead," Kenya threatened.

Trey turned. "Ah, there you are. I was beginning to think you were standing me up."

"Standing you up? What are you talking about? What are you doing here?" she asked as she walked farther out into the front of the shop. She smiled when she saw the twins standing beside him, each holding an animal cracker in their hands.

"Mamma Lou is on her way over and I—"

Kenya walked over to the counter and grabbed tissues from the box. She turned. "I thought you were going to take care of that?"

"Well, obviously I didn't. Besides, weren't you the one who didn't want me to lie to a sweet old lady?"

"That was before," she said, smiling at Jonathan and Johanna as she knelt down and wiped their faces and hands. She looked up at him.

"Before what?" he asked, penetrating into her eyes.

"Never mind," she said, looking away quickly to focus on the twins again. Her stomach quivered. Looking into his eyes was detrimental to her senses.

"Look, all you have to do is pretend for a few hours."

"No," she said and stood up quickly. "I can't."

"Why not? You had no problem with it this morning," Trey asked, reaching down to pick up Johanna.

"That was this morning. Things changed," she said.

"What changed?" he asked as Johanna reached out for her. Kenya smiled and shook her hand playfully.

"This isn't my problem, I have work to do, and I can't do it with you here. So I'm sure you can find your way out?" She turned to leave.

"That's not very hospitable, Kenya," Trey said as he sat Johanna back down on the floor next to Jonathan.

"I don't feel like being very hospitable, Trey," she said sternly.

"Ah, come on, you'd throw two adorable children out on the street?" Trey said as he lowered his bottom lip to pout.

Kenya smiled even though she didn't want to. "I've seen your house, remember? You're not exactly destitute. Bye."

"Hi, again," Shelly said, walking over with a stuffed animal in her hand. "Shelly Turner. I'm Kenya's partner."

"Sorry, Shelly, this is Trey Evans," Kenya said.

They shook hands. "I've heard a lot about you."

"It's a pleasure meeting you, Shelly. Gross exaggerations, don't believe everything you hear," he said, looking directly at Kenya.

"Funny, that's exactly what I always say. A pleasure meeting you, too, Trey."

"The pleasure is all mine, I assure you."

"Listen, do you mind if I show the children our kids' corner? It's just over there. It's enclosed with dozens of toys. I'm interested to see which toys are more entertaining. Call it a focus group survey."

"That won't be necessary, Shelly. Trey and the twins were just leaving and so were you, remember?"

"Oh, I can hang around awhile longer, no problem."

"Of course, Shelly. I think Johanna and Jonathan would be happy to participate in your focus group." Trey handed Shelly the small box of animal crackers.

Shelly leaned down and took each little hand. "It'll give you two a chance to talk privately," she whispered as they walked away.

"Thanks, Shelly," Kenya hissed through gritted teeth. Kenya turned to leave, as well.

"You're just gonna walk away and leave me like this. Isn't there something I can do to persuade you?"

Kenya turned and smiled. She decided to put everything on the table. "Let's cut to the chase, shall we? You obviously know who I am by now. So let's not insult each other's intelligence. You also know what I want from you."

Trey smiled—her directness was refreshing. He liked it. "I do."

"Good, we have that straight. So what are we going to do about it?" she asked.

Trey smiled. "We're both businesspeople. I suggest we come to an amicable understanding."

"Agreed. Give my father back his company, give him back his money and—"

"I'm afraid I can't do that," he interrupted.

"—I won't go to the SEC. End of understanding."

Trey laughed. Her outrageous request and threat took him

off guard. He was right—she was definitely going to be interesting. "I think maybe we can do better than that. What happened to negotiating?"

"That was negotiating," she informed him.

"Middle ground," he offered.

"There is no middle ground."

"There's always a middle ground."

"Not with me," she said firmly.

"I do enjoy a challenge," he stated, smiling.

"As do I," she replied.

"Okay, show of good faith. Help me out this evening and we'll discuss the matter in detail."

"My position would be firmer if I didn't, and we discussed the matter now." She smiled, deciding to take advantage of his need for her cooperation.

"I could come clean and you'd have no position at all," he countered.

Kenya bristled. He'd called her bluff. She turned to walk away.

Trey reached out and took her hand. "Kenya, I need you," he whispered softly. "Please."

She stopped, not because he held her hand, but because she felt his desperation. She wasn't sure if it was real or not. But for the time being, it put her on top again. It was Economics 101, supply and demand. He wanted something from her that only she could provide. Maybe this was her perfect in. Maybe there was a way to get what she wanted. She turned to him and smiled. "It's gonna cost you."

Trey returned her smile; the idea intrigued him. He also noted something had most definitely changed about her attitude. "Exactly what do I get for this cost?"

"Exactly what you asked for," she said. "My time."

"Fair enough. How much?"

"Two thousand, five-hundred fifty dollars," she said quickly before she lost her nerve.

"You're joking, right?"

"Do I look like I'm joking? I'm a businesswoman."

"Exactly what kind of business are you offering?"

"Look, my time is valuable. I'm sure you charge an exorbitant amount for your time, as well. Mine is just as important. If you want me to play nice this evening, then fine, two thousand, five-hundred fifty dollars is the price." He smiled as he considered her offer. "Tick tock, better hurry up," she said, smiling knowingly.

Trey didn't have to consider her offer. He knew he'd accept it. It wasn't the money or Mamma Lou's matchmaking this time that prompted his decision. It was the growing interest in a woman who obviously thought she played the game as well as him. What gave him pause was what she thought she was doing.

But he needed to be careful. Dumb luck. There was no set name for a novice chess player checkmating a master, or a seasoned fighter being knocked out by an amateur. But it happened. Her father was proof of that.

"So what do you think you know about me, Kenya?"

She smiled. There was a connection building. She knew they both felt it. "Quite a bit actually. You have a way of making news."

"That's unavoidable in my line of work," he offered.

"Ah, but it was your personal life that I found much more interesting—the parties, the women, the parties, the women. Shall I continue? It was a very detailed file."

"Let me guess, the Internet."

"That was one source. You like to play by your own rules."

"I play by the rules that were in place long before I came along."

"So you're saying that everything they say and what's

written in the press—the Iceman, coldhearted businessman, bachelor playboy…that not you?"

"Some of it is, some of it isn't. But that's not all there is to me. The rest you'll have to find out for yourself," he said softly, moving closer.

"I don't deal with bad-boys who have Peter Pan complexes. Been there, done that, never again. So you can save the charm thing. In case you haven't noticed, I'm not feeling it."

"You did this morning," he whispered.

She knew he was talking about her reaction to the kiss. She looked up at him. The depth in his eyes went straight through her. An overwhelming swell of heat began to generate deep inside her body. Her heart thundered and her stomach fluttered. She was on the verge of backing away, but then she caught herself. "Don't flatter yourself, Trey, I've been kissed before. You kissing me was really no big deal."

"Ah, but I think it was. There was something about the look in your eyes afterward. You see, that's my business, I read people. My job is to know and study tells. Like poker, it's not always what people say that's important."

He was obviously trying to bait her again. But unlike this morning, now she was prepared. She took a deep breath, then let it out, slow and easy. He wasn't going to do this to her again. She knew his game and she intended to play to win. There was no shyness or hesitation in her, not this time. She was ready for him. "So what am I saying now?" she asked.

"I'd say right now, you were bluffing."

"Is that right? Are you certain?" she asked, arching her brow. He nodded with assurance. She smirked. The idea of getting him back and beating him at his own game hit her instantly. On impulse, before a second passed, she leaned in quickly and kissed him.

As their lips met, an explosion of passion erupted. The kiss was force meeting force. Her hands reached up to hold his neck firmly in place. He leaned back against the counter and she molded her body against him. She felt his body respond in needful earnestness. He had something she wanted and she intended to get it. She opened her mouth to him, leading him exactly where she wanted him to go. He followed willingly.

When the kiss ended, she remained pressed against him and looked boldly into his eyes. His stunned bewilderment amused her. She had taken him by surprise just as he'd done to her earlier that day.

"How does it feel to not be so sure of yourself?" she asked. He laughed and nodded. "Seems you're not as good as you think you are." She moved to step back. He instantly pulled her back against his body, locking her in place with his strong arms. She felt the hardness of his desire reach out to her. She liked the sensation.

"Actually I am," he said, feeling her shudder.

"Do you ever get tired of being so sure of yourself?"

"I could ask you the same question."

"You like doing this, don't you?" she asked.

"What, this...? This is just playful banter," he said, loosening his grip on her body.

"Aw, now you're taking the fun out of this," she said. "It's not banter."

"And what would you call this?" he asked.

"This would be called foreplay, so I guess you'd better take notes." His eyes sparked. Kenya nearly shivered as the words left her mouth. She knew exactly what she was saying. She just hoped she knew what she was doing.

"I stand corrected," he said, licking his lips, tasting her again. The lights dimmed, then brightened, then fluttered. They looked up. "What was that?" he asked.

"That was a two-thousand-five-hundred-fifty-dollar invoice."

"Ah, so that's why you want the money," he said, releasing her fully.

She took a step back. "Yes, that's why I want the money."

"Check, cash or credit card?" he asked.

"Cash," she said. He pulled out his wallet and gave her the money. "Thanks." She took the money and put it in her jeans pocket. "Okay, Trey, for the next three hours, I'm all yours. So this is your party. When do we start?"

Trey glanced up to see Louise Gates looking up at the address. "I'd say now is as good a time as any." He pulled her back into his arms and kissed her. Just as her mind was turning to mush, he stopped and smiled. "We're on."

Chapter 7

The gentle knock on the door turned her head. An elderly couple stood smiling. On wobbly legs, Kenya walked over and opened the door. Her mind was still rattled, so putting distance between them was the perfect escape. "Hello, hello, hello," Louise greeted as she hugged the still-rattled Kenya.

"Good evening, all," Colonel Wheeler added, taking his cap off as he entered the building.

"Hi. Welcome," Kenya finally said. "Please come in."

Trey walked over and greeted the couple.

"Where are my little ones, Jonathan, Johanna?"

Two little heads popped up. Shelly stood from the tiny desk and chair and helped the twins get to their feet. She took their hands and walked them back to the front area.

"Hello, my darlings," Louise said, beaming at the sight of the twins running to her with papers flying. They grabbed her legs and she leaned down and kissed the tops of their heads.

"What do you have there?" Trey quickly reached down and scooped both up in his arms. He gently placed them on the wooden countertop and held them tightly.

They offered Louise their crayon-scribbled drawings. "Oh, my, did you two do these? I love them," Louise said as she hugged the two. Their little arms grabbed her tightly.

"Hey, what do you have there?" Colonel Wheeler asked, being offered a crayon from Jonathan.

Kenya moved as a smiling Shelly walked over. Kenya glared at her knowing that she must have witnessed the kiss a few minutes ago. "Groove on, my sistah," she whispered.

Kenya bumped her with her hip. "Mamma Lou, Colonel Wheeler, this is my friend and business partner, Shelly Turner."

"Hello. How are you, Mr. and Mrs. Gates," Shelly said as she shook their hands.

"Actually, Shelly—" Trey began to clarify.

"It's Louise Gates and Otis Wheeler," Kenya corrected.

"For the time being," Otis added, smiling at Louise.

Trey, never one to miss a hint, instantly picked up on his remark. He also noted the twinkle in Colonel Wheeler's eyes as he said it. There was something going on, he easily surmised. Maybe he wasn't the target after all.

"Oh, I'm sorry," Shelly said, looking slightly embarrassed.

"Not at all, but call me Mamma Lou, dear, everyone does," Louise said sweetly.

"And Colonel Wheeler here," he said.

"Well, it was good meeting you both, but I have to go or I'll be late for the theater."

"The theater?" Louise said.

"Yes, we do work for the local children's theater company when they need us."

"We?" Trey asked with interest.

"Yes, Shelly and I design costumes and help with scenery.

The childrens' theater is like our pet project. We donate our time," Kenya said.

"Plus, we just all have a lot of fun. It's very rewarding."

"I bet. How wonderful," Louise said.

"We enjoy helping out and the kids get a kick out of the costumes we design. They're putting on a production of *Peter and the Wolf.* And if I don't hurry, I'll be late. So I'd better get going. Again, it was great meeting you all, Mamma Lou, Colonel Wheeler, Trey. Bye, guys," she said to Jonathan and Johanna. They waved and said bye.

Kenya followed Shelly to the door. They stood quietly talking a few moments before she left. After locking the door Kenya sighed. She wasn't sure what she'd gotten herself into. She didn't realize this little game was going to get so complicated. Well, she was stuck now, so she might as well get it over with. She turned, ready to continue with the pretense.

"Well, I'm curious," Louise said as she looked around the open space. "I want to see everything. Tell me, do you actually design all of the clothes for the store?"

"Yes, we both will."

"So Shelly's a designer, too?" Colonel Wheeler asked, holding a twin in each arm. They laid their heads on his shoulder, making the sweetest picture.

"Yes. We have our workroom in the back."

"Can I persuade you to give us a brief tour?"

"Sure," she said, "but truthfully, there's not much to see really. Shelly and I just moved into the building a couple of weeks ago. It still needs a lot of work and sometimes it feels like the place is about to fall down around us. But the rent is perfect and the location is just what we were looking for."

"Did you consider renting a storefront in a shopping center?" Trey asked. "The foot traffic is constant and there is always security."

"Actually, no, we didn't, not really. This is a great part of town. There are three elementary schools in the area and dozens of day-care centers. Plus it's right by the Metro stop. It's a mommy-and-me haven."

"Yes, that does make a lot of sense. Plus the area is just starting to come back," Colonel Wheeler said.

"Exactly," Kenya added as she turned toward the workroom. Everyone followed. "Being a pioneer in an urban renaissance is a tremendous opportunity. We're excited about being here." She opened the door and held it. Louise, Colonel Wheeler and the twins entered the large open space.

Trey followed and nodded his head, obviously impressed by her business savvy. As he passed, Kenya looked into his eyes. She wasn't sure what she saw, but something was definitely there. He leaned in too close. His arm brushed against her breasts. "Thank you," he whispered. His warm breath tickled her neck and made her stomach flutter.

"Oh, my," Louise said, drawing Kenya's attention away from Trey.

"Sorry, it's not usually this messy," Kenya said and quickly picked up scraps of fabric from the floor. She'd forgotten all about the mess they made earlier. She folded one of the ironing boards and put bottles of silk-screen paint back on the shelf above the sink.

"Oh, don't mind us, Kenya. We know that the creative process is exciting no matter how you find it. The place looks wonderful. It's exhilarating."

"I agree, I'm stimulated just being here," Trey said, smiling. He stood between a mannequin and a dress form and watched Kenya in the wall-to-ceiling mirrors.

Kenya glared at him as she moved to the other side of the room. She needed to get as far away from him and his boyish charm as possible. "Shelly and I have been working on some new designs."

"For the opening?" Louise asked.

"No, those are already done. These are all for next season. We're still in the process of designing and cutting patterns. It's a slow, tedious process. Not at all like it seems on those television design shows."

"I can just imagine," Louise said. "May I?"

"Yes, of course, help yourself."

Louise, with Colonel Wheeler by her side, began looking over Kenya and Shelly's drawings. Floor-to-ceiling sketches were secured to the wall. There were dozens. Some were of hats or socks or belts. Others had notations written on them, some had complicated instructions. Some drawings were fully completed and colored, while others merely quick design sketches.

"These are marvelous," Louise said.

"Indeed. They're an art form all their own," Colonel Wheeler added.

"Thank you," Kenya said. Trey still looked at the illustrations, observing them more closely. He didn't say anything. Kenya found herself more than anxious and actually caring what he thought about their work. When he finally turned, he was smiling. She was relieved, smiled, then quickly looked away.

Louise finished looking at the design sketches on the wall and moved to the drawing table. She glanced at the open sketch pad. Colonel Wheeler, still holding the twins, stood behind her.

Sketches and completed design illustrations were scattered and spread out across the work area. "These are all so wonderfully different—the dresses, the skirts, sweatsuits, pants. The designs are so playful and fun, absolutely marvelous."

"I like experimenting. I think it adds excitement to everything."

"It does, to everything," Trey whispered in her ear. She

spared him a quick glance. He smiled seductively. She turned and ignored him as she inched away.

"Where do you find inspiration?" Colonel Wheeler asked.

"All over the place," she said. "It's mostly visualizing. For example, sometimes I'll see a shape, usually something ordinary, and I imagine it differently. I vary colors and fabrics or even try different positions to make it more exciting."

"Different positions, is that right? That's good to know," Trey whispered only to her. Kenya didn't even look at him this time. She already knew he was smiling.

They continued talking about the drawings as Trey continued with his seemingly innocent comments that Kenya knew were anything but. She moved away easily, following Louise as she and Colonel Wheeler walked around the two larger cutting tables. He walked toward her, his eyes dead on his target. They eventually maneuvered their way toward the wall where the forms were lined up on the platform.

"These are absolutely darling," Louise said admiringly. "Is this your new line for next season?"

"Yes, Shelly and I are very proud of it. Of course, these are just a few of the pieces. There are others already at our manufacturer."

"Where do you have the garments manufactured?" Colonel Wheeler asked.

"We use a place in Southern California. They're a bit more expensive but the clothes are sewn better and it's not a sweatshop."

"Yes, that is important. People should not have to work in conditions that are deplorable," Colonel Wheeler said.

"I agree. Years ago my great-grandmother was a seamstress in a sweatshop. She was nearly killed when she brought the union in and changed things. Shelly and I are particular about who we do business with."

"Good for you," Colonel Wheeler said.

"These pieces are absolutely adorable," Louise said.

"They are really nice," Trey added as he left her side and actually stood by one of the garments.

"So where did you attend school?" Colonel Wheeler asked.

"New York. Shelly and I were roommates at Parsons. We'd sit up late and talk about the boutique we were going to open someday."

"And here it is. When exactly is the grand opening?" Colonel Wheeler asked.

"We're still a few months away. We have a lot of cosmetic work to do. It's an old building, but as I said, it's a great location."

"Would you look at these," Louise said of the two antique sewing machines. "They're fantastic. Would you believe that I actually had one like that years and years ago?"

"Looks like they've been around a long time," Colonel Wheeler said.

"Yes, they're very old."

"Do you still use them?" Trey asked.

"They still work, believe it or not, but no, now they're just for inspiration. This one belonged to my great-grandmother, then my grandmother gave it to me. And that one belonged to Shelly's grandmother."

"Is that what got you started in the design business?"

"Probably. I remember my grandmother using this machine when I was a kid. I'd watch her for hours, cutting patterns and sewing on this old thing."

"Well, this is a wonderful shop and you and Shelly are very talented designers. I can see you having great success here," Louise said.

"Yes, yes, I completely agree," Colonel Wheeler added.

"I hope so," Kenya said. "We're trying hard."

"You will," Trey seemed to promise.

"So that's about it, end of tour."

Louise, with Colonel Wheeler carrying the sleeping twins, went back into the front area, leaving Trey and Kenya behind. "Mamma Lou's right, you are extremely talented."

Kenya looked at him suspiciously. "Wow, that's a bit disconcerting. If I didn't know any better, I'd say you were actually sincere."

"I am."

"A compliment," she joked, but the look in his eyes showed nothing but genuineness. She paused. "Thank you."

"You're welcome." They stood smiling a moment until Trey reached up and stroked the length of her face. "There's something about you."

"What?" she asked, leaning away nervously, then taking a step back.

"You don't have to back away from me, Kenya. I wasn't going to kiss you again."

"I'm not… I mean, I didn't expect—" she began, then moved back more, edging dangerously close to the pointed angle on the sewing machine table.

"Careful," Trey said as he grabbed her to him before she backed into the point. He held her close. "Looks like I just saved your life."

"Oh, really," she declared.

"Yes," he whispered as he tipped her chin up with his finger. "Yes," he repeated as his mouth descended. "In some cultures, that means you owe me your life." His head tilted as their lips nearly touched.

"Good thing we don't live in one of those cultures."

"Don't we? So what exactly are you up to, Kenya?"

"Telling you wouldn't be much fun, would it?" she said knowingly.

He shook his head. "I can't figure you."

"Is that a bad thing?"

"For me, yeah, it is," he said.

"No control, off balance and flying blind, not your style, huh?"

He nodded. "Something like that. You walk into my life and in one day turn it upside down."

"Maybe your life needed to be turned upside down."

He considered her assessment a second then smiled.

"Trey," Louise called out from the front.

"We're coming," he said, leaning back. "After you."

"No, you go. I need to finish picking up a few things." She turned to pick up a fabric bolt lying on the table. She shifted and slid it to the opposite side then hurried to grab it. Putting the width of the cutting table between them seemed to not be adequate enough. She looked up just as he walked toward the front room. Relief washed over her.

It seemed that they were both in the same boat. She was just as off balance as he was. She gathered a few scraps and picked up a spool of thread that had fallen and unfurled. Finally regaining her composure, she went out front. Colonel Wheeler, Trey and the twins were gone and Louise stood at the door.

"You're leaving so soon?" she asked.

"Yes, Kenya, we're going to leave now and let you get home before it gets too late. It was wonderful getting to know you. You are a gem. I must say, Trey has certainly done me proud."

"How so?" she asked curiously.

"He didn't tell you." Kenya shook her head. "I'll let you in on a little secret. The only thing I've ever known Trey Evans to be uneasy about is me."

"You… What do you mean?"

"Trey is an intelligent, very competent and very successful businessman who's smart as a whip about most things. But when it comes to love, he's a babe in the woods."

"I don't know about that," Kenya said.

"Oh, he pretends to be the playboy type, but really he's just a good guy playing a part. He's a kindhearted, generous man. But, of course, I don't have to tell you that. He has a heart as big as the whole outdoors. He just doesn't want anyone to know it."

"He keeps it well-hidden."

"Yes, he does indeed. There's only one thing that seems to unnerve him and that's my matchmaking."

"Oh, I see," Kenya said, finally understanding her role. "Trey's afraid of commitment."

"Oh, no, I wouldn't quite say that he's afraid of commitment. But you, my dear, have captured his attention and possibly—in my professional opinion—his heart."

"Me and Trey, no," Kenya said quickly.

"Oh, yes, I think so and I'm never wrong about these things. Between us girls, I'd say he's—"

"We're ready," Colonel Wheeler said as he opened the front door. Louise and Kenya turned. "All set?"

"Yes," Louise said, then hugged Kenya. "Thank you, dear, we thoroughly enjoyed ourselves."

"Me, too. Please stop by anytime you're in the neighborhood." Kenya led Louise to the door. She waited and watched Colonel Wheeler walk her out. The sight of them together was heartwarming. It made her wonder if she'd ever be blessed to have a man in her life. One who adored her as much as Colonel Wheeler adored Mamma Lou.

She considered her parents' marriage. It had been strained as long as she could remember. Her father's gambling addiction made it almost impossible to believe in him. Hence, she had grown up distrustful of men and always expected the worst of them.

She wondered about Trey. Everything she read about him all pointed to the same thing. He was coldhearted and uncaring. But Mamma Lou saw someone completely different. Maybe Mamma Lou was the exception. She was sure that a grandmother would always see the best in their grandchildren, even when they didn't deserve it. Her grandmother did. She always said that her father would come through. She was right, he did. Then he didn't.

Trey walked over to her. "Thanks."

"You're welcome. Just doing my job," she said.

"Your job… Oh, right, I almost forgot."

"I guess my acting skills were pretty good after all," Kenya said, thinking about her sister's recent comment.

"I'd better go. We'll talk. Good night."

She nodded. He turned and strolled to his car. She waved as both cars pulled away and drove off down the street. She sighed and locked the door.

"What a day," she muttered, more from amazement then exhaustion. There was no way she would have thought when the day began that it would end like this. But at least it was over. Everyone was gone and she was back where she started. She went into the workroom and began cleaning up again.

As she picked up scraps and swept the floor, she thought about Trey. This morning he was cold and impassive. But this evening, he was so different. It wasn't his grandmother's presence, because he was just as stilted with her earlier. So what had changed?

Of course, she had no idea. She smiled, remembering how he followed her around the room earlier whispering seductive and suggestive comments in her ear. She blushed at one particular remark that included painting her with chocolate then licking it off. Her smile broadened as she continued working and thinking about him. He was definitely an enigma. But she needed to stay focused.

A half hour later she was getting ready to leave when she

heard knocking on the front door. She cautiously walked to the front.

"Who is it?" she asked.

"Trey."

She hesitated a second, then unlocked the door. He stood there, half smiling. "What are you doing here, Trey? Where are the twins?"

"I realized I still have an hour and twenty minutes."

"What?" she asked.

"My time's not up."

"Actually, it is." She paused and swallowed hard. "You know what I want. I suggest you seriously consider my position." She began closing the door.

"Surrendering so soon. I'm disappointed," he said.

She opened the door again. "This isn't surrender, this is nonnegotiable." Trey smiled amorously. "And if you think your charm is gonna get you off the hook or into my panties, you're very wrong."

"Interesting offer. Is that a dare?" he asked.

"That wasn't an offer. This is business, nothing more."

"If I remember correctly, Whitakers don't play fair when it comes to business."

"You know you have a lot of nerve coming back here. You swindled my father out of his company and stole his money and you think you can charm your way out of it. I don't think so."

Trey's jaw dropped. "Sweetheart, I've been called a lot of things in business, but never a swindler."

"Maybe others don't know your true nature as I do."

"Or maybe you've been misinformed."

"Are you calling my father a liar?"

"I'm saying that you need to get your facts straight before you hurl accusations. Now if you want to discuss your father's actions over the last six months, I'll be happy to. In the meantime, I suggest you speak with you father and get the story straight."

She knew she was being baited, but she had no intention of responding. "Good night, Trey." She closed the door.

She walked back into the workroom and gathered her things. What was she doing? What was she thinking? All this craziness had gotten to her. She'd lost her temper. Now how was she going to get into his house to help her father? Who was she fooling? She couldn't sneak into a man's house and steal information. As soon as she picked up her purse her cell phone rang. Now what? "Hello?"

"Hi, sweetheart," Lynette said.

"Mom, hi, how are you? How's the trip?"

"Fantastic, we're having a great time. Cape Town is a dream. The colors are so vibrant. I'm so glad we have this opportunity to come here. It's more beautiful than I imagined. The people, the culture, the country, it's all so incredible. I wish you could see it."

"Maybe one day, Mom. Isn't it late there?"

"We're six hours ahead of you so yes, I guess it is late. I think my internal clock is still off. I couldn't sleep and I wanted to make sure everything was okay there."

"We're all fine. I spoke to Asia this afternoon and stopped by to see Sidney this morning. I'm glad you're having a wonderful time and I'm glad you called. How's Dad?"

"He's fine. As a matter of fact he's talking to Sidney. Hold on, we'll switch. But while I have you on the phone I sent you a few things to the house. The hand-dyed fabric here is breathtaking. I send you a few bolts."

"Thanks, Mom, I'll make sure to stop by the house to pick it up."

"Oh, and don't forget, we're headed out on safari day after

tomorrow and cell-phone reception isn't very good, so don't worry if you don't hear from us. We'll be fine."

"Okay, Mom. Did you talk to Dad more about the money?"

"Yes, we talked."

"Did he explain more about what happened? I mean, none of this makes sense. Why didn't he go to the SEC?"

"It's not that simple, Kenya. There's more to this than you know."

"Then tell me. What else is there?"

"I know your father wants to put a villainous face on his troubles, but the truth is just not that simple."

"Is he there?"

"Hold on, here's your father now."

A few seconds later her father got on the phone. "Hello."

"Dad, hi," Kenya said.

"Kenya, you're missing a great trip."

"Yeah, that's what Mom said. I'm glad you're having a good time. But there's something important I really need to talk to you about."

"Sure, what is it? Problems with the shop?"

"No, everything's good there. It's this money."

"Kenya, I told you, don't concern yourself with it. I'll take care of it when we get back."

"Dad, I already know that you were investing with Trey Evans. I need to know what happened exactly. You said that they stole money from you."

"Yes," he said plainly.

"How?"

James sighed. "After we invested with them, I realized that it wouldn't be easy to liquidate my assets. I needed funds for ventures I'd been working on. The idea of going to them and begging for my own money each time was ridiculous. I wanted it back. But there was a clause in the contract that I hadn't noticed. It's called a transmittal designation. It allowed them to transfer money out of the account at their discretion."

"What, so they just transferred the money out of your account? How can they just do that? It's illegal. So you confronted him about getting the money back, right?"

"Yes, of course. But he denied everything."

"So he just lied to you."

"Yes," James said. "He stood in his office and assured me that the money was all still in my account and that the investments the firm was making on my behalf were all sound and secure."

"But they weren't," Kenya said as a cold chill inched down her back. How could she be so gullible as to actually believe him? Her heart thundered. The idea that a so-called reputable firm could just steal from its clients was infuriating. And to think she was just starting to buy in to Trey's good-guy image. She felt her anger burn inside her. How could she be such a fool again? This was becoming the story of her life, misjudging and believing the wrong men.

"What happened then? What did you do?"

"I needed out of the contract so I talked to some other people."

"Who—the SEC?" she asked.

"None of them," he said.

"You didn't call them? Why not?"

"I just wanted access to the rest of the money. So I got together with Cal. He had an idea for a mortgage company. I knew the idea was a good one, plus it solved my problem with Trey. Cal needed investors so I signed on. According to my contract with Trey, I could withdraw the rest of the money for a major business investment."

"That's when you started working with Cal."

"Yes. When Trey found out he was adamantly against it. He

told me not to do it, but I could see it was a good investment. So with Cal's help, we got out of the contract with TE Acquisitions."

"Good, you don't have any investments with them at all," Kenya said.

"Yes and no. The account is closed, but they held on to a portion of the funds. It's called a DR allowance fund."

"A DR allowance. What's that?"

"It's a discretionary retirement fund. Your mother opened one with them before any of this happened."

"So Mom still has money invested with them? Why? After everything that happened with you? I don't understand."

"They can't withdraw from that account. It can only be added to."

"So if the DR allowance is a retirement fund, why would he care about holding on to your retirement account?" Kenya asked, more to herself than to her father.

"Your mother convinced me to let it go and let him hold it. After I invested in the company, I found out that Trey had also invested in the company. He had invested almost as much as I had. I knew what it meant."

"What?" she asked, having no idea.

"That's how he operates. He grabs a few shares then a few more until you realize that he holds the majority shares in your company. Cal confirmed that he stole his father's company without even a second thought. I wasn't about to let that happen."

"But why would he want your company? He makes millions."

"I believe it's a power thing with him. He can't resist a challenge."

"So you're saying that you posed a threat," she asked.

"I did a lot of research on Trey Evans and TE Acquisitions. I saw an opportunity."

"What do you mean an opportunity?" she asked.

"I found a way to outmaneuver him and buy a stake in his

firm. It was all just business. I was going to use it as leverage and keep him out."

"Dad, don't tell me that you went after Trey's company."

"It was just business. I wanted control," he insisted. "I saw an opportunity, that's all. It happens all the time."

"So what happened then?"

"Trey found out and offered Cal money to buy him out."

"Let me guess, Cal sold his portion to Trey."

"Yes, with what he already had, plus Cal's shares, Trey Evans is now the majority holder in my company."

"He stole your company. That's what you meant when you said it was gone. You don't actually own all of it anymore. Trey does, at least the majority of it. So the money's not all gone, it's just tied up."

"Exactly, but as the majority stock holder, Trey can decide to sell the company for as little as five dollars if he wants. All he has to do is give me a percentage and it would still be legal."

"He wouldn't do that to you, Dad."

"He did it to his father's company, so let me take care of this."

"But, Dad—"

"Kenya, let me handle this. Just wait until I get back. I'll take care of everything. Remember, your mother always says, nothing ever came from being angry and not thinking first."

"Fine." She lied to her father for the first time.

Chapter 8

But it wasn't fine. She had no intention of sitting back and doing nothing. Trey owed her father and she intended to make him pay him back. Shelly thought Kenya was joking, but now she was serious. She wanted to hurt Trey, just like he hurt her father.

Furious after her phone conversation, she got into her car and drove to Trey's. She had no idea what she was going to say or do. She just knew that she had to do something. She looked up at the Woodley Park home. This is where it all started. So the idea of coming back here made her uneasy. The one good thing was Trey had no idea what she intended to do. Unfortunately, neither did she.

She reached up to press the doorbell but stopped herself. She was opening a Pandora's box. Trey was too good at this. Plus, he stirred feelings inside her that she wasn't sure she wanted to control.

I can do this, I can do this, she thought to herself. *This is business, nothing else. I can do this.* But doubt quickly surfaced. Maybe this wasn't such a good idea. She was too angry. Mistakes happen when you're emotional. She needed a moment to think clearly and calmly. She turned to leave but then stopped.

He would expect her to be angry and hostile, like their last meeting. But as her mother always said, "Nothing ever came from being angry and not thinking first." She was absolutely right. An offer of honey would be unexpected. She needed to be amenable. There was nothing more devastating than an unexpected stab in the back. She turned when she heard the door open. Trey was fully dressed, this time in jeans and a shirt. "Hi," she said softly.

"Hi," he repeated.

She took a deep breath.... *Cold, unfeeling, emotionless.* "I stopped by—" She paused and swallowed hard. "I wanted to know if you found a nanny for the twins."

He nodded. "Yes, she starts tomorrow morning."

"And tonight?" she asked calmly.

"So are you back to being a nanny again?" he asked.

"No, but if you needed help, I was going to offer my baby-sitting services." *Stay focused, stay businesslike.*

"No need. The twins are out for the evening," Trey answered.

"Oh, I see." She nodded, curious as to where they were. "Back with their mother, I assume?"

"No, Madi's still away."

"I see." He didn't offer any more explanations so she didn't ask any more questions.

"Is there anything else?" he asked.

"No...well, yes, I want to apologize about earlier. I was rude. The things I said were out of anger and spite. I shouldn't have attacked you like that, I'm sorry."

"Apology accepted." He smiled easily.

Kenya was surprised by the quick acceptance. "That's it, just like that, apology accepted."

"I don't hold grudges. It's pointless." The charm was most definitely back.

"You realize that I'm not apologizing for what I intend to do to you," she said. He nodded, still smiling. "Make no mistake, Trey, I'm going to get my father's company back, and if ruining you in the process is what it takes, then so be it," she promised soundly, with unwavering determination.

Trey chuckled. A threat like that would usually give him cause for concern, at the very least put him on guard. But for reasons he couldn't begin to fathom, he welcomed her challenge. As a matter of fact, he wouldn't have it any other way. "Then let the games begin."

Cold, emotionless, unfeeling. She nodded then took a step back to leave. "Okay, well, so much for small talk. Good night."

"Wait," he called to her, "have you eaten yet? I just cooked a late dinner."

She smiled slyly, not too surprised that he'd called her back. "You cooked… You can cook?"

"I'm a very good cook," he declared.

She chuckled. "Really?"

"Yeah, come on in."

Yes! "So what is this, part of the 'keep your enemies closer' strategy?"

"Actually it's the 'I'm hungry and I hate to eat alone' strategy."

"Uh-huh, we'll see." She stepped inside and looked around. Other than the foyer and dining room, the house lights were dimmed. She walked toward the living room. The large area, softened by low lights, glowed with the muted blaze of the fireplace. Soft music flowed all around her. The setting was pure seduction. It was as if he'd been expecting someone. "Were you busy?"

"No."

"Expecting someone?" she asked. He smiled too wide and too bright. The knowing glint in his eyes told her everything. "You knew I'd come tonight?" He chuckled. "You do have a tendency to be very sure of yourself, don't you?" He began chuckling again. She looked around more carefully. The place was pure seduction. "You don't really think I'm going to sleep with you, the man who stole my father's company, do you?"

"Did I say that?" he asked.

"You didn't have to," she muttered. "The smirk is all over your face. You are so full of yourself."

Trey laughed out loud. "Come on into the kitchen, dinner's almost ready." He led. She followed. As soon as she entered, she smelled a heavenly aroma. "Have a seat. Can I get you something to drink?"

"Sure, thanks," she said.

"Champagne?" he offered as he grabbed another glass, filled it then handed it to her.

"Champagne? Are you celebrating?"

"It's Perrier-Jouet. It's perfect with this dish."

"The flower bottle, I know. I once got a bottle as a thank-you gift for a gown I designed."

"Must have been a really nice gown," he said.

"It was."

"But I thought you designed only for children."

"I do primarily, but once in a while the opportunity presents itself."

"I see. You're an opportunist."

"Aren't we all?" she stated.

He nodded.

"So what are you cooking?" she asked as she sat down at the counter. "Whatever it is, it smells incredible."

"Thanks, it's just pasta, something simple."

"You mean a can of spaghetti, right?" she asked.

"Actually it's grilled chicken with portabello mushrooms in a wine-and-cheese sauce over linguini." Kenya chuckled. Trey nodded sincerely.

She got up, walked around to the front of the stove, picked up the lid and inhaled. "Ohh, you gotta be kidding me. You cooked this?"

"Yes," Trey said.

"No, seriously," she said. "Not frozen, freeze-dried or takeout. You actually sliced mushrooms and everything?" He nodded. "Because I once dated this guy who supposedly cooked dinner for me, but I saw the takeout boxes in the trash can. He even had a pot of water boiling on the stove that he borrowed from his stepmom."

"You're not very trusting, are you?"

"Should I be, given our relationship?"

"Touché. By all means, check the trash can," he offered.

"No, that's okay, I believe you."

"No, you don't. You don't trust me."

She wanted to tell him that she didn't trust herself with him but she didn't. "You have questionable practices."

"Are you referring to business or personal?"

"Both, but let's talk personal for a minute."

"Sure, what would you like to know?" he asked.

"Actually, it's what I already know. You're a saint, a sinner, an angel, a devil, a philanthropist and, my personal favorite, a serial dater."

Trey chuckled through the entire list. "I need to update my profile. But wait, a serial dater, what's that?"

"It's a man who dates frequently, but after a few dates he dumps them, moves on, leaving a trail of broken hearts."

"Wow, you make it sound pretty bad."

"Yes, it is. So why do you treat women like that?"

"Honestly, I don't believe I do. Yes, I date often. And I'm smart enough to know what I want and don't want."

"You're saying that what you do to women is a good thing?"

"I'm saying women do it all the time. They date lots of men and they try to change, manipulate or improve them only to find out that it doesn't work. So they go out and start all over again. One date is enough to let me know if I want to be with a person. No wasted time, no expended energy. One date and I know. I don't want to change anyone into what I want. I accept people at face value, and go from there."

Kenya listened to his explanation and found herself agreeing. In all honesty, he made a good point. Spending time trying to change someone into something else was a waste. She knew dozens of women who did just that, and then complained when it happened to them.

"Maybe we should talk about something else. Tell me about the twins, you and their mother."

He nodded. "What do you want to know?"

"I know you're not married, so are the two of you still together or not?"

"The two of us… Oh, I get it. The twins aren't mine. They're my cousin's children. I'm babysitting."

"You're babysitting." She sighed, relieved. "Wait, but why? Who would do that? Let's face it, you're the last person I'd ask to babysit."

"Did you just insult me?"

Kenya laughed. "Come on, you're not exactly father knows best. You're a disaster. How in the world did you get tapped?"

"I probably shouldn't tell you."

"Tell me what?"

"You'd probably think we're all certifiable."

"Now you have to tell me."

"I lost a poker game. The last pot had babysitting in it. My cousin and her husband had to go out of town and I volunteered, called in my own marker to help out."

"What? And they let you?"

"They trust me," he said simply. "Trust is important in my family." Kenya took a sip of wine. The sincerity of his answer made her feel guilty. She was there for one reason and that was to find a way to hurt him—so much for trust. "Are you okay? You got quiet on me."

She smiled weakly. "I'm fine, just thinking."

Trey nodded, seeing her pensive expression. He decided to change the subject. "So, Kenya, do you cook...can you cook?"

"I can when I have to, but I'd rather not. I bake."

"Bake, like cakes and cookies?" he asked.

"Breads mostly. I love the smell of baked bread. It comforts me. My grandmother and Mom baked bread all the time. I'd sit in the kitchen and do my homework. I'm pretty sure that's what got me through algebra. I hated math."

"I loved math."

"I know. You're incredibly smart at both math and business. You're an insatiable reader, and your knowledge of capital markets and economic trends is unparalleled. An entrepreneur at a young age, you worked for your father at his company before striking out on your own. Undergrad at Georgetown, masters at Berkeley, then there's GWU and Wharton. You're six foot two inches, green eyes, black hair with no discernable markings." By this time Trey had turned to her.

"Discernable markings?" he queried.

"Tattoos. Did I miss anything?"

"No, that was impressive," he said. "Although my eyes are more hazel than green."

She nodded. "I'll make sure to make a note of that."

They laughed as Trey plated the food. Moments later he served dinner and added more champagne to her glass. They ate, laughed, talked and joked. She found out that he was born in Philadelphia and was a huge Eagles fan. She being a Redskins fan, they talked about football at length. She helped him clear the table and dried as he washed the dishes by hand.

"It's going to be a shame when I take you down."

"Still think you will?"

"Of course. I have no doubt."

"Interesting, very interesting," he said.

"Don't you have a dishwasher in this huge kitchen?"

"Yes, of course. But I seldom use it. It's usually only me."

"He cooks, he cleans, he babysits for family. What else does he do?"

"He offers dessert," Trey said. "You up for ice cream?" he asked.

She nodded then sighed heavily. This was wrong. Everything she read about him pointed to the fact that he was cool-blooded and calculating. But here he was scooping up chocolate ice cream for dessert and adding whipped cream and cherries. The contradictions were dizzying.

"Come on. Dessert is best in the living room."

"Chocolate ice cream and whipped cream, is this how you seduce all your women?"

"Of course."

"Does it work?" she asked. He smiled. "Never mind."

She followed and sat down on the sofa beside him. They ate ice cream and talked about music. He liked big bands. They joked that he had been born at least eighty years too late. They talked about politics and history and ended up talking about books they'd read.

When the conversation wound down, Kenya shook her head, completely stumped. "So why are you doing this, Trey?"

"What do you mean? Doing what?" he asked.

"This, being so nice and normal," she said.

"What did you expect exactly?"

Kenya shook her head. "Either you are the most talented actor in the world or you have terrible PR."

"You're talking about all the things you've read and heard about me?" he asked. She nodded. "Business is business. I make no apologies. I'm just a man doing what he enjoys. There are rules that I operate by and never break."

"What are your rules?"

"Let's not talk business," he offered, knowing that he wasn't ready for her to show her hand and end this game they were playing. "You know about me, now tell me about you. Do you have brothers or sisters?"

"My mom and dad are away traveling. I have two sisters, both younger. One lives in New York. She's an actress and the other is an international affairs major in her last semester at George Washington University."

"Impressive. My younger sister also went to GWU."

"You have a sister?"

"Aha, something you didn't know about me. Amazing. I also have two half brothers, several cousins, not to mention a few very impressive friends in high places. Impressed?" he asked. She laughed. "So does that make me more human or just less of a monster?"

"I never called you a monster."

"Just a thief and a swindler," he said.

"Both well-founded."

"You believe what you read, what you hear."

"When it's from a reliable source, yeah, I do. I guess I needed to get to know the real Trey Evans, decide for myself."

"And what do you think about him so far?" he asked. On impulse, she leaned over and kissed him sweetly. "I thought you wanted to chill on that, strictly business."

She smiled and leaned back. "I think I changed my mind."

He held his hand out to her. She grasped it and was pulled toward his body instantly. He kissed her, sealing his mouth to hers in one smooth action. She melted into his embrace, molding her body to his. To be wrapped securely in his arms was exactly what she wanted. She enfolded her arms around his neck and held him tightly. The kiss, hot and passionate, burned deep into her body.

Pressed hard, his body felt like coming home. Her thoughts whirled in dizzying directions. What was she doing? She'd just met this man and already here she was wrapping her body around his. She was losing herself as her body betrayed her. She wanted him as much as he wanted her.

There was a hunger. There was lust and there was an attraction that could no longer be denied. She burned for him and only he could fill her. She shifted her body closer to him and felt the hard readiness of his arousal. It excited her. He reached down and lifted her leg, encircling it around his thigh. She shifted her weight as he gripped her buttocks and raised her up. Face-to-face, she sat on his lap, straddling him as he relaxed beneath her.

Looking down into his eyes, she could see his need and desire for her. He wanted her, bad. She smiled. She had finally found the ultimate power over him. She leaned down and kissed him hard, then softened and leaned back. He leaned out to her, but she pressed him back against the sofa and then shook her head.

She slowly unbuttoned his shirt, then opened it wide. This was what she remembered all day. This was her first sight of him. Her fingers itched to touch him then. Now that she had him, she could do whatever she pleased. She ran her hands across his chest, feeling the smooth rich silkiness. She touched his nipples; he flinched. She smiled inwardly. Power was addictive: the more she had, the more she wanted, especially power over him.

He closed his eyes, obviously enjoying the feel of her teasing hands. She continued rubbing her hands across his chest, careful to only touch his nipples when she wanted his undivided attention. "Look at me," she instructed. He opened his eyes instantly. Ice-green eyes tinted with golden sparks stared up at her. She smiled. She stuck her finger in her mouth then pressed it to his nipple. Trey sizzled then shuddered. He grabbed her, then instantly let go. "I think you like doing that," he said.

"I do. Kiss me," she ordered.

He kissed her hard, locked in a passion that nearly raged out of control. Her mouth, her neck, her chest…all at his disposal and he ravaged her like a starving man. He pulled at her sweater, pulling it up from her pants. He kissed and licked his way down her chest until he came to her lace bra. The sweet swell of her breasts seemed to send him over the edge.

His breathing quickened and she could feel his heart racing. He buried his face between each peak and thrust his tongue beneath the lace. He reached up to undo the front snap.

"Stop," she whispered. He obeyed instantly, throwing his head back and closing his eyes. He licked his dry lips, and then looked at her, half smiling. Kenya returned his smile. They knew the game they played. She sat back on his thighs and ran her hand over her chest, slowly, seductively. She circled her lace-covered nipple and smiled wider, seeing the need in his eyes.

"Do you want to touch me?" she cooed. He nodded slowly. "Like this?" she said seductively, slowly circling her nipple with her finger. He nodded again. "Or like this?" she said, grabbing her sweet swell of flesh and squeezing tenderly. Trey's focus shifted to her hand. He licked his lips again and barely nodded.

"No." She pouted. "Maybe not. I don't think you want me."

He nodded breathlessly. "Yes, I do. I want you."

"Really?" she said, toying with him.

He nodded, nodding his head like a bobblehead doll. "I want you, I want you," he repeated.

"Nah, I'm not convinced." She unsnapped the front clasp on her bra, freeing her breasts, but keeping the lace material in place. Trey's eyes fastened instantly. She teased him by revealing more of her breasts each time she breathed deeply. The sweet swell of her nearly exposed breasts stoked the raging fire. He reached up to touch her then stopped and looked into her smiling eyes.

She shifted her body, grinding against his increasing hardness. Doling out torturous pleasure was her intent and she succeeded well. "Oops, is that you down there?" She reached down and unfastened his belt, then slowly pulled it free from the loops.

She took his hands and wrapped the belt around them. He was bound. She tightened the belt then pulled it up, raising his hands up behind his head. He looked completely helpless, but she wasn't fooled. His tightened muscles showed too much strength and power to think that he was completely trapped. He merely allowed her to play, so play she did.

"You know," she began as she unsnapped his pants as if it were the most normal thing in the world, "one of my favorite classes in college was drawing nudes." She shifted again. Trey groaned earnestly. "Um, there's something about the body that fascinates me. Most designers don't like the drawing part, but not me. I like seeing and drawing hard bodies. Not too muscled, but just right."

She scratched her nails over his tightened arms, feeling the curve of each sculpted muscle. "Mmm, I love seeing muscles work. Like the biceps and triceps. Did you know that they work together to control forearm movement?" She shifted her hands upward. "And the deltoid, thick and triangular, attaches here, to the scapula. And this is the trapezius." She reached her hands around his neck then leaned in and kissed his biceps, triceps, deltoids and trapezius.

Afterward she reached up and touched his face, and then slowly traced her fingers down his body, from his neck to his shoulders, his chest to his stomach, his navel to…lower. The tiny wispy hairs she remembered so well from before. They captured her attention now. She gently played with them, torturously dipping lower and lower and lower. She found the core of her hunger. The iron stiffness of his body moistened her. She held him secure, feeling his thickness. She smiled, assured of her victory.

"Kenya," Trey groaned, his voice deep and husky with passion. Each breath he took was measured and desperate. She continued toying with his body while sending chills into her own. She reveled in her newly found power. She felt him tighten his control. "Kenya," he repeated, even more strained.

"Yes," she answered nicely.

"Yes," he repeated automatically.

She placed one hand on his chest, and then boldly began to stoke him. Each tremor prompted her further. She could feel his heart pound. This was everything she wanted. She stroked and he gasped. She set a rhythm, pulsating to the beat of his heart. Then, without warning, like an iron vise, he grabbed her hands. "You have about five seconds to make your point," Trey stated in no uncertain terms.

Kenya smiled, still reveling in her power over him. "Five," she began, slowly moving her hips, grinding against him. "Four, three, two—" She never got to one. Trey grabbed her, removed her bra and reversed their positions. She straddled him again, although this time her legs encircled his hips. It happened instantly. In the blink of an eye she lay on her back, collapsed and reclined on the soft sofa pillows. He hovered over her. The smooth lightning-speed action took her breath away. "No fair," she protested in vain.

"Let's play my game now." The ominous way he spoke sent a ripple down into her stomach. She shuddered. She had taunted and teased him without mercy. There was no telling what he had in mind for her. But before she had the chance to even consider the possibilities, his mouth fell to her breast. He suckled long and firm, drawing her into the fullness of his mouth. Her body betrayed her and she arched up, meeting his heavenly pull.

The wondrous feel of his mouth sent shivering tingles all through her body. How do you despise a man who makes your body scream in pleasure? How do you resist the tempting call of your primal need? At that moment he was everything she desired and everything she wanted and so much more.

He gathered her breasts together, licking each nipple as his head turned from side to side. She moaned as her body ached for him. He was fierce in his assault and she savored every second. He rose up and kissed her, letting his hands wreak havoc with the rest of her body. He touched her there, slipped low, between her legs, still fully covered.

She felt his hips move as his hardness pleaded to enter. She was breathless and near panting. That's when he kissed her neck and shoulders and breasts and stomach, and the blinding thought of more made her call out his name. "Trey."

"Yeah, I agree, let's do this."

He leaned back and stood in one fluid motion. Then he reached down to her and helped her to her feet. She rose to stand in front of him. He tipped her chin and kissed her slowly, passionately. She didn't remember anything else, certainly not how she got up the stairs. When the kiss ended they were standing in the doorway of his bedroom. He glanced over to the bed, then back at her.

"I'm not sure what this is, or how we got to this point, but I'm glad we did," he said earnestly.

"I know, we just met this morning."

"A lot has happened since then," he said. She nodded, and then looked over to the bed. "If you want to wait, I'll understand."

"Do you have any?" she asked.

"Yeah."

She reached up and kissed him while pulling him into the bedroom. He guided her to the bed. She stood as he unzipped her pants and let them fall to the carpet. She stepped out and stood with heels and panties. Trey looked down the length of her, smiling. "You are a remarkable woman—beautiful, intelligent and incredibly sexy. You have no idea what you do to me."

She touched him gently. "I think I have a pretty good idea." She helped him remove the rest of his clothes. They stood there, him fully naked and her with panties and heels.

He sat down on the side of the bed and guided her to stand between his legs. He touched her breasts, the flat of her stomach and then down the backs of her legs and up over her buttocks. "You have no idea what your body does to me, or what I want to do to your body."

"Tell me. No, better yet," she corrected, "show me." He turned her around to the side and admired the rounded apple of her bottom. He caressed her cheeks then kissed her hip gently. He turned her completely around and ran his hands up to her shoulders, then down to her knees. Her skin was like silk and all he wanted to do was touch her.

He pulled her back closer so that he could easily feel the front of her. His hands, reaching up, covered her breasts, squeezing gently, feeling the rounded soft flesh. She fit perfectly into his grasp. His hands drifted down, touched the elastic lace, then slowly peeled it from her body. He released her.

"Turn around," he requested. She did. As soon as he saw

her completely naked his eyes sparkled. He took a deep breath and licked his lips, then nodded his approval. He was obviously awed by the gift.

Kenya smiled at his reaction to seeing her. She knew she was fit, of course, but it was always nice to take a man's breath away. "Where are the condoms?"

"In the drawer," he said.

She stepped away and walked to the drawer, perfectly comfortable in her skin, and knew that Trey was watching every step she took. She opened the drawer and took out two condoms. When she turned, his eyes were glued to her. He shifted back onto the bed as she returned. She climbed on top then reached to remove her heels.

"No, leave them," he muttered. She nodded at his request then opened the package and rolled the latex down over him.

He settled her hips and held her waist, guiding her close. On top, she kissed him, opening her mouth and accepting his tongue. Sweetly, gently, they savored the passion, kissing firmly and steadily. His hands roamed everywhere as she adjusted her body to hover over him. She reached down and placed him at the tip of her core. Then with steady ease she lowered her body and impaled herself onto him.

Long, hard and thick, he filled all of her. She gasped, nearly blinded by the sensation of fullness. She arched her back. He sat up. She instantly felt his mouth capture her breast. An instant later she began to rock her hips up and down. The slow easy motion was like riding. Each sensuous movement stroked her nib, while also deepening his arousal.

The pull of his mouth and the friction of his body built to a steady climax. The rapture had begun. She rocked into him and he rocked into her. The building fever increased in vigor and thrust. Soon they were mindless in passion. The throbbing strokes of sensual pleasure surged, unrestrained beyond their control. They had abandoned the calm, allowing the fierce pulsating hunger to build. Quickening the pace faster and faster, she gasped for air. Holding him tight, she felt her body begin to soar. Seconds later her body rocked with spasms. Then a blasting, blinding light of passion and ecstasy enveloped her.

She climaxed, shuddering as his body continued to thrash into her. She climaxed again. Seconds later he came, meeting her. The second orgasm was just as blinding as the first. She dug her nails into his shoulders and held on as she climaxed again. He grabbed and held her tight. An instant later she collapsed against him and he relaxed back, taking the full weight of her body.

They lay there, exhausted, deep in spent passion. Their competitive nature had tempted and prolonged their release, amplifying their lovemaking to reach higher. She was in control, he was in control, they had shifted and shared, yet neither one held power over their hearts.

Chapter 9

Dawn's morning light peeked low and embraced their naked bodies as they lay in each other's arms, basking in their recent lovemaking. Three empty packages attested to their passion the night before. Trey was awake but he kept his eyes closed, savoring the moment. The feel of her bare body pressed against his was too good to be true. Her breasts, soft and generous, flattened against his chest. Soft and supple. He liked the feel of them pressed to his body. Actually, he liked the feel of everything about her.

Initially he had no intention of making love to her. He was just curious as to what game she was playing and how far she'd go. She was her father's child, so trusting what she said was out of the question.

"I think I'd like to sketch you one day," Kenya said.

"That might work."

"Nude," she clarified.

"I don't think so," he said with his eyes still closed tightly.

"Oh, come on, your body is perfect for nudes." She ran her finger down the length of his chest and dipped into his navel.

"I don't think so," he repeated, stilling her hand before she went lower.

"Why not? I've already seen the family jewels," she joked, peeking beneath the casually draped sheet.

"I'd rather not have others see the jewels."

"You think I'd display it?"

"I think naked photos, video recordings and other embarrassing images have a curious way of becoming public."

"This sketch," she said, leaning close to his ear, "I promise will be strictly for my personal appreciation."

He smiled. "I'll tell you what, I'll think about it."

"Why do I not believe that?"

"I would never lie to you, Kenya."

"Really?" she asked skeptically.

"Yes," he said, opening his eyes, "never."

"Good." She almost believed him.

Kenya lay a while longer until she heard Trey's steady, even breathing. She knew he'd fallen asleep again. She figured he was tired. After all, he had been up most of the night. She smiled dreamily. She had no idea what had come over her. Sex, as a whole, was great and she enjoyed it, but with Trey it was truly amazing.

Maybe it was their competitive nature. All she knew was that she couldn't get enough of him. She craved him. As soon as they'd finished making love, she wanted him all over again. Her appetite for him was ravenous. He shifted position.

"Hey, are you awake?" she asked.

"Are you trying to kill me, woman?" he asked.

"Now why would I want to do that, when having you alive

and healthy is a lot more fun?" She inched against him, arousing his body again.

"Give me fifteen minutes."

"Come on, where's your adventurous spirit?"

"Exhausted," he confessed. "Fifteen minutes."

"Five," she countered.

"Twelve," he negotiated.

"Five," she still insisted.

"You don't surrender, do you?"

"Never."

"You know what, I have a better idea. Come here."

He nudged her closer as he rolled her over to drape across his body. "Turn around." She did. He reached down and moved her leg up over his thigh. Her legs were spread wide. He began touching her, first her breasts. He massaged the nipples to pebble between his fingers. Then he felt her full frontal, touching and exploring every inch of her body. Kenya closed her eyes and rolled her head back. It felt so good when he touched her. "Trey," she rasped. He was so attentive to her body, he didn't respond. "Trey," she repeated.

The man's playful hands needed to be classified as secret weapons. He teased her and she writhed beneath his skill. When he dipped lower she gasped and instinctively inched away, but he held her firm. "Where do you think you're going?" he whispered playfully. "Uh-uh, you're not leaving me now. This is the best part."

There was no way he was going to let her miss this. He caressed the soft delicate curls then pressed into her. She moistened instantly, surrounding his fingers. He repeated the stroking then began to tweak the nib of her passion. She gasped and jerked then strained to control her breathing. "Trey."

She squirmed away again, but this time he met her with more torturous pleasure. He began pressing rhythmically. She joined him, moving her hips to the cadenced of his fingers. The sweet relentless torment was divine. She writhed in sweet ecstasy as the intensity of the rapture swelled. Seconds later, she cried aloud, then again and again. Each blinding spasm eclipsed the last against his continued assault. She climaxed again, then once more, jerking stronger, harder, fuller, each blissful time.

"Okay, okay," she begged, stilling his hand between her legs. "I give."

"Do you surrender to me?" he asked triumphantly.

"Yes, yes," she whispered.

"Say it," he instructed.

"I surrender to you."

"Good. Now, woman, let me sleep," he whispered, wrapping his arms around her and holding her tight. She did for twenty whole minutes.

A half hour later Kenya got up. She grabbed some of her clothes and headed to the bathroom. When she returned Trey was still asleep. Seeing him lying there gave her a pang of regret. She had every intention of hurting this man. He had destroyed her father's dreams and made a fool of him. She was going to make him pay.

But being with him, and seeing him lying there now, softened her heart. Maybe she couldn't do this. No. She was going to do this. She needed to do this.

Steeling her emotions, she went downstairs and looked around the living room for her bra and top. She found her bra on the floor between the sofa and the coffee table. She put it on then picked up her top. As soon as she did she saw a briefcase sitting beside the side table.

Curiously, she looked around then sat down, picked up the briefcase and opened it. There were a few legal documents, several loose papers and a thick red presentation folder inside.

She pulled out the red folder and flipped through quickly. There was a listing of company names. She scanned down the list then stopped when she saw Whitaker Real Estate, her father's company.

She turned back to the first page, reading quickly. It was a listing of the company's current assets. She turned back to the listings page. She didn't recognize any other companies listed. But she did find the names of clients. There were senators, judges and a few names she knew from the newspapers. She figured that he probably stole from them, too. They just didn't know it yet.

She grabbed her purse and pulled out her cell phone. Adjusting focus, she quickly laid the folder out and began taking photos. She saved each one and then sent them to her e-mail address. She was almost finished when she heard a car alarm beep twice outside. She quickly began putting the papers back into the folder. Just as she finished and closed the briefcase, the front door opened. "Hello, Trey, it's me."

Kenya hurriedly placed the briefcase back where she found it. Just as she stood up a young woman walked into the living room. Kenya's top fell from her lap to the floor. She quickly picked it up and put it on.

"Well, good morning," the young woman said, smiling knowingly. It wasn't too difficult for anyone to imagine what had happened the night before.

"Good morning," Kenya said calmly then smiled at the obvious awkwardness. The last thing she needed to deal with was baby-mamma drama but it appeared that it was unavoidable. "Insert uncomfortable moment here," she joked.

The young woman chuckled. "Sense of humor—" she smiled and nodded "—that's good. Awkward moment, yeah, just a bit. But don't mind about me, I don't really count." She tossed her jacket and purse down, then perched her hip on the arm of the sofa. "So you're new, right?" she asked.

"New, as opposed to not so new?" Kenya asked.

The woman chuckled again. "Funny. Excuse me for staring, but you look really familiar. Have we met before, at GWU maybe?"

"No, I don't think so," Kenya said, figuring she might have seen her sister Sidney there.

"That's funny, 'cause I seldom forget a face."

"Sorry, we've never met, and I was just leaving." She reached down and grabbed her purse.

"Don't leave on my account. I'm just passing through. I'm Regina, Trey's sister."

"Oh," Kenya said. She remembered Trey talking to someone named Madi when they first met. She was instantly relieved that this wasn't the baby mamma, Madi.

"Hi," Kenya said, breathing a sigh of relief, "I thought you were… Never mind."

"Someone else, Trey's girlfriend?" she asked, amused.

"The twins' mother," Kenya said.

"Nah, that's Madi."

"Right, um, I'm Kenya. I met the twins yesterday. Your brother was looking for a nanny and I—"

"You're the nanny," Regina said, obviously amused.

"No, actually I'm a designer."

"What kind of designer?"

"I design children's clothing."

"That's nice, interesting. Do you like doing it?"

"Yes, very much. But like everything else, it has its ups and downs," Kenya said, half smiling, seeing Regina's frozen smile and cold green eyes. She looked a lot like her brother at that moment. "Anyway, as I said, I was just leaving."

Regina nodded. "It was nice meeting you."

"You, too," Kenya said as she walked around her and headed to the front door.

"Uh, I presume Trey's here?" Regina asked.

"Yes, he's upstairs still asleep," Kenya said.

"Is there anything you'd like me to tell my brother?"

"No," Kenya said as she turned the doorknob then paused. "Actually, on second thought, yes, you can tell him that I enjoyed doing business with him." She opened the door and left.

Regina smiled. She had no idea exactly what had happened the night before, or who Kenya was, but there was something about her that she instantly liked.

Upstairs, Trey awoke a few minutes later. His eyes still closed, he smiled reflectively as his body yearned for the woman he'd spent the night with. Their evening together had been one of the best he'd had in a long time. It wasn't just the physical that had intrigued him. She was spirited, intelligent, knowledgeable and a lot of fun to be with. They'd laughed and joked and even argued, mainly about football. A Redskins fan, well, she was allowed one fault.

He still wasn't sure why she was doing what she was doing. He could only assume in the end she intended it to benefit her father. That part he admired. She obviously loved her father and family. In the same position he'd probably try to do something to help, as well. Of course, his father was very different from James Whitaker, but lately, not by much.

Trey reached out to her, but she wasn't there. He sat up, fully awake, to an empty bed. He looked around the bedroom—she was gone. He grabbed his robe and opened the bedroom door. The smell of coffee immediately welcomed him.

Assured his coffee would be waiting for him downstairs, Trey showered and dressed and went downstairs. He looked in the living room. There was no sign of her, but there was a

jacket and purse on the sofa. Still smelling coffee, he went into the kitchen.

"Good morning," Regina said, looking up from the newspaper and coffee as soon as she saw Trey enter.

"Morning. What are you doing here?" he asked, looking around the kitchen for Kenya.

Regina smirked. "She's not here."

"Who's not here?" Trey asked, playing off his curiosity as he walked over to the pot of coffee. He grabbed a cup and poured.

"Don't tell me you didn't even get her name."

He turned around to his sister and glared. "Her name is Kenya."

Regina smiled. "Yeah, I know. We met. I like her."

"You met her?" he asked.

"We had a quick chat before she left."

"When was that?"

"A few minutes ago," she said. Seeing his disappointed expression, she chuckled. "Wow, she must have been something special. You actually look like you care. Usually you're relieved when they leave. I'd say that you look almost disappointed."

"Don't you have coffee at your place?"

"The entertainment's better here. I can't wait to tell J.T., Tony and Raymond about this. I might finally win the bet."

"Then by all means take the coffee with you."

"You like her, don't you?" Regina challenged.

"Exactly why do you have my front-door keys again?"

"Don't change the subject, you like her. Well, I'll be. This is definitely a Trey first and cause for celebration. Trey Evans's ice-cold heart finally melted by a woman, I can see the headlines now."

"When's the last time I fired you?" he asked.

"Two weeks ago," she said, smiling happily.

"So I guess it's about time I fired you again."

She laughed. "Come on, big brother, you know that Iceman stuff won't work with me. Remember, I know you too well. You're all mean and stern outside, but inside, where it counts, you're a softie. Wait…is Mamma Lou involved in this?"

"No, at least I don't think so. Why, what do you know?" he asked, his voice strained with added concern.

"So tell me about her. Was this the urban-legend third date or something?"

"What do you mean urban-legend third date?"

"Come on, you know that you can barely stand two dates at most with any one woman. Anything more than that and it's an urban legend."

"It wasn't a date."

"A booty call?" she questioned. Trey looked at her fiercely. "And touchy about her, hmm, interesting. But a nanny, really, Trey, isn't that a bit clichéd?"

"She's not a nanny," he said as he sipped his coffee. He instantly grimaced.

"Oh, that's right. She's a children's clothes designer."

Trey glared again. "Don't you have a job to get to?" he asked, then turned to put cream and sugar in his cup.

"I just got fired."

"You're hired again, now go to work."

Regina smiled. Working for her brother wasn't exactly what she intended to do for the rest of her life, but it was something until she decided what she wanted. He was an impossible boss, demanding and intimidating. Those fortunate enough to work for him did it at one hundred and ten percent every day. "Keep that up and I won't give you her message."

Trey instantly turned. "What message?"

"Tell me about her first," Regina said.

"You can be such a brat sometimes."

"That's what younger sisters do. So tell me about her. She designs children's clothes. What else?"

"What else did you talk about?"

"This and that, you know, girl talk."

"Girl talk again, huh. Could you be a bit more specific?" he asked.

"You're stalling," Regina said.

Trey sighed, knowing that even after all these years, he'd never get the best of his sister. "Fine, we met yesterday. Mamma Lou thinks we're dating."

"So Mamma Lou *is* involved in this," she said, chuckling. "Okay, tell me, what would make Mamma Lou think you're dating?" Regina asked.

"Kenya was here when Mamma Lou stopped by to see the twins. She assumed, so I let her. What's the message?"

Regina looked at her watch. "You're right. I need to get to work. I've got a conference call first thing." She stood, walked over to the sink and rinsed out her cup. "Thanks for the coffee," she said then left.

Trey shook his head as he watched her walk out of the kitchen. His sister could be the biggest pain at times. She constantly insisted on butting into his life.

He grabbed his cup and sat down at the counter. The newspaper was in shambles, as usual, when Regina read it first. He sorted through the jumbled pages and found the business section. As soon as he settled to read the financial review, Regina stuck her head back in. "Tell him that I enjoyed doing business with him."

Trey didn't bother looking up, but he did smile. It sounded just like her. Then, remembering the night before, his smile broadened. Her impetuous, insatiable appetite was unexpected, but well-received. He never expected to find himself so completely taken with a woman. But there was something about her that had captured him. Yeah, his sister was right, she was definitely something special.

He sipped his coffee and made a few phone calls. The peace and quiet afforded him a few minutes to attend to business. Afterward he turned on the kitchen television and watched a few early-morning business programs. But to his surprise he found the complete silence distracting. He missed the twins already.

A few minutes later the doorbell rang. He hurried to answer. Louise and Colonel Wheeler stood with Jonathan and Johanna.

"Good morning, we're here," Louise said enthusiastically.

"Hey, come on in," Trey said happily. "Hey, little guys, how are you? Did you have a good time last night? Where's my hug?" He opened his arms. Both Johanna and Jonathan, dressed in pink and blue rain slickers, respectively, grabbed him. Slightly damp, he stood up and bounced, causing them to squeal and laugh. He turned them around quickly then headed inside.

Louise followed Trey and the twins, and Colonel Wheeler followed her, carrying several overnight bags. Trey placed the twins on the floor beside two toy rocking horses. The twins immediately ran over and jumped on.

"So how were they?" Trey asked.

"They were little angels, of course," Louise said, helping them remove their rain slickers. Colonel Wheeler started chuckling. Louise glanced over to him. "Although they had poor Otis here running around all morning."

"It was my pleasure," he said. "But remind me never to play ball with those two again. They're like little Energizer Bunnies. They never get tired."

"Yep, made that mistake yesterday," Trey said, laughing. "I finally tossed the ball behind the sofa. I believe it's still there."

"Now you tell me," Colonel Wheeler said.

Johanna got off the horse and ran into the living room. Jonathan followed her. Louise followed them both. "How about some coffee?" Trey asked Colonel Wheeler.

"Now that's what I'm talking about," Colonel Wheeler said happily. "Lead the way."

They went into the kitchen. Trey poured Colonel Wheeler a cup of coffee and topped off his own. They sat down at the kitchen table and talked about the twins, then politics, then business and sports. The exuberant conversation finally slowed as Trey poured two more cups. "You know she adores you, don't you?" Colonel Wheeler asked in that respectful fatherly tone he had.

"Who?" Trey asked, taken off guard by the sudden change in topic.

"Louise. She wants the best for you."

Trey smiled. "I adore her, too. She's a sweet lady, but don't tell her I said that. It might ruin our ongoing opposition." Colonel Wheeler chuckled and nodded. "I know she adores and wants the best for me, but does that necessarily have to mean marriage?"

"You sound just like I did at your age. Man, I fought like the devil to stay single. It worked, too. No complications, no drama and no commitments. I loved being free as a bird to come and go as I pleased."

"See, that's it right there," Trey declared. "Freedom—is that too much to hope for? Yeah, I see my family and friends all getting hooked up, but it's not for me. I'm not that guy."

"Want to hear a word of wisdom from an old freedom seeker?"

"Sure."

"We're all that guy. Sometimes we just don't realize it in time to do something about it."

"Regrets?" Trey asked.

"No, no—no regrets, just missed opportunities."

"What do you mean?"

Colonel Wheeler smiled and shook his head pensively. He signed heavily. "I've known Louise for a lot longer than most realize."

"Really? I presumed you met years ago on the island after her husband died. How long have you known Mamma Lou?"

Otis smiled. "I don't remember not knowing her."

He paused. Trey smiled, letting his comment rest with both of them. The simple words held power—*I don't remember not knowing her.* For the first time he actually saw how much Otis Wheeler loved Louise Gates.

"Yes, we did meet after her husband died, but that was our second meeting," he finally continued. Trey looked surprised. "Yes, we'd known each other years before that, before she married Jonathan, before she moved to Crescent Island."

"You were lovers," Trey surmised, less surprised than he expected to be.

Colonel Wheeler sighed then looked away. "*Lovers*...the word sounds so inadequate. That summer we had something so strong it defied words. Boyfriend, girlfriend, lovers—those words couldn't nearly describe our love. What we had was far more than that, than anything. I loved her with a passion that was more than my life. The sun rose and set on her as far as I was concerned. She was—*is*—everything to me. But the military was my life and foolishly my freedom was too important to me. I thought loving her meant losing it, so I panicked. I was a fool."

"Wow, that's deep."

"Oh, yeah, it was deep, all right. We had that kind of love that most people only dreamed about—all-consuming passion. I burned for her. From the first instant I laid eyes on her." He paused again.

"What?" Trey asked curiously.

"I saw her but she didn't see me. Tuskegee, Alabama. She was with some friends at a restaurant. I watched her damn near the whole time she was sitting there. Man, she was a vision. Dressed in lavender, I'll never forget. She laughed and the beauty of her spirit captured me instantly. Just as she was about to leave, I walked up and introduced myself."

"And it was love at first sight, right?"

Colonel Wheeler laughed. "Hell no, she nearly ripped my head off. Oh, she had a temper that day. See, opening lines weren't exactly my strong suit back then. There was no manual on pickup lines." Trey joined in the laughter. "No, she disliked me on sight, had something to do with a small thing called reputation."

"You were a player," Trey guessed.

"I handled my business," he said tactfully.

"So what did you do?"

"I wooed her. Man, I spent every cent I had on flowers and candy. She sent every last thing right back to me. I didn't know what to do. She was in my blood by then. I couldn't think of anything but her."

"How long did all this take?"

"Three, maybe four days," Colonel Wheeler said.

"That's all? Four days doesn't seem like a lot of time to know that it's really love," Trey said, astonished by the short duration of time.

"Trey, if you hear nothing else, hear this—love, real love, when you feel it inside won't be about time or duration or opportunity, it's about knowing."

"Knowing."

Colonel Wheeler nodded. "Knowing without a doubt, with every fiber of your being, that that person is put on this earth to be with you and only you. You can mess it up with foolish nonsense. But believe me, you will never experience the joy of true love without trying."

Trey nodded his understanding. "So what happened?"

"I stopped running around like a fool. I realized that I'd fallen in love the first time I saw her. She didn't need all that stuff I was sending. So one afternoon I grabbed a couple of vending machine sandwiches. I found her sitting on a park bench reading. I sat down and honestly talked with her. We must have sat there for hours. I'll never forget that day, it rained cats and dogs."

"Did it work?"

"It wasn't meant to work. You see, I didn't do it to win her, I did it to know her. I just needed to hear her voice. We spent the rest of the weekend together. In three days I knew I was in love."

"Three days."

"That's all it took. Love isn't about time, it's about the heart."

"But then you lost touch," Trey said. "The war?"

"No, I walked away, too scared to commit," he said.

"But what about being in love?" Trey asked.

"Louise wanted a future with me and I wanted my freedom. It was the worst decision I ever made. I kept up with her life over the years, her marriage and children. Then Jonathan died. I retired and moved to Crescent Island."

"So when are you headed back?"

Colonel Wheeler laughed out loud. "Subtlety isn't exactly your strong suit, is it?"

"That's not exactly how I meant it," Trey said.

"No need to apologize, it's not the first time I've been asked that question. I remember your cousin J.T. had that same idea in mind. Every time Louise showed up, he'd break into a cold sweat. She has that effect on men."

"Yes, she certainly does. This may be a crazy question, but have you ever considered asking her to marry you? Maybe she's been playing matchmaker setting people up because no one ever did it for her."

"I asked a few times, about a thousand or so. She always says the same thing. Our time is past."

"I don't think so," Trey said.

"Neither do I, but I'll keep asking."

"And one of these days maybe she'll say yes."

"Careful there, Trey, you're beginning to sound like a romantic."

Trey laughed. "Yeah, I guess I am at that."

"So enough of this ancient history, what about you and your young lady? Been together four months, is it?"

"Actually, it's only been a day," he confessed. "We met yesterday morning shortly before you arrived. I hated to lie to you and Mamma Lou but—"

"Desperate times call for desperate measures."

"Exactly," Trey said.

"I figured as much."

"You did? How? Does Mamma Lou know?"

"No, I don't think so. All she saw were her sparks."

"Her sparks," Trey repeated.

"Yep, she seems to think that true love comes with sparks. When she saw you and Kenya together, she saw sparks. But don't underestimate her, she saw these same sparks with just about every couple you know."

"Sparks, huh. I don't know if they were sparks or not, but something."

"What do you mean?" Colonel Wheeler asked.

"Neither one of us is being very honest about our intentions. She has an ulterior motive and, well, me, I guess I'm just playing the game."

"That doesn't sound good."

"That's how it started, anyway."

"And now how is it?"

"To tell you the truth, I have no idea. I'd been sitting here thinking about that all morning. She stopped by late last night. We talked, really talked, and got to know each other. She's smart, talented and funny and everything I always complained I couldn't find in a woman. But is it really her or is this all part of this game she's playing? She stayed over. And, not to sound like a couple of locker-room jocks, but I've never met anyone like her. The woman is amazing. But I keep wondering."

"The game thing, are you sure it's just a game?"

Trey nodded. "It involves her father. In brief, he tried to take over my company so I got to him first."

"Revenge, is it?" Colonel Wheeler asked.

"I'm sure that's how it started but now I hope—"

"You need to make a move. Nothing ever comes from sitting on the sidelines watching. If this is more, you'll know it. If you want it to be more you need to show it."

"Sparks?" Trey offered.

Colonel Wheeler nodded then caught himself. "Oh, no, did I just suggest that?" he asked, chuckling. Trey joined in.

"What are you two doing in here laughing and talking like two old housewives over a back fence?" Louise said as she came in with the twins. "I think we're ready for a morning snack."

"Coming right up," Trey said. He went over to the counter, picked up a box and shook it. "Who wants Cheerios?" Jonathan and Johanna came running.

Chapter 10

The day was miserable, rainy and wet. But Kenya didn't even notice. By the time she got into her car her breathing was erratic, her heart was pounding and her nerves were on edge. Asia was so wrong, she was a good actress, 'cause she had no idea how she kept her calm when Trey's sister walked in and nearly caught her. They talked casually, but all the time she was panicking inside.

She hadn't expected Regina to show up. Who would have thought that Trey's sister would just walk in like that, no warning. She was just thankful it wasn't Trey. There was no way she could have explained going through his briefcase and taking pictures. She just got lucky.

"Okay, it's over, calm down, relax," she told herself while still glancing in the rearview mirror every once in a while. After a few minutes driving, her nerves finally settled down. She continued home in a self-imposed fog centered mostly on Trey.

"You did it," she whispered, then squealed, "I did it." The elation she felt inside spread wide across her face. She did it.

After a night of mindless bliss, she'd been shocked back to reality. How could she be so stupid? How could she even think about trusting him? She actually had second thoughts about getting back at him. But not anymore, all bets were off. Trey Evans deserved everything he got, and she intended to give it to him.

She glanced up in the rearview mirror again. This time she caught a glimpse of her reflection. Her smile faded.

So why was she still so conflicted? On one hand there was what she'd seen in the folder and on the other hand there was her time with Trey. But the reality of what Trey had done was right there in black and white. She didn't read all of it, but she did note several passages concerning her father's company. It implied that TE Acquisitions & Associates intended to implement plans to shut down Whitaker Real Estate Investment Company permanently. It was dated six months ago.

Trey had swindled her father just as he'd told her. But six months ago, how was that possible? Yet all her doubts had been silenced. The proof had been sitting right there beside the coffee table the whole time. Seeing it took her breath away. She looked down at her purse. Her camera cell phone was in there. How could he? How could anyone be so malicious as to steal when they already had so much? But it was okay now. One night was all it took and she'd gotten what she needed.

Of course, last night wasn't what she expected when she went over there, at least not all of it. She was going to make him want her, not the other way around. Her plan was simple when she arrived—seduce him, then drag him along and keep him wanting. She needed him to trust her. After all, there was no way she was going to actually sleep with the man who ruined her father. But she had.

A slow smile spread across her face as memories of the night flooded through her. The night before had been unbelievable. She'd done it. Where countless others had failed, she had successfully melted the coldhearted, detached Trey Evans, at least for the night. The exhilaration of her success made her smile again.

She had to admit, he was amazing. He was nothing at all like she imagined. As a lover he was open and generous and patient, far different from the insensitive businessman.

When she opened his shirt and saw his chest, everything—her plan, her common sense—vanished. Then she touched him. It was as if her fingers were on fire. Sure, she went to his house for the sole purpose of revenge, but somewhere along the way things changed.

She pulled up in front of her building and got out. Walking to her condo, her thoughts finally centered on the day ahead.

As soon as she got home she jumped into a hot shower, got dressed and headed to the boutique. She struggled through the morning, creating one disaster after the next. Nothing went right and it appeared the afternoon was headed in the same direction.

"Okay, enough of this, you've been acting weird all morning and now you're just creepin' me out. You've sewn, ripped out and then resewn the same thing again. It's a wonder there's any material left on that one pair of jeans. I've never seen you this jittery. What's going on with you?" Shelly asked.

"Nothing," Kenya said innocently, "I'm just preoccupied."

"Girl, please, who do you think you're fooling. Does it look like I just got off the banana boat yesterday? This isn't preoccupied, this is downright spooked. What happened, what did you do?" she asked. Then it dawned on her and her jaw dropped. "You didn't. Kenya," she said. Kenya didn't look up. "I don't believe it. You did, you slept with him last night, didn't you?"

"I am not justifying that with an answer," Kenya said.

"Don't even think about taking the high road with me. It's all over your face. You slept with him and you just met him what, yesterday morning? I can't believe you did that. Since when do you get your passport punched like that?"

"Shelly, please, don't start, this has nothing to do with anything."

"It has everything to do with anything. Kenya, stop this now before you get in over your head."

"Nothing's changed. I know exactly what I'm doing."

"Oh, please, you don't have a clue. Since when do you sleep with a man after just meeting him? Never, that's when," she said, answering her own question. "And all this crap about conning him is ridiculous. Don't you see this is all wrong? You can't win in the end. Revenge isn't right. And what you're doing is for all the wrong reasons."

"He deserves it, Shelly," Kenya said firmly.

"You've got revenge on the mind. And it's obvious that ever since that drama with Craig, you've been on this man-hating thing."

"I have not. I don't hate men."

"No, not all men, just men with power. The rest you just don't trust thanks to Craig."

"This has nothing to do with Craig."

"This has everything to do with how he made you feel. He hurt you and you're using this to get back at him. You want to use and hurt Trey Evans like Craig hurt you. So last night you slept with him."

"I didn't do anything that I can't live with."

"You made love to him," Shelly said.

"I had sex with him, there's a difference."

"Semantics. Just because you didn't actually feel anything for him doesn't mean that it was any different," Shelly said, then saw Kenya's face. "Wait a minute, you do feel something for him."

"No, it was nothing."

"Like hell it was nothing. Look at you."

"Okay, okay, yes, I did it. We did it, over and over again. It's not what I expected. He wasn't how I expected. But I didn't mean to do it. It wasn't the plan when I went over there."

"Where men and women and hearts are concerned, there is no plan."

"Fine, then all's fair in love and war," she recited.

"You really think you know what you're doing?"

"I know what I'm doing," Kenya said firmly. But that's as far as the words got. Inside, deep in her heart, she didn't have a clue.

"Okay, if you say so."

The conversation stopped. In silence they each continued doing their work. Shelly was on the sewing machine and Kenya was at a form altering a jumper bodice again. She put pins in her mouth so that she wouldn't speak. She had had enough of talking about Trey. It was bad enough that she'd slept with him, but now she was thinking about him differently. Being with him had altered her perception, and she couldn't afford that.

She stiffened her back and sat straight up, in hopes of maybe physically affirming her position. She had to stay focused. That's what he'd do. She needed to be like him, coldhearted and unfeeling. Her resoluteness had to be unshakable. Revenge didn't work if emotions got in the way. *I can do this, I can do this,* she silently chanted. Moments later she slumped.

"Girl," she said quietly when Shelly walked over to the ironing board, "I swear I was climbing the walls. I couldn't get enough of him. Okay, I'm not exactly overly sexual, but I swear I wanted him all night long. I have no idea what came over me."

"Maybe because it's been such a long time," Shelly suggested. "You and Craig broke up almost a year ago, right?"

Kenya nodded. "I woke him up twice just to be with him. I was uncontrollable, like a sex maniac. I don't know what came over me."

"Lust."

"Yeah, a whole lot of that."

"Affection, desire, trust."

"No, not trust. Not after what he did to Dad."

"Kenya, you had to trust him in order to sleep with him the first day you met him."

"No, not trust," she still insisted.

"Okay then, let me make sure I have this right. What you're saying is that you met this man in the morning, hung out a few hours and then wound up sleeping with him last night. All because you don't trust him and your master plan is still to ruin him."

"Not exactly, plus when you say it like that, it sounds wrong," Kenya said.

Shelly sipped her coffee. "That's 'cause it is kind of wrong. What are you thinking?"

"I know what I'm doing."

"No, you don't. If you did you wouldn't have done something so out of character. Look, Kenya, I know you're pissed about your father and believe me, I am, too, but you can't just go around hurting people like this. Stuff like this always backfires."

"Believe me, he won't hurt for long. It's not in his nature."

"But it's in yours. Okay, say you get him and he falls for you and then you break his heart. The SEC investigates. Then what? It's not in your nature to be so cruel. If you succeed you're gonna remember this and feel guilty if you're lucky."

"What do you mean, if I'm lucky?"

"I mean you'll be lucky if that's all you feel. Knowing you, you'll wind up just as brokenhearted as him. But you'd beat him in the end. And after all, that was the plan, right?"

"I hate it when you do this."

"I'm just saying," Shelly said quietly.

"I'll be fine and so will he."

"How do you know?"

"He's the Iceman, remember? No feelings, that's how he can destroy people like my father so easily. I'm just beating him at his game. It's just that the stakes are different."

"And what if your heart gets broken in the process?" Shelly asked.

"It won't. I remind myself that it's just business all the time."

"Even when you were with him last night?" she asked. Kenya paused. No, she couldn't honestly say that it was all business. The feelings she experienced being with him went beyond revenge. Her anger had turned to want and her want to need. She needed him last night. "One more question," Shelly said. Kenya looked up at her. "What if he doesn't call you and you don't hear from him again? Then what? You said he usually only goes out with a woman once, maybe twice, right?"

The idea of him not contacting her again was a definite possibility. He'd gotten what most men wanted. She'd made it too easy for him. There was no challenge, no real need for him to see her again. But hopefully the message she sent by way of his sister would pique her curiosity and she would initiate a conversation with Trey.

But nothing was completely set where Trey was concerned. Everything she'd read told her that he was unpredictable. Shelly was right—what if he was through with her?

"Is that someone knocking on the front door?" Shelly asked.

"Are we expecting a delivery today?" Kenya asked.

"I'll go see who it is," Shelly said. She went into the front area then came back. "Kenya, it's for you."

"Me? Who is it?"

"You wouldn't believe me if I told you."

Chapter 11

It was the end of a very long and strange day. Shelly had gone home early and now Kenya was more than ready to go home. She'd just finished adding miniature crystal beads to a christening gown and her eyes were beginning to droop. She was exhausted.

She stuffed the satin bodice with tissue then wrapped it in muslin and put it in a small garment bag. After turning off the overhead lamp, she gathered her things. She dropped her sketch pad into her portfolio and headed to the front. Just as she got there, she looked up, posted on a smile then unlocked the door. "Hi."

"Good evening. I presume you were expecting me?"

"Of course, come on in." She opened the door wider and Trey walked inside. She smiled, seemingly ready to trap her fly. "We got your gift this morning, thank you. It was unexpected but most welcome."

"I hope it was okay." He turned to her, his expression calm and serene.

"Yes, as a matter of fact it was perfect. Everything was taken care of. Apparently it wasn't as bad as we were originally told. Your electrician was very thorough."

"Good, I'm glad. I considered sending flowers and candy but they just seemed a bit ordinary." He leaned back casually against the countertop.

"Oh, of course, and you're anything but ordinary," she said as she leaned back on the counter beside him. "But you're right, if I'm not mistaken, a paid-in-full electrician is definitely a more appropriate next-day acknowledgement for a one-night stand."

"Oh, a one-night stand, you make it sound so dispassionate. If I remember correctly we were anything but passionless."

"Last night was a—" she began.

"Please don't say a mistake."

"Last night was a lapse in judgment on my part."

"A lapse in judgment would imply once. We lapsed three times, if I remember correctly."

"Four, but who's counting," she said, stepping away. "But that's what it was for all practical purposes. Calling it a one-night stand makes it civilized."

"Lapse in judgment, um, that's disappointing."

"Were you expecting something more?" she asked, turning to him.

He looked around, nodding. "Oh, I don't know, maybe a plumber, drywall hanger, carpet, heating and air-conditioning person, a couple of painters, maybe a few furniture deliverymen."

She had to laugh. "You don't quit, do you?"

"No, and apparently neither do you," he said.

"Where are the twins, still out?" she asked.

"Mrs. Thatcher is caring for them."

"Your new nanny?" she asked. He nodded. "So how's she working out?"

"She's pretty good, very professional, stern, but fair. She's taken care of the twins before."

"I see."

"You know, you could have had that position."

"That would mean me moving in for the week. After last night I hardly think that would be appropriate."

"Maybe not appropriate, but interesting," he said.

"You have a very naughty mind, Mr. Evans."

"Let's see, you sleeping just down the hall. I think I like that idea. No, actually down the hall would be a bit far, given your appetite."

"Okay, enough, you win. So what are you doing at this end of town? It's not exactly your usual hangout, is it?"

"How do you know what or where my hangouts are? Oh, that's right, you read up on me."

"Obviously I missed a few articles."

"Obviously, but to answer your question, I came to see you," he said, his eyes softened with purpose. "You look particularly pleased with yourself this evening."

"I am particularly pleased with myself this evening."

"Aha, you think you have something on me, don't you?" he asked, stretching out a broad net of possibilities. She flinched. He smiled and chuckled with a knowing nod.

"I gave myself away, didn't I?" she asked. He nodded. "No problem. Yes, I do have something interesting."

"Intriguing," he said. "Now am I to guess, or will you be surprising me?"

"No need to guess, but be assured that I will use it, when the time comes." She arched her brow for added meaning.

"Cryptic." It was obvious that Trey loved this game.

"What happened between us last night doesn't change anything," she told him.

"I'd be very disappointed if it did," he said.

"I'm still going to get my father's company back."

"You can try."

"Would you like to give up now?" she asked. "Offer a mea culpa?"

"No. You?"

"Hardly," she said.

"Good, then shall we begin negotiations?"

Kenya smiled coyly and looked away. "Actually, I was just about to call it a night. I'm a little tired. I didn't get a lot of sleep last night."

"What a coincidence, neither did I. Are you going home?" She nodded. "May I escort you home?"

"Sure, why not." She grabbed her purse and garment bag from the counter then turned to pick up her portfolio. Trey picked it up for her.

"I missed you this morning," he whispered too close. Her heart skipped as her stomach fluttered. This was so unfair. Why did it have to be him that took her breath away? What do you say to someone you're supposed to despise, when all you can think about is how much you want him? "Come on, let's go."

They stepped outside and he waited as she locked the door and secured the gate. "It's raining again. Where's your car?" he asked.

"Down the street," she said.

"We'd better make a run for it. Let's go," he said, preparing her for a quick dash to the car.

"No, not necessary. I usually walk home."

"Where do you live?" he asked. She looked straight up above them. Trey looked up to see apartments above the boutique and other storefronts along that side of the street. It never occurred to him that there was more to the building.

"This way," she said as the rain fell heavier. They hurried a few feet and came to an iron gate. She unlocked it with her key then they entered a small covered alcove. They passed through and entered a secluded enclosed garden area. There, a stone pathway encircled a small fountain. They hurried across to a narrow doorway. She unlocked it. They entered the lobby then headed to the large freight elevators. She unlocked the elevator and pushed the button for the fourth floor. Moments later the elevator door opened at her condo.

"Come on in. I'll get some towels," she said quickly before disappearing behind a screen.

When she returned with towels Trey was standing at the window looking down on the street. She walked over and handed him a towel. He turned to her.

"I think I like seeing you wet."

The hope of not blushing wasn't even plausible. It seemed whatever this man said, innocent or not, she blushed. "Thanks. I think. Speaking of negotiations—" she began.

He leaned down into the curve of her neck and inhaled deeply. "Did I mention that your scent is intoxicating?" He lingered too long and a tingle of desire began to inch into her.

"We're negotiating, not smelling."

"Attractive, intelligent, sexy, seductive…"

Kenya swallowed hard as she closed her eyes to stay her pounding heart and fluttering stomach. She was just about to grab and kiss him when she felt him lean back and walk away.

"Great view. I never imagined," he said as he looked at her and not at the large windows behind him.

"Yeah, it's not bad," she said quickly, then walked over and stood near the ledge. "It's better at sunset. The building faces west so there's a show every night. Also it's the general direction where they do fireworks in town. I can just sit back, relax on the sofa and be amazed."

"It sounds pretty good. Maybe I can get an invitation to check it out one of these days."

"We'll see," she said evasively.

After drying off, she made tea and they sat on the wide cushioned windowsill and watched the traffic crawl beneath them.

"Your home is really beautiful," he said and looked at her admiringly.

"It's not exactly Woodley Park, but it's home."

"It's comfortable, warm and inviting—it's you."

"I liked it the instant I saw it. I know it's the typical artist loft and it's such a cliché. But it's perfect, close to work and everything."

"So what have you got to eat in this artist loft?"

"Eat?" she questioned.

"Yeah, you know, food," he said.

Kenya stood and walked over to the kitchen area. It was large and modern but empty. She opened the refrigerator and looked in. Trey stood right behind her. "Okay, I have eggs, bacon and a bunch of other stuff."

"What do you usually eat after work?" he asked.

"I usually grab something on the way in."

"That's terrible. Oh, that's right, you don't cook, you bake bread."

"Of course I cook, it's just boring cooking for one."

He removed his jacket, grabbed the eggs and bacon and some other ingredients from the refrigerator. He placed them on the counter then looked around. "Cheese, butter, onions?" he queried. She nodded then began to gather the ingredients. Once collected, she brought them to the counter.

"No onions. How about shallots?"

"Even better," he said. "I need a cutting board, a sharp

knife, a skillet, a spoon and a spatula." She delivered everything as he rolled up his sleeves and washed his hands. She handed him a paper towel then washed her hands, too.

Trey stood at the stove while Kenya cut up the ingredients. She got out a bowl and he began mixing everything together. She was amazed how comfortable he seemed in the kitchen. He looked more like a sous chef than a businessman. Eventually Kenya relinquished her kitchen duties. She turned on the CD player and poured two glasses of wine. When everything was chopped and added, Trey poured the ingredients into the hot-buttered skillet. The mixture sizzled, instantly sending a heavenly aroma into the air.

"Yum, that smells fantastic. I haven't had an omelet in forever."

"Not just an omelet, sweetheart, it's a frittata, an Italian omelet. That makes it special." He grabbed the chopped herbs and more cheese and sprinkled them on top of the bubbling egg mixture.

"That's a work of art. Where did you learn to cook like this?"

"I wanted to be a chef."

"What?"

"Aha—see, not everything about me is on Google. And some things you hear might not be the whole truth."

They looked at each other for a second. His eyes captured and held her. Kenya quivered inside. If she didn't know any better she'd swear he knew what she was up to.

"But a chef?"

"A pastry chef to be exact. You should taste my pastries and pies."

She opened her mouth but was speechless. The man insisted on surprising her at every turn. Just when she thought she had him figured out, he changed up on her.

Kenya just shook her head and took a sip of her wine as

she looked over at the stovetop. "Don't you need to flip it or something?"

"No, not with a frittata," he said as he turned the oven's broiler on. Moments later he placed the skillet on the top shelf right beneath the fire. Within seconds the omelet was perfectly toasted. He pulled it out then added a sprig of parsley. Kenya busied herself setting the table. Trey walked over and looked at her handiwork—candles, china and wine. "Mind if I make a suggestion?"

"No, not at all," she said.

He looked over to the large windows. The rain had stopped and the last of the day was fading in the west. The sky had brightened, the sun had peeked through and the color pallet was breathtaking. "How about dinner with a view?" he asked.

She nodded. "Perfect." She reset the coffee table, adding the bottle of wine. Trey brought the sliced frittata and set it down. Kenya looked at him as he placed a slice on each of the plates then added a small salad with his special vinaigrette dressing. He poured more wine to top off their glasses. *It's business,* she tried to tell herself, but it just didn't work.

She bowed her head and said grace. When she looked up Trey was smiling at her. The truth and emotion in his eyes made her feel guilty. Her heart opened up, against everything she read and heard and believed. Against her mind, her head and her reason, she knew right then that she'd fallen for him.

"To you, Kenya, you're an incredible woman." She nodded her gratitude as they touched glasses. "Come on, dig in."

He cut a piece with his fork and took a bite, then nodded. She did the same. The food melted in her mouth like heaven. It was beyond delicious. "I can't believe all this was in my refrigerator."

"Yeah, about that, we're gonna have to pick it up a bit. We'll go shopping for some real groceries."

"No way, it'll just sit and rot. There's no way I'm going to come home every night and cook like this. You can do it, but I can't. Give me a microwave dinner or takeout any day."

"I guess that means I'm gonna have to be around to cook for you, at least for a little bit. Is that all right with you?"

Kenya refused to look at him even though she knew he was looking at her. One turn in his direction and she knew she'd completely abandon her plan. "I'll think about it."

Two slices of frittata each and a bottle of wine later, and they were full, relaxed and comfortable. They cleaned up the kitchen at his insistence. She was just too relaxed to bother so he did most of the work.

"Why do you do that?" she asked as she sat on a stool at the counter and watched him load the dishwasher and wipe down the stove and countertop.

"Do what?" he asked as he turned to her.

"Be so nice, so wonderful," she said in a near whisper.

"Kind of hard to hate me, huh?" he asked.

"Yeah, something like that," she said.

He walked over and stood between her legs. He reached up and stroked her face gently. She looked at him. Her eyes begged for redemption. "Your eyes are glassy. You had too much wine."

"No, I didn't. I'm fine. I'm just—"

"Just what?" he asked as he slowly leaned in to kiss her.

"Falling..."

"Don't worry, I'll catch you," he whispered instantly, surprising himself as the words held tight.

"No, you won't."

"Yes, I will," he promised. "Remember, I told you I'd never lie to you." She nodded. "Believe it." She nodded again. He kissed her again. "Now come on and walk me to the elevator."

"You're leaving?" she asked as she held on to him and pulled him back to her. He nodded. "Stay."

"No."

"Why not?" she asked.

"Because if I stay, I'll want to make love to you and I can't do that."

"But I want you to," she said truthfully as she pulled his hips closer. "I want to be with you tonight. Stay." He shook his head. "Why not?"

"This is moving too fast for both of us. We have to slow it down. I'm not interested in a one-night stand with you, Kenya," he said as he gently kissed her temple. "Let's get to know each other, not from what you read on the Internet or from files, but for real, the real us. Can you do that?"

She laid her head on his chest and felt the comfortable rhythm of his heart. It wasn't made of ice after all. It beat and pumped just like everybody else's. She wrapped her arms around him and held tight. The feeling of falling came to her again. All she had to do was let go. But she couldn't. Letting go would mean walking away and she couldn't do that yet.

She was no fool. She knew that as soon as he found out exactly what she was up to and intended to do, he'd hate her. So holding on only prolonged this feeling. He was right about everything. They had happened too fast. She did want to know him aside from all the drama. And she did believe that he would catch her when she fell. It was the last part that made her sad.

He'd never lied to her, yet she'd done nothing but lie to him from the moment they met. It was doomed from the start. She'd gone into this with her eyes wide open and it was nobody's fault but her own. She'd made her bed, now it was time to lie in it. "I don't know," she said softly, then hopped down from the stool. She took his hand and walked him over to the sofa. They sat down. "Let's talk."

"Okay," he said. "Me first. I have one sister, younger, you met her. She just completed a graduate program at GWU a few years ago. She's a pain and insists on spending more time in my personal business then she should. I got your message, by the way."

Kenya smiled. "Yes, we met. She seemed nice."

"She is."

"Brothers?" she asked. He didn't answer right away. He seemed to be debating the question. "It's not that difficult a question, or is it?"

"I have two half brothers."

"Oh."

"Parents," he said.

"My mom is a sweet, kind and generous woman. She loves her flowers and would rather go to a flower show than a stage show. She'd give her last penny to help someone or intervene to save a stray cat. She has a loving, trusting spirit. Too trusting sometimes but then again, I wish I was more like that, like her."

"Aren't you?" he asked.

She shook her head. "She's forgiving, too. I'm not like that. I wish I was."

"Maybe you just need to work on it."

"Yeah, maybe," she said thoughtfully. "We never really talk anymore. We don't have a whole lot in common. I guess if anything I wish she was more proactive about her life."

"How do you mean?" he asked.

"She's not that old, but she's like a product of the fifties. She gives my father full rein to do everything. Even when he clearly has no idea what he's doing."

"Is that a bad thing?"

"Yes, it is."

"She lets him be a man. Sometimes that's important."

"No, she gives up her power. My dad does whatever he pleases. She never says a word. He makes all the decisions about money. My mom wouldn't know a thing about what to do with money."

"You'd be surprised what people know."

She looked at him. "What do you mean?"

Trey smiled. "I've learned never to underestimate people. They have a way of surprising you."

"I guess you're right," Kenya said, and then paused. "She loves him, I get that, but when is love weakness?"

"You think her love for your father makes her weak?"

She nodded. "Sometimes."

"You don't want to be weak," he surmised.

"No, never again. She completely lost herself. I don't ever want to be like that."

Trey nodded. It explained a lot. "I can't believe I'm about to say this, but love isn't about losing yourself in someone else, it's about finding yourself."

"Is that off a ninety-nine-cent Valentine's Day card?"

He smiled. "No it's a theory I've been working on lately."

"Well, it is for the women in my family. It's a curse, I think. My grandmother was the same way. My grandfather finally left her. And she had to fend for herself and their daughter. And I, believe it or not, almost gave up everything the same way."

"But you didn't?" he asked.

"No."

"You know, being strong is fine. Having power is great but love is the ultimate high."

"And you know this how? By all accounts you're not exactly a poster child for happily-ever-after."

"But it's all around me, my family and friends. I see their joy and sometimes I'm just a bit envious."

"Have you ever been in love?" she asked.

"I'm not sure," he said honestly.

The way he looked at her made her insides melt. He was

saying something but she didn't want to hear it. "Okay, your mother," Kenya said.

"My mom is special. She's loving and the most caring woman I know, present company excluded. She's like a superhero, she believes in honesty and courage and standing up for what's right. She's not afraid to fight the good fight if she thinks it's for a good cause. She's got a strong sense of right and wrong and a keen business sense. My sister is a lot like that. I'm not."

"Funny, I would think you were describing yourself. Aren't you supposed to be brilliant? Businesswise, I mean." Trey laughed.

"Let's just say I'm skilled."

"Okay, what about your father?" he asked.

Kenya tensed. "You first," she said, stalling.

"Okay, what do I say about a man I grew up hating?"

"What, you hated your father?" she said.

"Correction, I didn't know my father. There was a man who showed up on occasion with presents and money. He'd come in, talk about business, money and power, and then he'd leave."

"I presume your parents were divorced."

"Thankfully yes, they divorced a few years after my sister was born. She didn't even really get to know him at all."

"But you did."

"I knew enough."

"Do you still see him?"

"No, not since I took over his company."

"So that part is true, you took over your own father's company?" she said slowly. "Why? How could you do that?"

"I had my reasons."

"And that justifies what you did, taking a man's life's work, stealing his company. Fine, maybe he wasn't the greatest guy in the world, and maybe he was a lousy father, but taking everything he had, I don't think so."

"You're taking this personally. It wasn't personal, it was business."

"Like with my father, too. Was that just business? I know my dad's not perfect, but he didn't deserve what you did. You just can't arbitrarily make a business decision and change a person's life."

"Yes, I can," he said.

"Just like that, cold and calculated," she said.

He nodded. "When I have to be."

"When you took over your father's company, is that when they started calling you Iceman?" she asked. He nodded. "I wondered about that. I guess under the circumstances, it's fitting."

Very few people knew the absolute truth behind the takeover of his father's company. Usually he didn't care one way or the other what people thought or believed. But for some reason he didn't want Kenya to think any less of him than she already did.

"The truth is he was ruining the company. He'd already taken some of the employee pension money, he didn't pay taxes and the federal government was about to toss him in jail. I bought the company, revived it and got the government off his back. So of course he wanted me to sell it back to him, at a very reasonable rate. I refused."

"Why would he want it back, to keep doing what he was doing? What about the employees?"

"I don't think they really mattered. He sued me for misrepresentation of intent. The headlines during the court case were pretty sensational. He was the poor pitiful father and I was the cold-blooded son. I'm sure it sold a lot more papers."

"Did the courts give him the company back?"

"No."

"So you saved the company, paid his debts, saved him from going to jail and still became the bad guy."

"All in a day's work, ma'am," he joked. "Your turn, tell me about James Whitaker."

"Please, you know all about James Whitaker."

"I know the basics. James Whitaker, previous owner of Whitaker Real Estate Investment Company, a small real estate investment company. Six months ago he came at me sideways with a takeover bid."

"A takeover bid," she repeated.

"He made a few amateur mistakes. One being, he sent a letter of intent prematurely. I was able to outmaneuver him. I made a deal with his partner, then bought all his available stock. Bottom line, his company is now my company."

"Couldn't you have given him a break?" she asked.

"Your father played and lost, that's the game. Although, an interesting maneuver, I'll give him that. None of us actually even saw it coming," Trey said.

"So what are you going to do with his company, sell it, strip it?"

"I haven't decided yet," he said smugly.

"Sell it to me."

"What?"

"You heard me. I want it—sell it to me."

"You're going to be a real estate investor now? What about your designs, your boutique?"

"That's not your concern. This is business."

"You can't afford it."

"I'll have Shelly buy me out and get a bank loan," she said.

Trey, knowing better, half smiled while shaking his head. "You can't afford it."

"One good thing about having dated a stock broker is I got really great stock tips."

"I never gave you any stock tips."

"I'm not talking about you."

Trey realized that she was referring to an ex from her past. The sting of jealousy bit him hard. "No, I'm not selling you the company."

The firmness is his tone was final, but there was no way she was giving up. She decided to relent for now, but this was far from over. "Okay, round one of negotiations done."

"Agreed. Now what?"

"Now, how would you like to see what I'm working on?"

"Sure, what is it?" he said, relieved to change the subject.

She got up, grabbed the garment bag and brought the muslin-wrapped garment to the sofa. She laid it on the coffee table and opened it up. His eyes lit up instantly.

"It's a christening gown, right?"

"Right," she said, surprised that he knew what it was.

"It's beautiful," he said, then looked closer. "How long did it take you to do all this?"

"Designing the gown was pretty simple. But the double-knot hand-stitching took a while. Then attaching each bead and crystal was really time-consuming. Every pearl seed and every crystal bead has to be knotted and individually stitched on. But I'm almost finished."

"It's beautiful. You really are very talented."

"Thank you," she said offhandedly.

"No, really, look what you've created. It takes a very special person to create something like this from a few scraps of fabric."

"Okay, okay, stop being nice. It's out of character. Remember you're supposed to be a hard-as-nails businessman, unfeeling and cruel."

"What if this is my true character? What if everything you've read and heard about me is a lie? What would you do then?" he asked. She looked away. "No, don't answer. I don't think I'm ready to hear it. Let's just enjoy the moment."

"So you said before that your cousin Madison and her husband and a lot of your family and friends are away—why didn't you go?"

"I have a very important business deal in the works. It's pretty fragile. The owner selling is skittish. I need to personally see it through. I'll head over in a few weeks."

"Head over where?"

"Africa."

Kenya's heart skipped a beat. She feared that whatever it was might concern her father. "Why is everybody in Africa?"

"My mother's brother, Jace, is married to Taylor Evans. She's an—"

"An artist, I know, I love her work. She's brilliant. I didn't know she was painting again. I thought she retired."

"Semiretired. She only paints for a select few. But this is a special show. Aunt Taylor and Kennedy, my other cousin, are opening an exhibit at the Nubian Art Gallery. It's to raise money for the local area. Kennedy's husband is Adarah and Maurice Mebeko's son."

"Wait, that would make your cousin a princess?"

"Technically, yes," he said.

"That's totally amazing."

"It's a strange, long story. I'll tell you about it one day. But the short version is, it all began with Mamma Lou."

"Your grandmother," Kenya said.

Trey laughed. "No, Mamma Lou is Tony and Raymond's grandmother. Tony is married to Madison."

"Your cousin?" she asked. He nodded. "So she's not really your grandmother, or for that matter, even related to you?"

"Correct."

"I don't get it. Then why were you going out of your way to fool her into thinking that we were together?"

"I wasn't trying to fool her. I'm trying to protect myself."

"Protect yourself? What do you mean? She seems really nice. Why would you need to protect yourself?"

"Make no mistake, Louise Gates is a sweet, wonderful woman as long as she's on Crescent Island."

"Crescent Island? I've never heard of it."

"It's located off the coast of Virginia, so when she's there, she's wonderful. But when she's here, that's another story. Here she's dangerous, sneaky and downright hazardous to your health." Kenya started laughing. "Yeah, it's funny until you wind up with a bull's-eye on your back. She's the worst kind of matchmaker. She's successful."

"So you thought that since she was off the island, she was targeting you?"

"I know she was."

"Was, as in past tense?" she asked.

He nodded. "I'm pretty sure I'm off the hook, but I'm sure not for long." Kenya laughed again. "You don't know Louise Gates, she's unbelievably persistent. Once you're targeted, that's it."

"Well, is she any good at least?"

"She's never failed as far as I know. She has to her credit Tony and Madison, Raymond and Hope, J.T. and Juliet, Juwan and Kennedy, Randolph and Alyssa, Dennis and Faith—and those are only the ones I know about."

Kenya continued laughing. "Wait, wait, let me get this straight. You, a big, strong, powerful businessman, are afraid of a sweet little old lady just because she likes to play matchmaker?"

"Of course not." He paused. "I'm not afraid of Mamma Lou, I'm terrified of her."

They laughed. Kenya shook her head. "You have some kind of family."

"Yeah, tell me about it."

"So how is it that you and your sister have the last name Evans? Did your mother not change her name when she got married?" she asked.

"She changed it. But she changed it back when she got divorced. She also changed our names after the divorce. My birth name was Trey Phillip Garfield."

They went on to talk more about family life, about past experiences and future dreams. Hours passed without them realizing it. "You know what, I'm having a really good time," she said happily.

"You know what, me, too, but it's getting late." He looked at his watch and saw that it was already well after midnight. "Actually it's early."

Kenya glanced at the clock in the kitchen. "Wow, I can't believe we talked all evening."

He nodded. "Maybe we could do it again sometime."

"You mean like on a date."

"Yeah, I guess we really haven't had one of those."

"A date would imply we're seeing each other—we're not. This is business. I have every intention of getting what I want from you."

"I like the sound of that. Okay, we'll negotiate, then. A business date tomorrow night, or rather tonight."

"Negotiate, huh?"

"Yes," he seemed to assure her.

"Okay, call me."

He stood and held his hand out to her. He raised her up easily and held her for a few moments. "I most definitely will. Good night," he whispered in her ear.

"Good night," she said softly.

The evening ended with a sweet good-night kiss.

Chapter 12

Kenya overslept and awoke to her house phone ringing. She jumped out of bed and hurried to grab it. "Hello? Hello?" There was no one there. She hated crank calls early in the morning. She quickly showered and started rushing to get dressed when the phone rang again. She grabbed it quickly. "Hello?"

"Kenya, it's me," Sidney said.

"Hey, Sid, what's up?"

"Listen, I just tried to get money out of the house account and I was told that there were insufficient funds. What's up with that?"

"Insufficient funds? What?"

"Yeah, that's exactly what I said. I mean, Mom and Dad have, like, hundreds of thousands of dollars in the account, right? I don't get it and I checked it three times. Anyway, I have one of those can't-get-out-of lectures and labs this morning, so I was gonna go down to the bank this afternoon after class and see what's up. I don't want Mom and Dad coming back to this stupid drama. Do you want to meet me down there around one o'clock?"

Kenya was almost too shocked to speak. The words *insufficient funds* still had her stunned. "Um, no, listen, you go ahead to class. I'll swing by the bank this morning and take care of this. How much money do you need?" she asked. There was a very pregnant pause on the other end. "Sidney, you there?" Kenya asked.

"Yeah, a couple of hundred," she responded.

"Okay, I'm getting dressed now. I'll meet you at the bookstore on campus in about half an hour. Can you make it there before class starts?"

"Yeah," Sidney said slowly. "Why?"

"To give you the money, Sidney," she said. "I gotta go. See you in a few."

"Wait, one more thing. You need to check your cell. I've been calling it all morning. The message says that there's something wrong with the service."

"Okay, see you in a little bit."

Kenya finished dressing. She went into the living room and saw the christening gown still lying out. She recovered it and carefully placed it back in the garment bag. After a quick stop at the boutique, she dropped off the portfolio, locked up and kept going.

The GWU campus was massive, and finding a place to park was always like playing Russian roulette. She had a choice, illegal, with the possibility of getting a ticket or being towed, versus walking a half mile. She decided to chance it. She parked illegally right in front of the bookstore and ran in.

Before she got to the entrance, Sidney called out to her. She turned to see her sister waving to come back to the car. Kenya hurried back just as a campus police car turned the corner. "Come on, get in," Sidney said.

Kenya got in and they drove off just as the police car got there. She pulled out an envelope and handed it to Sidney. "Okay, here's the cash. Let me know if you need more. Where do you want me to drop you?" Kenya asked, pulling over again.

"Oh, no, you don't, whoever you are. Where's my real sister."

"Stop playing, Sidney. I'm not driving you around in circles all day. Get out, go to class."

"No, not until you tell me what's up with you."

"Nothing's up with me. Would you just go? I have a ton of things to do today."

"Girl, please, I've either lost my mind, you fell in love or the bank is right about Mom and Dad's account. You never just hand me money, no questions asked," Sidney joked, but she scanned her sister's face and noted her reaction. "Oh, crap, please tell me that I've lost my mind."

"Okay, okay, you've lost your mind," she said hurriedly.

"Try it again," she said.

"Fine, I'm head over heels in love. Now would you please get out of the car," she said. Sidney stared at her, seeming to assess the truthfulness of her remark. "Sidney, I'm just being a good sister—satisfied?"

"Fine," she said as she opened the car door, "let me know what the bank says. Oh, and don't forget to check your cell phone. I might need some more cash later. Bye."

Kenya watched as Sidney got out and ran across the street. She turned and waved then entered a building. She sat watching until she heard a horn sound and saw a campus police car in her rearview mirror. She waved then pulled off. On her way back to the boutique, she dug in her purse for her cell phone. It wasn't there. She couldn't remember the last time she used it so she figured she'd left it on her drawing table as usual.

Kenya stopped at the bank and had a lengthy conversation with the bank manager. Assigned power of attorney, she was able to access her parents' accounts. He informed her that there had been money in an account, but that it had been diverted to a secondary account.

"Diverted to what account, and by whom?" she asked.

"I'm sorry, I'm not at liberty to say," he said.

Kenya sat a moment as he did more checking. Although he couldn't give details, he did say that the secondary account had been set up by a third party. Trey instantly came to mind.

After the bank, Kenya drove to the boutique and parked down the street. She unlocked the door just as a smiling Shelly met her. "You'll never guess what," she said excitedly.

"What?"

"We just got a call from Youngin's retail store in New York. They want to meet with us tomorrow."

"What, are you kidding me?" Kenya said, half smiling, almost afraid to get excited.

"I know, can you believe it?" Shelly said eagerly. "They called this morning. They said that they heard about our work and they want to talk to us. I set up an appointment with them for tomorrow afternoon. We can catch the train up."

"Oh, man, this is fantastic. It's unbelievable. If they like our designs, we can have garments in every one of their retail stores. That's nationwide exposure."

"I know, I know, I can't believe this. We have a ton of things to do today. I don't even know where to start," Shelly said, heading back to the workroom.

"But wait a minute, they said they heard about us. How did they hear about us?" Kenya asked with suspicion, although she was still delighted by the news.

"I don't know. Who cares, it's Youngin's. They want to meet with us," Shelly repeated excitedly.

"Yeah, right." Kenya smiled then laughed along with Shelly. "Okay, I guess we have a million plans to make."

"Yeah, I already started. I reserved our train tickets. Come on."

By midmorning the workroom had been completely demolished. In preparing for the New York meeting, they pulled out every sketch and design they had. They painstakingly reviewed each one. Finally they chose the top twenty design sketches and set them aside to review again later.

That afternoon they did the same with the sample garments. Afterward they took photographs then created a Web presentation. After selecting several pieces they dressed the forms to get a better idea of the fit and range of the collection. They were discussing options when they got a delivery. Kenya answered the door. It was flowers from Trey with a note about their date that evening. He also mentioned that her cell wasn't working.

"Ooh, nice. Who sent the flowers, Mr. Iceman?"

"Yes."

"Don't tell me you and him did it again."

"No, no, nothing like that, although trust me, I wanted to. Hell, I came real close to just pouncing on him. But he said he just wanted to talk. He also said he thought this was moving too fast."

"Ya think?" Shelly said sarcastically as Kenya reread the card.

"All right, I get the point," Kenya said. "He asked me out on a date tonight."

"Aw, now that's nice. Where're you going tonight?"

"I have no idea, but listen to this card—'Thanks for last night. I had an interesting time. Maybe one day we can both let down our masks. In the meantime, negotiations this evening. Dress formal. Trey.'"

"Negotiations, dress formal. Interesting. So what are you gonna wear?"

"Are you kidding? I can't go, not after the message from

Youngin's. We'll probably be working all night long to get ready for tomorrow."

"Kenya, chill, we're ready. Remember, they called us. They must already have some idea of our work. We've already finalized the sketches and chosen some of our best garments. We got this, go on the date. I know I have no intention of staying here panicking all night. It'll be the perfect distraction. And tomorrow we'll—"

"We'll blow them away," Kenya added, finishing her statement as they high-fived, knocked hips and laughed.

"Yeah, that's right, we bad, we bad," Shelly said as she strolled around the table. Kenya laughed.

"Come on, if we're taking the night off, we'd better get back to work."

Shelly leaned over and smelled the flowers. "You know what I think? He really likes you."

"Don't start, Shelly."

"He likes you," she affirmed again.

"No, what he likes is a challenge, and that's what I am. Telling him that I intended to bring him down only whet his appetite. The only reason he's playing this game is because it's a competition."

"You, too."

"Nah-uh," she said quickly.

"Nah-huh," Shelly replied just as quickly.

"I don't want to even think about all that now. Besides, I'm already in the middle of it so I can't really turn around. The best I can do is see this through."

"No, the best you can do is tell the man the truth. Maybe together you can come up with a solution to suit both him and your father."

Kenya shook her head. "Once he finds out what I did, he'll want nothing do with me."

"What, you mean the revenge thing?"

"No."

"What, then?"

"The other day, at his house, after we spent the night together, I got these." She opened a saved file on her laptop and showed Shelly the files she'd copied.

"What are they?"

"Copies of documents from files I found in Trey's briefcase."

"How did you get them?"

"I took pictures of them with my cell phone."

"Please tell me you're joking. You didn't really do that, did you?"

"I did."

"Kenya."

"Shelly, I told him that I wanted my father's company back. I wasn't kidding."

"So you snuck into his briefcase and copied personal papers."

"One of them mentions my father's company."

"Girl, you know you're wrong."

"It doesn't matter. It's too late, it's already done. I just have to read through the documents, find the most damaging and then send it to the SEC. They have a whistle-blower form on their Internet Web site."

"You are not the same person."

"Tell me about it," she said sadly.

"I still vote for telling him," Shelly said, dipping her nose into the aromatic bouquet.

"Girlfriend, this is not a democracy. Come on, let's get back to work," Kenya said as she began shifting things around on her desk.

"Fine, whatever. What are you looking for?"

"My cell. I think I left it here last night."

"Call yourself."

"I did—no service. It must be on mute."

"Or the battery is dead. Are you sure you had it here? I don't remember seeing you with it yesterday."

Kenya started thinking. "I know I had it the day before yesterday. I talked to Asia and my mom. Her and Dad were going on a safari and wouldn't be in contact for a few days. So it must be around here somewhere."

They spent the next fifteen minutes clearing her desk and looking around the workroom. "Well, if you left it here, it's not here now," Shelly said. Kenya stood with her hands on her hips. She had no idea where it was. "When's the last time you used it?"

"I don't know, yesterday I think. No wait, I took some pictures. But I know I dropped it in my purse after that."

"Well, it's not here now. So look, it's late and we pretty much have this under control. Why don't I run out and grab us something to eat and you run over to the phone store and have your phone replaced. You're gonna need your cell phone for tomorrow. Neither one of us will be here."

"Good idea," Kenya said, still wondering about her missing phone. An hour later she walked out of the phone company with a brand-new phone. She and Shelly ate up front while discussing the best strategy for New York. They each decided to take advantage of the trip and do a bit of scouting and shopping in the garment district.

The rest of the afternoon went by quickly. They settled on the perfect sketches and garments to bring along. They refined the computer presentation and decided that each would also bring their personal portfolios. By five o'clock they planned to meet at the boutique, pick up their samples then drive to the train station together. They closed early with confidence that the trip would be a complete success.

Kenya hurried to her condo and got ready for her date. She

showered, dressed, then looked at herself in the mirror. She wasn't the raving beauty Asia was or the smooth-talking home girl Sidney was, but she held her own, too.

She used a bit of makeup and then sprayed on her favorite perfume. She was just finishing her hair when the doorbell rang. She buzzed the opener, releasing the outside gate's security latch. A few minutes later the bell rang again. She pressed the elevator button, sending it down. When the door opened she stood waiting.

Chapter 13

Trey smiled automatically at seeing her. Then a second later he paused, admiring her more fully. She was a vision and she took his breath away. "You look sensational. Is that one of your designs?"

"Yes, it is. Do you like it?"

"I love it. It's gorgeous," he said, encouraging her to turn around. "Wow, you are truly a vision in that gown." He stepped closer as she turned back around to face him again. "I'm tempted to cancel our plans and see how it looks off."

Kenya blushed. He was definitely a charmer. "I thought this was supposed to be a business date."

"It is," he assured her.

"I'm sure you wouldn't say that to Bill Gates," she admonished.

"Probably not," he said, chuckling. "I can't see him filling out that dress as well as you do."

"Business date, remember."

"Aw," he said in mock disappointment. "But, sweetheart, you take my breath away. You look stunning."

"Thanks. You look very handsome in your tuxedo. Are we ready to go?"

"I am if you are."

She walked over to the sofa and grabbed her shawl and evening purse. The aromatic smell of the bouquet of fresh flowers on the coffee table scented the air. "The flowers are beautiful, thank you. But the card was a bit cryptic. Where exactly are we going this evening?"

He held his arm out to her. "You'll see."

They got into the waiting limo and headed south. Kenya still couldn't believe the evening, and it was only the beginning. "So, do you call yourself trying to impress me?"

"No, not particularly. You already know how I live, what I have and probably how much I'm worth. What would be the point?"

"Exactly, so why the limo?" she asked.

"Simple, I'm too lazy to drive."

She chuckled, caught off guard by his response. "You are so silly sometimes."

"Yeah, I get that a lot," he confessed. "You know that old saying—don't judge a book by its cover?" he asked. She nodded. "Well, it's very true, especially in business. I'm not saying that I'm some mild-mannered Clark Kent. But make no mistake, I will take care of business when I have to," he said as the chilling tone in his voice left no doubt.

Kenya nodded then turned to look out the window. A heated flush embraced her as her heart began racing. This was the perfect time to confess, but she couldn't. How did you tell the man you were trying not to care about that you were about to destroy his world? "So where are we going this evening?" she asked softly, changing the subject before she weakened.

"We're going to a political fund-raiser."

"Really? I've never actually been to one, but I've always been curious about them."

"This one might not be the best example."

"Why? What hotel is it being held at?"

Trey smiled. "No hotel. We're going to the circus."

"The circus? I didn't even know one was in town."

"Well, actually it's Cirque du Soleil."

Kenya gasped. Like a switch that had been turned on, she nearly jumped on top of him. "What, really?" she asked. He nodded. "For real, no joke?" she repeated.

"Yes, why, you don't want to go?"

"Are you kidding me? I'd love to go. I've only seen their performances on television, but what I've seen is awesome. I can't believe it. The artistry, the costumes, they're phenomenal. I can't believe we're going," she said excitedly.

"Wow, if I knew I was going to get this response, I'd have gotten tickets sooner."

"It's just a wonderful surprise, that's all. I've always wanted to go. I just never got around to it."

"I'm looking forward to it, too."

The limo pulled up in front of the theater. They got out and breezed into the lobby. They were escorted to their private booth just before the performance began. The show was everything she imagined and more. It was awesome. Kenya's eyes were glued to the stage as Trey's were glued to her. She had the perfect reaction. It was thrilling just seeing her so happy.

Afterward, they went backstage. There Kenya was completely enthralled. She spoke to the costume designers and seamstress and gathered as much inside information as possible. Afterward they ate dinner at a small restaurant then drove around the city the rest of the evening. Kenya relaxed and sat back against Trey. He wrapped his arms around her and she laid her head on his chest. "I don't remember having so much fun. It was an incredible evening. Thank you for this."

"You're very welcome. I had a great time, too."

Kenya closed her eyes. "Tell me about her."

"Tell you about whom?"

"The woman in your last relationship," Kenya said.

"My what?" he asked, taken completely off guard.

"The woman in your last relationship," she said.

"Are we at that point already?"

"Uh-huh," she answered.

"Why do you want to know?"

"I'm curious. What was she like?"

"Truthfully, I haven't had a quote-unquote 'relationship' in a long time. I've dated, obviously, but there's been no one steady woman in my life for some time. There was a woman a long time ago, but it didn't work out."

"Did she break your heart?" Kenya asked.

"No, why?"

"As I said, I'm just curious."

He paused a moment. This conversation was hitting too close to the mark. He needed a good old-fashioned diversion. "The business fast track doesn't leave a lot of time for emotional entanglements."

"You mean relationships, don't you?"

"Semantics. At any rate, I find it hard to sustain a meaningful long-term relationship with my schedule. I just don't have time."

"You take time for what's important and for what really matters to you," she said.

"I guess you're right, because here I am out with you this evening."

"How about that," she said.

"So tell my why you asked."

"I wondered if you'd ever had your heart broken."

"Is that what you intend to do to me?" he asked.

"No one ever intends."

"Not true. To answer your question, no, not yet. But there's always a first time, right?" he offered. She nodded silently. "What about you? Tell me about your last relationship."

She sighed heavily. This wasn't what she wanted to talk about but in all fairness she started it. "We met in New York. He was a businessman, very determined and very focused on his goals. He was strong-willed and charming and well on his way to being very, very successful. I believed in him and I thought I knew everything about him. He was everything I thought I wanted."

"But?" he asked.

"But he wasn't. He asked me to give up my work to be there for him, totally devoted and attentive."

"Did you?"

"Yes, for a while I did. We moved in together and I was the perfect girlfriend."

"Then," he prompted.

"Then I realized he wasn't the man I thought he was. Everything I thought I knew was a lie."

"What do you mean?"

"I found out that I wasn't the only woman in our so-called monogamist relationship. His reasoning was that he needed more than I could give."

"I see."

"Unbeknownst to me he had a child by one woman and had gotten another woman pregnant, after I put aside my career for him. I found myself in the middle of baby-mamma drama. So that was the end of that. Oh, one last thing, he was a stock broker."

"Figures."

"Yeah, figures," she said.

"He lied to you, cheated on you and played you."

"Yes. But that's long over now."

"Good, I'm glad," he said.

"Good, I'm glad," she repeated. "Insensitive much? I just poured out my soul to you and all you can say is 'good, I'm glad'?"

"Yes, because had you not gotten rid of him, we might never have met."

The genuine sweetness of his remark made her smile. He'd caught her off guard again. Every time she thought that she had a handle on him, he turned it around. "What have I gotten myself into with you?" she questioned quietly.

"I've been asking myself that same question."

"Is that bad?" she asked sleepily.

"I sincerely hope not."

She yawned, covering her mouth. "Excuse me. Do you know that since I met you, I have yet to get to bed before twelve o'clock?"

He reached over and pressed a button on the side panel. "Driver, take us back, please."

"I really like being with you, Trey. I know I'm not supposed to. You're so wrong for me."

He kissed her forehead. "With that said, shall we test the waters again? How about dinner tomorrow evening?"

"I can't. I have plans tomorrow."

"Another man? Should I be jealous?"

"Definitely," she joked.

"Who is this rival?"

"Manhattan."

"I think I know him. Tall guy, beard and mustache?" She poked him gently as he chuckled. "So you're headed to New York tomorrow."

"You should know. I have a feeling you set the whole thing up."

"What whole thing?"

"Shelly and I got a call this morning from Youngin's retail stores. They want to see our work. They're interested in selling us through their stores."

"That's wonderful. Congratulations. But how would I know about it?"

"You didn't set this up?" she asked.

"No, sorry, I wish I had. But it wasn't me," Trey said.

"Well, then I wonder how they heard about us."

Trey shrugged. "I have no idea. It wasn't me, unfortunately."

"Hmm," she said, seeing the familiar landmarks of her street as the limo pulled to a stop in front of her building. The driver got out and opened the door. Trey helped Kenya out and walked her through the alcove and to the elevator. "I hate to keep being redundant, but thank you, I had the best time."

"I'm glad."

"So I guess I could invite you up for a nightcap."

"You could," he said, smiling, "but we both know where we'd be two seconds later, especially after seeing you in this gown." He touched her bare shoulder and slowly traced the curve of her breasts down to her hip. He breathed deeply. "You realize, of course, that I'm going to dream about this dress tonight."

She leaned close and whispered, "That was the whole idea."

He instantly grabbed her waist and drew her close, pressing her against his hard body. He didn't speak or kiss her, he just stood there looking into her eyes, holding her tight. The piercing gaze took her breath away. Then he closed his eyes, released her and walked away.

"Trey," she called to him. He stopped but didn't turn. She walked and stood behind him. She leaned her body against his back, molding as close to him as she could get. She reached around and held his chest, laying her cheek on his back. "What do I say?" she asked herself out loud. "How did I let this happen?"

"It sneaks up on you," he told her.

"Yes, it does."

"You're not alone." He turned, grabbed her in his arms and kissed her until she forgot who she was. All she knew was that she was his for as long as he wanted her.

Chapter 14

Trey sent the driver away.

He walked back to the building and met Kenya at the elevator. She pushed the button as soon as he got in. They stood across from each other, their eyes staring into each other. The doors closed. The silent hush of the mechanics jerked the elevator's motion. It began to rise. With each floor they passed Kenya's heart beat harder, faster, stronger. The anticipation of being with him made her whole body quiver. Her breathing increased and her body, already on fire, was tingling.

She watched him watch her. He didn't move, yet the muscle in his jaw flexed tight. She slowly lowered the shawl from her shoulder, letting one end hit the floor. His eyes didn't waver. She leisurely reached up and released the clip holding her hair in the loosened French twist. Loose waves and ringlet curls dropped to her shoulders.

By the third floor, her breasts seemed to expand, nearly

bursting from the bodice. She arched her back, giving him full view of her offering.

The elevator arrived on the fourth floor. The doors opened. She pushed away from the side and walked out. But before she got two steps into the loft, Trey grabbed her hand and pinned her back against the inside of the elevator wall. He pressed the hardness of his body firmly against her. He leaned in, parted his lips but didn't kiss her. Just inches away, she waited, feeling only the sweet grind of his body against her. Her breathing was labored as his fiery eyes blazed hot with passion.

Then, in an instant, he took her mouth, pressing his lips to hers forcefully. The kiss was intense. She stopped breathing and her heart raced, but she was too overcome to notice. She felt the steel-hard shaft of his manhood press into her. Her stomach fluttered as her desire surged. She moaned as his kisses fell to her neck, her shoulders, her chest. The elevator beeped. She pushed him back against the button panel. The doors closed again.

Moments later, the doors opened. They were on the building's roof. The warm breeze blew around them as they barely even noticed. He touched her body freely, caressing her shoulders, arms and breasts. She reached behind him and pressed the fourth-floor button again. The doors closed. When they opened a short time later they were back at her apartment. She pulled away from his embrace. Breathless and overcome by passion, she staggered into her apartment. Trey followed.

She turned, grabbing his tuxedo jacket and removing it. He held her and kissed her hard. She pulled the end of his tie then started unbuttoning his shirt. Midway down, she ripped it open. With the shirt opened she touched his chest, running her palms over his nipples. He hissed and moaned, pressing her against the back of the sofa. Her fingers tantalized his nipples and his hands stroked her breasts.

They were mindless in their pursuit. "I don't want to rip it. Take it off," he muttered huskily. She turned away from him, revealing the indiscernible zipper in the back. He found the tab and pulled down. The fabric separated, revealing her smooth, even skin. "Take it off," he ordered. She turned, holding the bodice up just over the tips of her nipples. The abundant swell of her breasts teased him. "Take it off," he repeated. She let the garment fall.

Kenya was now standing there in just lace panties and stiletto heels. Trey stepped back and stared, admiring his prize. "Yes?" she asked teasingly. "See something you like?" He nodded needlessly. The very definite protrusion in his pants proved his eagerness. But to her surprise, he just stood there, staring at her body.

"Woman, you have no idea what you do to me."

She ran her finger around the top of her black panties and smiled at him, tilting her head suggestively. "Tell me, what do I do to you, Trey?"

He smiled, eyeing her seductive actions. She continued toying with the elastic, dipping it down teasingly. "You set my body on fire," he said.

"Is that all, Trey, or is there more?" she coaxed slowly. She walked over to him and traced her finger over his chest, each nipple, over his shoulder and then down his back. He closed his eyes and tipped his head up. She leaned in, resting her bare breast on his back. Her nipples pebbled and she moved back and forth.

She reached around front and loosened his pants, then slowly undid the zipper, feeling his hardness the whole time. His pants dropped. She pressed her body, molding tightly against the back of him. "What else do I do to you, Trey?" she whispered just over his shoulder.

He turned instantly and kissed her, holding her with one

hand while stroking her body with the other. He touched the elastic all the way around, ending with his hands caressing her buttocks. She pulled back breathlessly. "Trey, right here, right now," she muttered.

He shook his head. "No. Where's the bedroom?" he rasped faintly. She turned, looking over his shoulder. He leaned down and grabbed something from his pants pocket. Then in an instant he whisked her up in his arms and went in that direction.

Moments later she fell on the bed with him kneeling on top. Her panties disappeared, as did his briefs. He covered himself, and then hovered an instant before delving deep inside her.

The one smooth motion made her gasp as she dug her nails into his back. Her body quivered and quaked as spasms of release began to take her. The thrusts came quickly, repeatedly, in rapid succession. His divine fullness swelled, filling her completely. She wrapped her legs around his body, holding on tight against the intense pleasure.

He pulled out then thrust again, repeating the action over and over. She arched upward, begging for more. His mouth found her nipple. He licked and suckled, sending tremors of pleasure through her body. The penetration deepened. She writhed beneath him. She fell into his tempo, rocking her hips against his. The frenzied tension surged stronger and harder until the intense eruption exploded. In a blinding light they climaxed.

He quivered and stiffened, she spasmed and released. Moments later he rolled to her side. She looked at him, dreamily breathless, eyes hooded. He smiled mischievously. "You don't think I'm done with you yet, do you?"

Before she could respond, he reached down and captured her tiny nib, and she climaxed instantly. He stroked her again. She gasped, holding her breath, then quivered sporadically, jerking her body like a rag doll.

He repeated the action, and then awaited her release. She didn't disappoint. Her body shook with unrestrained rapture. The madness of his torture was pure ecstasy. Again. Another orgasm shot through her body like a bolt of lightning. She shrieked, abandoning all modesty. She grabbed his hands breathlessly. "Enough," she rasped unevenly. He stopped.

It took ten minutes before her heart slowed and her breathing returned to normal. "If I didn't know any better, I'd say you were trying to go for some kind of Guinness world record," she said.

"Um, that sounds like an interesting idea. How about if I—" he began as he reached down between her legs.

"No, no, no." She rolled away from him only to have him bring her back to his side. "I already think my heart stopped beating. One more climax and I'm pretty sure I'll pass out."

He encircled her tighter, bringing her close to the side of his body. "We wouldn't want that," he muttered. "Then again, the things I could do with your unconscious body might be very interesting."

She closed her eyes, exhausted. "Shh. Sleep."

They did.

A few hours later Kenya opened her eyes. She was lying on her stomach and Trey was sitting up beside her. She felt his hands touching her back and rear. "What are you doing?" she asked.

"Nothing?" he said innocently.

"That doesn't feel like nothing."

He continued massaging her buttocks. "I love that right now, you're mine. So these belong to me." He smoothed and rounded her cheeks, kissing and licking the tops.

"Possessive?" she asked, twitching as her body moistened in response.

"Oh, definitely, I'm very protective of what's mine. Ever since I was a kid, I didn't like the whole idea of sharing."

"I bet your kindergarten report card read, 'doesn't play well with others.'"

"How did you know?" he asked, nibbling her neck.

"Lucky guess?" she asked as her stomach fluttered.

"Kindergarten, right?" she muttered in a haze of sleep and arousal.

He chuckled softly. "What? You sound distracted."

"Distracted, me? You have no idea." This slow, melodious torture was too arousing. "Mmm, that feels good," she muttered as he continued to rub and caress her back and shoulders. His hands flowed down her thighs then back up to her rear, centering again on the rounded cheeks. His fingers dipped between her legs and she moaned out loud, feeling her love come down. "Trey," she muttered. "Trey."

The sensual fog of desire draped heavily over her. He had a way of making her want him without even trying. And when he was trying, like now, Lord help her, she was just putty in his masterful hands.

"I could do this forever," he said, "be here with you."

The pang of guilt that had plagued her for so long surfaced again. It was now or never. She took a deep breath, rolled over then sat up to face him. "Trey, wait, I need to tell you something. You're not going to like it and you'll probably be—"

"Tell me later, not now," he interrupted.

"I have to tell you now, it's important. I may not have the courage again later. That first day we met—"

"Shh," he said leaning over to kiss her. "I know it's important, and we'll deal with it another time, I promise. But right now let me love you."

With his hands on her rear, he lifted her up to sit straddling his legs. She sat, wrapped her arms around his neck and looked down into his sparkling eyes. She wanted to say so much, to explain everything. But his expression muted her to silence. He was right, another time would have to do. He continued touching her and she continued basking in the wondrous flow of his undivided attention.

As passions continued, Kenya felt her need escalate. She leaned back. "I don't have any…any…"

"There's more in my jacket pocket," he said knowingly.

She got up and staggered into the living room. She picked up his jacket and found several more condoms. She brought them all. Watching him watch her with his seductive smile amplified her excitement. She tossed all but one on the nightstand, then climbed up on top, straddling him. She opened the package and rolled it down easily. Their eyes connected and held. Then, as smooth as silk, she reared up and lowered herself onto his firm, hard body.

She opened her mouth wider and wider as she filled herself. Seconds later she sat, satisfied to be completely filled. Neither one looked away or moved an inch. Then, smiling, she tensed and clinched, tightening her muscles around him. She could feel his jerking movement inside. His eyes widened. She had obviously surprised him.

She leaned down and kissed him leisurely, letting her tongue roam freely. His mouth opened, devouring her instantly. Their tongues savored the taste and feel of each other. Passion surged in an easy longing pace. She leaned up from the kiss. He reached up, cupping and covering her breasts. The perfect handful was his bountiful pleasure.

He massaged her swollen mounds while tweaking her nipples with his thumbs. Her back arched and she wanted more. He lowered her and captured a mouthful, squeezing both breasts together, nipples just inches apart. His tongue licked lustfully as he moved his head from side to side. Kenya moaned her arousal. It felt so good watching him work his magic.

He released her and took one breast into his mouth as he

fingered the other and massaged her rear. She was blinded by the rapture. Unable to take much more, she pulled back, breathless. He didn't release her; instead he sat up with her still in his mouth.

She pulled from his pucker and rose up, then began pumping her body onto him slowly. Her arms loosely encircled his neck as he held tightly to her hips. The distance between them was just enough for her breasts to tease his nipples, four together hard and pebbled. She pumped slowly, drawing out his pleasure. She felt his body stiffen and tense. She smiled. She could rock her hips on him all night long to watch him come.

Intently, she watched the strained pull of his dwindling restraint. He obviously had no intention of releasing without her. She quickened her pace, raking her lower lip with her teeth. The delight in pleasing him as he had pleased her was her catalyst. She could see his climax coming in his eyes.

Then he shifted beneath her and she gasped. He had found her out. He knew exactly what she was doing. Shifting back, she slowed her pace. Eye to eye, he shook his head and held her hips as she continued her quickened rhythm. Each downward motion tantalized her, stroking her throbbing nib until the last second. In blinding ecstasy they both exploded. She shrieked, grabbing and holding him tight. The fervor of their rapture surged again, spiking another climax for each of them.

Holding each other tight, they waited until their breathing returned and their heartbeats slowed.

"Kenya, don't do that," he whispered in her ear. "I'll never come without you by my side. That's a promise."

She smiled. There was nothing more to say.

They stayed in an embrace for a long time. When she finally got up her body ached. She grimaced. "What's wrong?"

"I'm getting old. My body's stiff."

"Come on, let's take a shower." He got up and led the way to the bathroom. He turned on the water while she stood at the large mirror and pinned her hair up. He came up behind her and placed his hands on her hips. He looked at her reflection and smiled. "You are so beautiful."

She smiled. "Thank you." She stepped aside, revealing his full-frontal nudity. Looking at him was her secret pleasure. "So have you thought about it yet?" she asked as she pulled out several candles.

"Thought about what?"

"My sketching you," she said, bending over.

"Are we back to that again?" he asked as he watched her bottom. His body hardened instantly.

"Will you trust me?" she asked, lighting the first candle.

He looked into the reflection of her eyes. She was genuine. "Okay, okay, after the shower."

She beamed excitedly. "Yeah," she squealed then turned and headed out the bathroom door.

"Whoa, whoa, hey, come back here," he said quickly, grabbing her hand and pulling her back to him. "Where are you going?"

"To get ready…pencils, charcoal, pad."

"Later," he said seductively, arching his brow menacingly. "Right now I want to do a little artistry with your body." She smiled and backed up. He stepped forward. She backed into the shower stall, giggled as he picked up the bar of soap and lathered her front and back.

After the hour-long shower she hurried out, dried off, put on sweats and grabbed her sketch pad. By the time Trey finished drying off she was ready for him. He walked out of the steamy bathroom with a towel over his shoulder. She smiled. The man was too exquisite.

"Oh, no," he groaned, seeing her intention.

"Oh, yes, you promised me and Trey would never break a promise to me."

"How about if I—"

"Nope, no bargains. It's been a long time since I had a model to draw. And I intend to take full advantage of you."

"Really, a long time, huh?" he began. She nodded, prepping her pencils and charcoal. "So who was your last model?" he asked.

"Never mind that, get on the bed and lie down," she ordered happily. He did. She got up, repositioned him, then draped the sheet precisely as she wanted it. "Perfect, now don't move." She grabbed her pad, sat on the other side of the bed and began sketching.

"You know this would be a lot more fun if you were naked, too."

"Nude," she corrected, sketching happily.

"What's the difference?" he asked.

"*Nude* is an artistic expression. It's purely aesthetic, devoid of sexuality. While on the other hand, *naked* is more like a strip club or *Playboy* magazine layout. I believe the professional term is *butt naked.*" He chuckled. "Ideally it's the same thing but a vast difference in perception. Now shh, stay still."

"Nude, naked, I'll take you either way." Trey laughed as he reached out to her.

"Models do not try to grab the artist. Do you think Mona Lisa grabbed Leonardo da Vinci?"

"If Leo was naked, she might have."

Kenya laughed. "Just hush and stay still." He reached out to her again. She blocked his hand away with her sketch pad. "Stay still."

"How long is this gonna take? 'Cause I have a better idea of what to do nude."

"That, sir, would be naked," she said.

"Can't you do this in the nude also?"

"The model is nude in a drawing, not the artist. Now if you don't want this to turn out looking strange, stay still."

He reached out to her again.

"Patience," she muttered, focusing on the sketch.

"Are you almost done?" he asked.

"Almost. Three more minutes." She grabbed another few pencils and began shading the drawing. A few seconds later Trey cleared his throat. "It's only been two seconds."

"It's been three minutes. Are you almost done yet?"

Without answering, she glared at him over the sketch pad. "You have the patience of a two-year-old," she said then refocused on the sketch. She lowered her head to define the details of the drawing. Without looking at him, she refined the edges, deepened the shadows and added the finishing touches. When she finally looked up again the sheet had been moved. He was no longer nude and he was very definitely ready for her.

After half an hour of looking at his nude body, she had to admit, she was very definitely ready for him, too. She tossed the sketch pad aside and unzipped her sweatsuit jacket. Her breasts, full and swollen, perked out instantly.

Trey smiled, enjoying the strip. "Now that's what I'm talking about, the perfect nude."

"No, sweetheart," she said seductively, "this is most definitely butt naked." She hurried out of her pants and lunged at him. He caught her and within an instant they were dancing that most intimate, ancient dance of love.

Chapter 15

The next few days turned out pretty well for Trey, especially since Louise Gates was back on Crescent Island. With her out of the way, he found himself able to relax a lot more. Knowing that she'd pop up at any time, at any place, was definitely distracting.

For the most part he worked from home, leaving Mrs. Thatcher, a real godsend, to care for the twins. The morning schedule was simple. Mrs. Thatcher got them washed and dressed while Trey cooked breakfast. Afterward, they all ate together, then when he went into his home office, they went about their day.

They played, mostly with learning games, at playtime. The twins adored her and she definitely took a load off Trey's mind. He was able to focus on his business deals with few interruptions, although he still found his mind wondering at times.

Kenya was the main reason for his lack of focus. She was

still away in New York. He intended to see her when she returned the same day, but was disappointed when she didn't come back right away. She called him instead. She said that she had extended her stay a few days. His first impulse was to fly to New York to be with her, but he resisted the urge. He was sure he could go a few days without seeing her. If nothing else, he'd get some much-needed sleep.

Three days and only a few hours of sleep. No wonder he wasn't himself. He sat at his desk, smiling, thinking about their last evening together. First Cirque du Soleil, then dinner and then... He stopped and smiled, shaking his head. That woman was too much and he loved every inch of her.

When he finally got home from what was technically their first date, he'd been completely exhausted. Neither one of them had slept much, if at all. Either they were making love or laughing and talking, or making love again.

He didn't even recognize himself lately. For once, he was smiling and genuinely happy. She was the reason why. She changed him. Thankfully no one else noticed because he knew it wouldn't last for long.

Enough. Just as he reached over to call her, his computer conferencing monitor beeped. He hit the open key. Joshua sat with his back turned. He was feeding papers into the fax machine and pulling something from the printer on the credenza behind his desk. He turned, then looked up at his monitor. "Hey," Trey said.

"You called earlier," Joshua said.

"Yeah, I e-mailed you a few prospectuses. I need you to look them over and get back to me. I think we should put them back on the front burner."

Joshua hit a few keys on the keyboard then nodded. "Got 'em. Check your fax. You need to sign off on the agreement, but look it over first. There were unsanctioned changes made.

I'm not exactly impressed. Also check out the new proposals I included. I think they'll work to our advantage."

Trey grabbed the papers coming out of his fax machine. He quickly looked them over as Joshua reviewed each one with him. It took about ten minutes. "I'll look them over in more detail and get them back to you."

Joshua nodded. "I'll have a contract coming your way this evening. Regina is taking care of the formalities."

Trey nodded. Having his sister with him was better than he imagined. She was professional and talented. Her knowledge of international finance and market strategy was exceptional. Plus her naturally bossy nature made her perfectly suited for the position as project manager. "Okay, anything else?" Trey asked.

Joshua leaned back in his chair. "New York's a bit shaky today." Trey looked up more intently. For an instant his focus shifted. "Chances are they'll close further down than anticipated. On the flipside, London, Nikkei and Osaka closed well."

"Yeah, I got that. See if we need to do a short-range dump to correct the forecasted numbers."

Joshua grabbed his pen and wrote a note to himself. "Got it. One more thing, Cedric is panicking. He hasn't seen nor heard from you in five days. He wants to know where you are and what you're up to. The man actually sounds paranoid. He thinks you're gonna bail on the deal."

"Interesting," Trey said, tapping his pen on the desk.

"You know, Trey, I'm still having second thoughts about this deal. I did another check and everything still looks good, but the last few days he's been really shaky."

"It's a huge deal, he should be stressing. When this goes through he'll be sitting on a nice sum of cash plus a quarter interest with TE stock."

"Trey, again—"

"Yeah, I know, you didn't like that little incentive from the beginning. But it was my idea, not his. It's not like he planned it. He had no idea I'd put that on the table."

"He wants to meet with you."

"I'm not coming in today."

"He said he'd go to wherever you are."

Trey chuckled. "He really is stressing, huh? Please relay my apologies and inform him that I do not entertain clients at my home."

"He'll be disappointed," Joshua said, chuckling.

"I can't help that. Anything else?" he asked.

"Nope, we're all set. How's it going there?"

Trey looked around his home office. "Extremely quiet."

"You're lucky," Joshua said just as his phone rang. "Catch you later." He pressed the key and disconnected the link.

Trey looked over the papers Joshua faxed over. He worked for about an hour, made corrections and additions, then finally signed off. He faxed them back to Joshua with additional notes to consider. Taking a break, he got up and went into the living room. There was no one around and the place was just too quiet. He continued to the dining room and then into the kitchen. He found the twins and Mrs. Thatcher out on the patio playing ball. They tossed and rolled it between them.

Trey stood at the door and watched for a few minutes. He laughed seeing Johanna try to toss the ball then see it go backward. She laughed and ran to get it. Jonathan was much better. Trey eventually opened the sliding glass door and stepped out. "Hey, there, everybody having fun?" he asked.

"We didn't disturb you, did we?" Mrs. Thatcher asked.

"No, not at all, I needed a break. This is perfect." He picked up an extra ball, tossed it into the air and caught it. Jonathan took his ball and tried to mimic Trey's toss. He tossed it so hard that it curved behind him. He ran as it rolled away.

Johanna ran and grabbed Trey. He picked her up and gave her the ball. She hit it then tried to hold it with her little hands. As soon as she grabbed hold, she tried to toss it but it just dropped to the ground. Jonathan, with his ball, ran over and tried to pick it up. He dropped both, accidently kicking them in opposite directions. He immediately chased them.

Trey sat Johanna down inside a miniature climbing toy. Jonathan hurried over and crawled inside one of the large openings also. He found his way to the top as Johanna slid down laughing. She sat there at the bottom as Jonathan came sliding right down behind her. Trey quickly whisked her up just as Jonathan landed and jumped up laughing. Johanna laughed at being picked up and Trey laughed at them both.

"You're gonna miss them, aren't you?" Mrs. Thatcher said.

Trey nodded. "I definitely will. When my cousins dropped them off six days ago I didn't think I would survive."

"But look at you now," Mrs. Thatcher said, smiling. "You're turning into a professional, Mr. Mom. I think I might be out of a job soon," she added.

"I wouldn't say all that," he joked. "I guess I just learned that not everything stays perfect or is perfect. With toddlers, you have to loosen up."

"Just a bit, and that's true of adults, as well," she said. "We're not perfect and I don't know anybody who couldn't use a second chance or two. Some of us need to have a bit more patience to get where we need to be."

"You're absolutely right," Trey said thoughtfully. He considered her words. Six days ago, after a few hours alone with the twins, he'd all but given up. Then Kenya showed up and calmed everything down. He had never professed to be a patient man. He was used to everything running smoothly.

"Well, now, we'd better get cleaned up. We had a nice

lunch earlier and a bit of playtime. Now I believe it's time to take a nap," Mrs. Thatcher said.

"Sounds good, and while they're doing that, I'm gonna grab something from the kitchen then get back to work," Trey said. He grabbed Johanna before she ran for the slide again. Mrs. Thatcher took Jonathan's hand and the four of them went back into the house. Trey went into the kitchen while Mrs. Thatcher and the twins headed up to the bedroom.

He made a sandwich and grabbed a soda and took them into his office. He ate and watched the business report then afterward he opened the Caine Enterprises file on his computer and grabbed the leather folder he'd been reading over the past few days. Moments later he was deep into reviewing the files.

There was a knock. He looked up. Mrs. Thatcher stood in the office doorway. "Hi, come on in, Mrs. Thatcher. Is everything all right?"

"Oh, sure, of course. The twins are taking their afternoon nap. I just wanted to give this back to you. Johanna has been playing with it and it really isn't good for her."

"What isn't?" Trey asked, just as Mrs. Thatcher placed a working cell phone on his desk. "A cell phone. Whose is it?"

"I don't know. It was in the playpen with the toys," she said.

"Thank you. I'll make sure to take care of it."

"Good. I'll be out in the yard reading. I have the monitor if the twins wake up early."

"Okay, thanks, Mrs. Thatcher."

She walked out and Trey picked up the cell and looked at it. It certainly wasn't his. He opened it. The screen was black. He pressed the on key but nothing happened. Assuming it belonged to Regina, he plugged it into his phone charger and went back to work.

He spent another few hours working on various projects. He had another computer conversation with Joshua and a few other associates. He was deep in concentration when he heard another knock on the door. "Hey, you busy?"

Trey looked up and smiled. "Hey, no, come on in, grab a seat. I could use a break." Regina walked in and sat in the chair opposite his desk. "How's it going?" he said, glad to take a break. "What time is it?" he asked as he stretched his arms wide.

"A little after six," she said as she pulled a file out of her briefcase. "Joshua asked me to drop these off on my way home. They're the final copies of the Caine proposal."

Trey took the files and glanced at them.

"How was the business trip?" he asked without looking up at her.

"Good, productive, I got everything accomplished. I still have to put a few things together, but you'll see all that later in the report." He nodded. "I see you're going ahead with this merger."

"Yes, I think it's a promising step," Trey said.

Regina shook her head slowly. "Trey, I still don't like it. There's something not right about it."

"Regina, we've gone through this a dozen times. Everything we know, everything detailed in the prospectus, is exactly as it should be. Cal, to his credit, was more than thorough. We couldn't have asked for a better opportunity. To walk away and pass it up would be ludicrous."

"Trey, to have this just fall in our lap, at this point, is too fortuitous."

"Fate, luck, fortuitousness, call it what you like. It's what success is based on. Being in the right place at the right time has always benefited those with the foresight to see the possible outcome."

"Trey, this isn't my first picnic, I know business," Regina said firmly.

He smiled and nodded. "I didn't mean to sound condescending."

"Then don't. You asked for my opinion, I gave it to you. I expect you to take it under consideration."

"I have. We did our homework thoroughly, you know that. We've checked, double-checked and triple-checked. Believe me, everything is exactly as it should be. We've noted your dissent and I have taken it under consideration. But, Regina, you yourself signed off on the original prospectus."

"Fine," she said, tossing her hands up in surrender. "So what are you up to these days, other than the obvious?"

"The obvious?" he questioned.

"Experimentation with facial hair," she said, then crinkled her nose. "What's up with that?"

Trey rubbed at his three-day beard growth. "Not me, huh?" he asked.

She frowned and shook her head. "No, not particularly. Although you might want to try a platinum rinse if you just feel like you need a new look," she joked.

"Never mind, I think I'll shave."

"Good idea," Regina said, standing. "Okay, gotta go."

"Hey wait, you got a minute?" he asked.

"Just. I have a date tonight."

"A date?" Trey questioned.

"Yes, a date. Unlike some people I don't let my drive for success overtake my private life."

"With whom?"

"You don't know him, so don't start getting all big brotherly on me. I just got the same thing from Joshua. He's a nice guy and I don't want you or Joshua scaring him off."

"When have we ever scared off someone you were dating?" She looked at him and shook her head. "All right, all right, maybe there was that one time." She opened her mouth, but he confessed to a few more times before she said a word.

"So tell me about Kenya, what did you do to her?"

"What do you mean, what did I do to her?"

"Three days straight you and she were attached at the hip, no pun intended, and now for the next three days she's MIA and you don't even leave the house."

"I didn't do anything to her," he assured her. "Kenya's in New York on business. Okay?"

Regina nodded. "Okay, I'm just checking, don't get all defensive. 'Cause you know how you can be when it comes to women."

"And how is that?" he asked, slightly insulted by the implication.

"Never mind, all I'm saying is that I kind of liked her for you. I mean, I don't really know her, but first instinct, I liked her. She was different from the other hangers."

"Hangers?" he asked.

"The women that hang around you for one reason or the other," Regina explained.

"Maybe she's a hanger, too. Everybody wants something."

"At least she's chill about it. And, of course, since she's been around, you've changed."

"You think I've changed?"

"Yeah, usually with you it's business, business and more business. Granted, on occasion the hangers are there as a temporary distraction. But they never seemed to mellow you."

"Mellow me?"

"I think so. Or maybe it's the twins. Either way you're different, big brother. So is she gonna be around a while?"

Trey frowned. "I'm glad you liked her, but I doubt she's going to be around much. She's very busy with work."

"See, that's what I'm talking about. You go through women like a box of tissues on prom night. They keep popping up and you just keep tossing them away. Even the good ones."

"This tune sounds familiar. Apparently you've been hanging out on Crescent Island too much. But, I assure you, with Kenya, this is a very different case."

"Okay, whatever, I'm out," she said, looking at her watch. She headed to the door then stopped and turned back around. "Oh, I just saw the twins and met Mrs. Thatcher. She's nice and great with the twins. I can see Madi wanting to keep her on."

"It's been good having them here this week," Trey mused.

"Are you ready to relinquish the Mr. Mom role? Everybody's coming back in a couple of days."

"The house is going to be empty when those two little guys leave."

"I bet. Okay, I'm out."

"Wait, here, you left one of your phones here the other day. I already charged it for you," Trey said as he grabbed the cell phone and disconnected the charger cord, then tossed it to her.

Regina caught it, looked it over then shook her head. "Nope, this isn't one of mine."

"It's not?" he said.

She shook her head. "Not mine. I gotta go, see you later."

"Have fun tonight, but not too much," he called out as she waved her hand and left. Curiously, Trey opened the cell. The screen was black. Just as he moved to press the on key, his phone rang. Moments later he and Joshua were back to work.

Chapter 16

"Do you see her yet?" Asia asked.

"No, but we still have a few more minutes before the train boards," Kenya said as she looked around the upper platform for Shelly. She checked her watch. "But she should be here by now."

"She's probably just running late. Traffic is always crazy this time of day," Asia said, looking around. "I'm gonna run over and grab a cinnamon bun. Want one?"

"Girl, I have no idea how you can eat like that and still not gain a pound or an inch."

"I gain. Are you kidding me, my butt is huge," she said and walked away.

"Oh, please." Kenya laughed as she watched Asia. Then she saw two businessmen bump into each other as they nearly broke their necks checking her out. Another man stumbled and nearly fell. Kenya shook her head. Asia didn't even notice.

She never did. Her acting career always came first. Kenya admired her focus.

She looked around for Shelly one last time, then grabbed a seat. She placed her suitcase and shopping bags on the empty seat beside her. At least she wasn't as tired as she was the day she arrived. She remembered that she could barely think straight, even after her nap on the train. But it was her own fault.

She and Trey hadn't slept all night. There was the occasional cat nap, but that was about it. She smiled, remembering. That was definitely a mistake knowing that she had an important meeting the following day. But it was well worth it, and unquestionably a night she'd never forget.

Thankfully, she had regrouped and the meeting with the Youngin's design team went extremely well. They loved everything she and Shelly showed them, including their new line. Afterward, they decided to stay in town a few extra days. Shelly visited her family in Brooklyn, and Kenya stayed with Asia in Manhattan. They met and shopped in the fashion district, then hung out on Fifth Avenue, checking out the store displays. They finished the day at Bergdorf Goodman.

"Did you see her yet?" Asia asked as she sat eating her bun. She handed Kenya a bag. "Here, for the ride home."

"Thanks. No, not yet," she said as she shifted her bags.

"I can't believe you're leaving already," Asia said, leaning her head on her sister's shoulder. "You just got here yesterday."

"It was two days ago," Kenya corrected. "I had to leave sometime."

"I know, but we barely got a chance to hang out, not to mention talk. I wish I knew you were coming in advance. I could have gotten out of my rehearsals."

"Are you kidding? No way. I loved seeing you onstage in rehearsals. You were absolutely brilliant. You had me laughing and crying at the same time. You are so talented."

"Thanks, sis, that really means a lot. Okay, have you heard from Mom or Dad lately? Last I talked to her she said they'd be out of touch for a while."

"She told me the same thing. I lost my cell phone the other day, so I'm still changing things over. I called and I left a message anyway but that was a few days ago."

"They must be back by now. You don't think anything happened."

"Of course not, Asia, don't even think that."

"Yeah, but for real, how long does it take to go on a safari?"

"They're fine, don't worry."

"Did you find out anything new about the money thing? I'd hate for them to come back home to that drama."

"I'm still working on it."

"You'll figure it out. You always do. Oh, before I forget, Sidney called yesterday when you and Shelly were out shopping."

"Please don't tell me you two are arguing again?"

"No, but she told me that you were seeing someone."

"What, she told you that?" Kenya said.

"Yes, so who is he?"

"I'm not seeing anyone," Kenya lied.

"Remember that conversation we had about you not being a good actress," Asia said, implying the obvious.

Kenya sighed heavily. "It's nothing, trust me."

"Anybody I know?"

"No, he's just some guy," Kenya said. Asia smiled. "Don't get all excited. I told you it was nothing."

"But nothing from you is major. Do you realize you haven't actually dated in almost a year?"

"Why are you keeping tabs on my personal life?"

"Somebody has to. You're not. If you're seeing someone, I think that's great. It's definitely about time. I was afraid that after Craig, you were gonna become a nun."

"Hey, guys," Shelly said, rushing over. "Sorry I'm late, traffic is brutal out there. We ready to go?"

"All set," Kenya said, shifting the bag and grabbing her purse.

"I thought we mailed everything to the boutique yesterday."

"We did. This is something else."

Shelly was just about to respond when their train was announced over the loudspeaker. "That's us," she said.

Kenya hugged Asia and said goodbye then the three of them hugged. "Be safe. I'll call you when we get there," Kenya promised.

"Okay, bye," Asia said and waved.

Shelly and Kenya got on the crowded train and actually got a seat together. They stored their overnight bags and prepared for the train ride home. As soon as they settled in, they started talking about the Youngin's meeting. They were both still excited. By Philadelphia, they were talking about the items they'd purchased and the different new ideas they had for the boutique and the new line.

By the time they got to Baltimore, the conversation had shifted again. "I forgot to ask you the other day, how did your first date with Trey go?"

Kenya smiled instinctively. "It was a business date and it was incredible."

"Really?" Shelly said. "Okay, details, details."

Kenya's smile broadened. "The note read formal attire, so I wore the champagne-colored strapless gown with a shawl. Trey, in a tux, picked me up in a limo."

"Ooh, elegant. Where did you go?" she asked.

"We went to a political fund-raiser for a friend of his, Senator

Randolph Kingsley. I met his wife, Alyssa. She was really nice. We had a private booth at the Cirque du Soleil performance, and then we slipped backstage to the costume workshop."

Shelly's mouth dropped opened as she gasped. "For real, are you serious? You went backstage and saw the costumes up close?"

Kenya nodded. "Girl, up close and personal. They were unbelievable. The actual costumes are just astounding. They took my breath away. The colors and the textiles were unreal. I found out that eighty percent of the fabrics are treated and dyed in-house. They employ over three hundred professionals in the workshop. I spoke to a couple of the designers in the show. They were great. One of them told me about the dyeing process they use."

"What process do they use?" Shelly asked excitedly.

"They use a mixed-media mixture of silk-screening, bath-dyeing and a few others—even hand-painting. I was speaking with one of the designers and she told me of a technique she learned while studying in Ghana. She was wearing a shirt she designed using the technique. It sounded pretty easy to duplicate and her shirt looked amazing. The colors were so vibrant and incredibly rich."

"From Ghana, for real. Great. You know I love African dyeing techniques. They change the whole look of fabric."

"I know. Anyway, I got her e-mail address. You two need to chat. Maybe she can give us some new ideas."

"That would be fantastic," Shelly said. "We seriously need to try that."

Kenya chuckled. "I know it was tacky, but I took some serious notes."

"Tacky? Don't even try it. I would have grabbed somebody's camera and got all Coppola on them. That was a once-in-a-lifetime experience."

"I know, I still can't believe it."

"That's too awesome," Shelly whispered softly in true amazement.

"Anyway, afterward we had a nice quiet romantic dinner in town."

"Aw, that's so romantic, talk about a perfect first date."

"Yeah, it was. It was amazing."

"Then what?" she asked, smiling.

"We went back to my condo and after a while, he let me sketch him," Kenya said. Shelly smiled. "And before you say anything, don't."

"I didn't say a word."

"Good, because I feel guilty enough as it is. You were right. I shouldn't have started this whole thing. It's getting way too personal."

"So have you given up on the revenge thing?"

"Yes, maybe, I don't know," Kenya answered. "To tell you the truth, I don't know anything anymore, everything's all confusing. The man depicted in the press isn't really made of ice. The truth of the matter is so different. He's not like that at all. It was all PR and I fell for it."

"Kenya, we all did. That's what newspapers and lawyers do. They shift sympathies. They make the bad guys the good guys and vice versa."

"Well, it's wrong. They made Trey out to be this cruel monster that stole his father's company out of spite. In reality, the truth is nothing like that."

"But isn't that what you thought he did to your father's company?" she asked.

"Is it, but I don't know anymore."

"That's what your dad told you."

"I know, but…"

"Kenya, the only way you're gonna find out what really

happened is to talk to him. Get both sides of the story, and then go from there. Tell him now before it's too late."

"I can't, Shelly, not now. I'm too far in."

"Kenya, you obviously really like him," she said. "Just make it right."

Kenya half smiled. "It's a trip, isn't it? I was gonna get him to fall for me, then dump him. And now look at me. I didn't even see it coming."

"Love sneaks up on people."

"Love, no way," Kenya said.

"Yes way, girl—love. It's all over your face."

"It's not love," she vowed. "I like him, that's all," Kenya said firmly. "So much for my diabolical plan, I should have just talked to him and told him everything after the first night."

"You can still do that. Just call the man when we get back home. You two can have a heart-to-heart and clear the air," Shelly said.

"No, it's too late for that. I think I'll just leave well enough alone. It's been three days since we were last together."

"Call him, get it over with. It may not be as bad as you think."

Kenya looked out the window. The train was coming to Union Station in Washington, D.C. The next move was hers.

Chapter 17

Work had long since ended as early evening found Trey at home sitting at his desk considering the past few days. His thoughts were muddled with everything that had happened. He mindlessly looked over the reports Regina brought by earlier. They pertained to the merger, a business proposition that had once been the sole focus of his days. But that was before.

A concerned Joshua had called several times and questioned a few things Trey hadn't yet attended to. They were inconsequential so he told Joshua to let them wait. He let everything wait. That was the problem. Nothing held his interest anymore, including business.

He wasn't sure when it happened, but something had definitely changed. He wasn't himself. He could feel it and he knew that everyone around him was starting to see it, too. On any given day, business was his life. It came first and foremost, always. It was the heartbeat and pulse of his world, and he never let his focus waver, until now.

He wondered if this was what had happened to J.T., to Tony and to Raymond? Was this what it felt like to be consumed? Having never felt the spark of love, Trey was lost. He still couldn't believe he'd let her sketch him nude. He grabbed his phone and pressed the auto-dial. It rang twice then the call was forwarded to the message center. He left a quick message then hung up.

He touched the mouse pad, bringing his computer to life. Then he arbitrarily grabbed some paperwork and began reading. Moments later, hearing laughter, he stood and walked over to the window. Mrs. Thatcher and the twins were outside playing in the yard. He watched them awhile as she blew bubbles and the twins watched in amazement as they floated above them.

When the delicate crystal orbs drifted down, he watched as either Johanna or Jonathan would run to a bubble and hit it. The bubbles burst and they laughed and rushed to another. The dancing bubbles game went on for a while. Trey watched, enjoying the entertainment, until his phone rang. He picked up. "Hey, cuz, how's it going?" J.T. said.

"Fine," Trey said, relieved. "How's everything there? How's Kennedy?"

"She's great. The baby's perfect and Juwan is as nervous as a cat at a dog show."

"I'd love to see that."

"It's funny, all this time they thought she had a stomach virus. Then they flew all the way to Africa and found out she's pregnant."

"Will she be able to come home?"

"Yeah, the doctor said that she could possibly go home next week, if she takes it easy and gets right back in bed."

"That's great news. Tell her I'll call her later. In the meantime do me a favor and give her my love and well wishes."

"Of course," J.T. said.

"How was the opening?"

"Everything's great. The show opened last night and I think it's going be a huge success. The museum looks incredible. They did a great job on promotions, because the place was packed."

"How's Aunt Taylor doing?" Trey asked.

"Mom was great and her work is remarkable. She had quite a few pieces I hadn't seen before. They were very impressive. I have a feeling she might be coming back," J.T. said.

"I figured that the second she opened the gallery doors here a year ago. Once an artist, always an artist. Isn't that what she always says?"

"You're right about that," J.T. said.

"So when are you headed back this way?" Trey asked.

"Tony, Madi and I will be leaving tomorrow. Dad's staying over and of course Mom will be here. Oh, before I forget, everybody says hello."

"Send them my greetings," Trey said.

"So how are adventures in babysitting?"

"Challenging to say the least, but I finally got it down pretty good. Mrs. Thatcher is a godsend."

"Have you heard from Tony or Madison today?" J.T. asked.

"Are you kidding me? They called me every half hour the first two days. Now I get at least five calls a day."

"It sounds like they're beginning to trust your babysitting skills."

"Nah, they know I have Mrs. Thatcher here with me."

"Yeah, I heard about her. Juliet is really anxious to meet her. I wouldn't be surprised if Mrs. Thatcher might have herself a full-time job," J.T. said.

"Not surprising. She's the best. But you might have a battle with Madi for her," Trey said.

"Okay, okay, I get it. So what's going on?"

"What do you mean?" Trey asked.

"I mean what's up with the panicked message?"

"What panicked message?" Trey asked. "I don't panic."

"That's very true and ordinarily I'd agree one hundred percent, but not today. Granted, I have never heard you panic in my life," J.T. said, then paused. "Until now." Trey didn't respond. "All right, man, here's the deal, we can dance around this for the next fifteen minutes, or you can just tell me what's going on. Remember, cuz, I know you too well. So what's up?"

J.T. was right. He was the older brother Trey never had. He was his confidant, mentor and best friend. Whenever he needed a voice of reason or a clear point of view, he went to his cousin. J.T. always had the answer.

"Tell me something, with you and Juliet, was it a love-at-first-sight thing?"

"Interesting question," J.T. said, then paused. "No, we weren't exactly falling into each other's arms, if that's what you mean. But then our first meeting was pretty unique. It was during the New York City blackout. We shared a moment of opportunity."

"So when did you realize you had feelings for her?"

"Feelings for her or loved her?" J.T. asked.

"Either, both," Trey said.

"To tell you the truth, it happened fast. At first we were just hanging out. I had my agenda, she had hers. Remember I was trying to fool Mamma Lou."

"Yeah, I remember."

"Well, after a while I couldn't get enough of her. She was in my blood. Man, I had it bad. I couldn't focus on work. She was all I thought about. Food was bland, sounds were muted, everything was slightly off. But when she was around, it was a different thing."

"Huh, interesting," Trey said.

"I suppose all this is leading to something."

"Just curious," he said.

"I don't buy it. You don't do curiosity," J.T. said.

Trey sighed heavily and breathed out a single word, "Kenya."

"Presumably a woman and not the country?" J.T. asked.

"Yes, a woman," Trey interjected. "Long story, short version—I took over her father's company. He somehow found a way to get to me, but I got to him first. He wasn't happy."

J.T. chuckled. "So needless to say, she wants to grind your bones into the dirt. That's an interesting way to start a relationship. I suppose she wants retribution for her father."

"She thinks he deserves it."

"Any thoughts on an amicable settlement?" J.T. asked.

"What fun would that be?"

"So you've been negotiating."

"In a manner of speaking," Trey said evasively.

J.T. started laughing. "Why don't you start from the beginning and tell me what's going on." Trey gave J.T. the particulars of his relationship with Kenya without going into too many locker-room details. "So it's like a revenge thing with a twist."

"Yes. Although the thing is, she has no idea what's really going on."

"So enlighten her."

"I can't, that would be breaking a confidence. She needs to learn the truth elsewhere."

"So she's trying to beat you at a game that she doesn't know the rules to and she has no idea who all the players are."

"Exactly, but to her credit, she's doing a great job."

"I bet. So, what now?" he asked.

"Well, we've both been as up-front as we can, given the circumstances, but—"

"But what?" J.T. prompted. Trey didn't reply. "But something changed," J.T. finally said, answering his own question.

"Yeah, something changed," Trey said. "The game is getting a bit too—"

"Let me guess, getting a little serious, too close to the heart, perhaps."

"Yeah, you could say that."

"On her part or yours?" he asked.

"Both," Trey admitted. J.T. paused a moment. "Well?" Trey prompted an answer. J.T. began chuckling. "You gonna laugh all evening or you gonna help me out?"

"I'm not the person to help you out."

"What are you talking about?"

"Trey, you already know the answer to all these questions. If you need help, I suggest you speak with a professional."

"Mamma Lou?" Trey said slowly.

"She's the one."

"No, there's no way I'm going to go to her and tell her all this. First of all, that would be admitting that I initially lied to her. Then she'd take it as her cue to play matchmaker."

"Are you sure she hasn't already?"

"You mean her and Kenya planned this?"

"No, absolutely not, that's not how she works. Mamma Lou isn't about trapping someone. She just opens the door and allows others to freely walk in."

"And you're asking me to invite her in. Are you insane? This is Mamma Lou we're talking about. Do you have any idea what that means?"

"I know exactly what that means. Lifelong happiness, a woman that I love and adore by my side, our child on the way—yes, I know exactly what that means."

"You're blessed, J.T., no doubt about that. And the part Mamma Lou played with uniting you and Juliet was substantial, but that's you. My freedom—"

"Do you see me lacking freedom?" J.T. asked. Trey didn't respond. "Well, do you?"

"No, not at all."

"Man, love isn't about what you lose—it's about what you gain. Love isn't an invitation for pain—it's a promise for the future."

"No, you're supposed to tell me that this is just infatuation, a momentary distraction."

"Can't do that. Bottom line, Kenya sounds like a remarkable woman. She challenged you, kept up with you and will more than likely succeed in getting her father's company back from you. She's your other half, your perfect balance. You can't walk away from that now."

"In any case, that solution is out of the question."

"Is being with her that important?"

"Yes."

"Is being without her unimaginable?"

"Yes."

"Can you breathe without her?"

"No."

"Okay, then you need to take a long hard look at what you want out of this," J.T. said. Trey didn't respond. "So if it was a game, what is it now? It sounds to me like somewhere along the way this game of yours got personal, more than personal."

"I don't know what it got," Trey said truthfully. "All I know is that I can't stop thinking about her. She's in New York for a few days and all I can think about is jumping on the next flight to see her."

"Yep, that's definitely more than personal," J.T. said.

They talked a while longer then made a plan to get together

when J.T. got back to the States. Trey hung up just as troubled as before. The clarity he hoped to find didn't materialize. What he wanted from J.T. was an affirmation that this was nothing serious. That what he was feeling would pass. That's not what he got. Exasperated, he grabbed the paperwork on his desk and forced himself to focus.

Thankfully, a few minutes later Johanna came charging into his office. She ran over to him and he lifted her up immediately. She laughed brightly as she laid her head on his shoulder and wrapped her hands around his neck. Trey smiled in amusement—if only the other woman in his life was just as accommodating.

Moments later Johanna reached to his desk and grabbed the cell phone. "Oh, no, you don't," Trey said, taking it from her. She immediately wiggled down and ran out of the office. Trey sat holding the phone. He'd forgotten all about it. He turned it over and flipped it open but closed it when his phone rang.

Kenya unpacked slowly then sat on the side of her bed. She looked back at the fluffed pillows and smiled. It wasn't surprising that her thoughts shifted to Trey. They usually did lately. The last three days in New York gave her time to think. Unfortunately, though she expected her thoughts to be clearer, they were just as muddled.

She lay back and closed her eyes, remembering Trey lying there beside her. The feel of his body pressed to hers was heavenly. And unfortunately for her, the memories just wouldn't subside. Shelly was right, all this was wrong, she had fallen into a trap of her own making. She had fallen for Trey.

She reached over and grabbed her sketch pad. After flipping a few pages she was surprised to find the unexpected: a drawing by Trey. It was her. It was rudimentary, but still a really good likeness. She lay asleep, her hair tossed back and a simple smile on her face. She had no idea when he drew it, but the thought that he'd done it for her was touching. She laughed out loud then tears dampened her face. Why did he have to be so perfect?

After wiping her tears away, she flipped and found what she was looking for—her sketch of Trey. She touched the drawing gently. She still couldn't believe he'd let her sketch him. Although she'd only sketched his portrait, the fact that he was willing to completely give to her had touched her. That was seriously an act of trust. *Trust.* The word hung in the air heavily like the sword of Damocles above her head.

Her phone rang—it was Shelly. They talked briefly about an idea she had, then went on to discuss plans for the next day. After they hung up, she noticed a text message from Asia. She'd gotten the soap opera and had to end her engagement with the play. Kenya smiled and made a mental note to send her congratulatory flowers. She'd also gotten a missed call from her mother. She called her back and left a message.

She thought about the photos she'd taken with her cell phone, the ones she didn't have anymore. Maybe it was fate that made her lose them. Suddenly a cold chill shot through her. She sat straight up. She'd lost her phone right after she took the pictures. The possibility that she'd accidently dropped it at Trey's house suddenly occurred to her. What if…?

"Oh, no," she muttered. Trey was meticulous. He had to have found it by now. As soon as he opened it he'd see what she'd done. He would be devastated that she'd used him. Sure, she'd warned him that she was after him and even promised that bringing him down was a possibility, but that was before.

Maybe he hadn't found it. She glanced across the room at the toys she'd picked up for the twins. If she dropped them off she could possibly check and see. She was just about to call Trey when her cell rang. "Hello?"

"Kenya."

"Hey, Mom, how are you? How was the safari?"

"Oh, it was wonderful, absolutely wonderful, I had an incredible time. Touring the backcountry, meeting the people and seeing the animals truly left me with a real appreciation for life."

"I'm glad."

"The scenery was breathtaking and the people were delightful. The adventure really gave me a sense of family and sharing."

"But you always had that, Mom."

"I know, but now even more so. I just wish your father had enjoyed it more."

"Why didn't he enjoy it?"

"Oh, I guess he enjoyed it well enough. But you know your father, his thoughts were miles away."

"Is Dad there now?"

"He's asleep. Did you need to speak with him?"

"No, actually, Mom, I wanted to talk to you."

"Sure, what about? Is everything okay?"

"Yes, everything is fine. You know Trey Evans, right?"

"Yes, of course. Has he called?"

"No, actually I contacted him. I didn't want you and Dad to come home to the mess you left. I went to his house to get the money back."

"Kenya—"

"I know, Dad wanted me to wait. But I couldn't."

"So impatient, just like your father," she said warmly. "Did you speak with him?"

"He told me that if I wanted to know what happened I should speak to you and Dad. Dad told me his part, now I need to know the rest. It's important."

Lynette signed heavily. "First of all, your father is a wonderful man and he's always provided for this family and always will. But that's the caring side of him. He wants the best for you and your sisters. When he won the lottery, there were two winning tickets, not one."

"But I thought—"

"It's not always publicized. I won the other half of the jackpot."

"Are you serious?" Kenya asked in amazement.

"Yes, very. Of course your father knew, but we thought it would be best if you girls found out after the dust had settled. Your father was the face of the winner and that's what mattered. He took the one lump sum and I went with the yearly annuity."

"I can't believe this. You won, too."

"Only one other person knew, other than your father, a friend, a woman whom I've gotten quite close to over the years. She suggested that I get help from a friend of hers. I did."

"Trey?" Kenya questioned.

"Yes. Your father took his half of the winnings and invested in his dreams."

"But you gave your portion to Trey."

"Yes."

"So when Dad lost everything," Kenya began, "that's why you weren't all that upset about what Dad said after the picnic. Dad's a gambler. You knew this was going to happen."

"No, of course I didn't. Your father, you, your sisters...everyone needs the freedom to spread their wings. The winnings allowed him that opportunity. Sometimes we win, and sometimes we don't. But there's always something put away for a rainy day."

"So that DR fund that Dad told me about. That's what it was for, the rainy days."

"Yes."

"Mom, I thought you didn't know anything about business.

You don't even have a checking account. How did you do all this? Dad takes care of everything."

"Does he?"

"But I thought—"

"Kenya, just because I don't work outside of the home, doesn't make me naive when it comes to business or thinking for myself. I'm no fool. I have the good sense God gave me and your grandmother taught me to always be able to take care of myself."

"But I thought that when you and Grandmom chose to be housewives you let Dad and Granddad take over everything. I thought you surrendered yourself."

"Where would you get an idea like that? Honey, never stop thinking for yourself, you hear me. Being in love and being married isn't about turning yourself off. It's about going full volume," Lynette said.

"When Craig wanted me to stay at home, I stopped working and stopped thinking. I totally surrendered."

"I know, but your good sense kicked in, and all that foolishness is behind you now."

Kenya felt a deep appreciation for her mother. The woman whom she always thought cared more about her flowers than her finances had apparently always taken care of the family. "I went to the bank the other day. The manager told me that the account was closed and that the money was transferred by a third party. I think it was Trey."

"It was. I asked him to."

"When Dad bought the business and didn't have enough, he didn't borrow it from a bank or Trey, did he?"

"No, he borrowed from the DR account."

"But Trey still deceived Dad about investing."

"No, I asked Trey to help him with the business. That's why he invested with your father and Cal. Unfortunately, I had no idea that it would make your father so angry to try to get back at him."

"That's when Dad went after Trey."

"And Trey protected himself."

"What a mess," Kenya said. "Does Dad know all this?"

"He does now."

"So Trey didn't take the money or the company."

"No. The company is still there, Trey has a larger share, but then so do I."

"I wish I knew this before I butted my nose in."

"You were always an inquisitive child."

"This is all my fault."

"No, it's not your fault. Your father and I forget that you and your sisters are grown women now. We still want to protect you, even from ourselves. You girls have grown up. I guess it's hard to accept that sometimes."

"Mom, I need to tell you something, but I don't want you to get upset."

"Tell me what?" she asked.

"It's about Trey."

"What about him?"

"After you and Dad left, I went to the house and checked out some of Dad's paperwork. I had to do something to help. You and Dad have always been there for me and I needed to do this for you."

"Kenya—"

"Wait, there's more. When I went to Trey I intended to force him to give me Dad's company back. But I soon realized it wasn't going to work. So I had this plan to get something on him, some kind of damaging proof to give to the SEC. I wanted to ruin him and take everything he had."

"Kenya—" Lynette began, sounding more astonished.

"It was stupid, I know. He wouldn't budge and he wouldn't

tell me what happened. So I assumed that it was what Dad said. I knew he wasn't telling me something. I didn't know he was protecting your confidence.

"We didn't argue or fight or anything like that. It was more like a battle of wills. But in all that, we started having a relationship. It started by accident. I don't think either one of us planned for it to happen."

"What kind of relationship?"

"A physical one, a personal one," Kenya said, pausing, waiting for a response. There was no response. But she could sense her mother's surprise. "It got emotional. And I know what you're gonna say, it's only been a week. But, Mom, this so much more. It's like I've known him and I'd been waiting for him all my life. I think about him constantly and I want to be with him all the time. It's crazy, I know. This is the man that hurt Dad. But my heart won't listen to my head. I love him."

"Kenya, I fell in love with your father the moment I saw him. A week sounds like forever to me now."

"I never knew that."

"I don't think we ever talked about it before. And as far as Trey being the man who ruined your father, I wouldn't give him that much credit. Your father is a grown man responsible for his own choices. You can't blame others for his actions. So tell me more about you and Trey."

"I'm in love with him. It sounds so odd saying that. I never thought it was possible that I could feel this way. After everything, I wasn't sure I was even worthy. But he fills me up inside. No matter what, he seems to make everything all right. I feel safe and trusted and loved. He's exactly the man I always wanted."

Lynette sighed sweetly. "Oh, sweetie, I'm so happy for you," she said, her voice quivering with emotion. Kenya told her mother about their first date, minus certain particulars.

They talked about things they'd never talked about before. She hung up a few minutes later feeling a lot better about things. Without thinking about it, she grabbed her cell and called Trey. He answered on the second ring. "Hello."

"Hi," she said cautiously.

"Hey, are you back in town?" he asked happily. The subdued tone of his voice hummed strong through the receiver.

Kenya relaxed. His voice was even and encouraging. Maybe she still had a chance. "Yes. We just got back an hour ago. I hope I'm not disturbing you."

"I think you know me better than that by now," he said.

"Yeah, I guess I do." She relaxed. He didn't sound any different. "It's good to hear your voice. I missed you."

He chuckled. "Is that right? Well, I missed you, too."

"So what are you doing this evening?" she asked.

"Nothing much. Mrs. Thatcher and the twins hung out at the park all day, so it's an early night for them. Why?"

"I was hoping we could talk."

"Negotiate?" he questioned.

"No, talk," she corrected.

"Sure, I can come over—"

"No, I'll come over there, if that's okay. I'll be over in about twenty minutes."

"Perfect, see you then." After hanging up, he smiled. He couldn't wait to see Kenya. He pressed the on button of the cell phone. The screen instantly lit up. He froze.

Chapter 18

Kenya was thrilled. She'd have a chance to talk to Trey and hopefully put all this behind them. She was sure they could work out a solution with her father. She drove over, parked, got out of the car and rang the doorbell. Trey answered almost immediately. She smiled happily. "Hi."

"Good evening, Kenya. Come in."

"Thanks," she said as she walked in and headed to the living room. One quick look around told her that everything was exactly the same. She glanced at the sofa, hoping that the phone had fallen between the cushions.

"What's in the shopping bag?" Trey asked, seeing two colorfully wrapped presents in the clear bag.

"I picked up something for the twins while I was in New York. I know they'll be leaving soon so I wanted to get it to them before they went back home."

"That was really nice of you," he said calmly.

"Actually it was the perfect excuse to walk through the toy store." She sat down in the same spot where she might have dropped her phone. "There's something about toy stores that brings out the kid in me. I think that happens to everyone. What do you think?" She paused a moment when he didn't respond, then continued. "Are you okay? You seem different, distracted."

"Business. It was a long day," he said as he sat across from her.

"Really, is everything okay?" she said.

"An unexpected situation has developed needing my immediate attention. I initially hoped to avoid it or at best resolve it much later. But it seems that I have no choice but to deal with it now."

"That doesn't sound like it's a good thing."

"It's an unfortunate inconvenience. But it's nothing I can't handle. How was the meeting in New York?" he asked.

"Great, they loved us. I think we're gonna hear from them soon." She paused a few seconds then continued. "This is such a major step in my career and a very exciting business opportunity. But to tell you the truth I'm a bit apprehensive."

"Why is that? It's what you want, isn't it?"

"Yes, it is."

"You should always get what you want," Trey said, remembering the cell-phone photos. They ranged from family photos to sketches and garments to business documents from his personal folder.

"I don't know about that," she said solemnly. "I think sometimes what I want isn't what I need, or what's right for me at the time."

"Really? Tell me, what do you need, Kenya?"

"Enlightenment, forgiveness," she whispered in the next heartbeat.

Trey paused a second, looking into her guarded eyes. "Why do you need enlightenment?" he asked.

"I think things aren't always what they seem. It's hard to know what's right, who to trust, who to believe in."

"You believe in yourself," he said simply enough.

"I do, but that's not enough. Family and friends can change all that. Doing the right thing, or what you think is the right thing, may not really be the right thing after all. Enlightenment would help that process."

"You sound confused, almost like you're confessing."

"I guess I am in a way, and therein lies my dilemma."

"And what about forgiveness?" he asked.

"I think we could all do a bit of that, don't you?"

"You're probably right," he said.

"Sometimes I don't know what to think anymore. I guess it's like you said, I'm just confused. What I know and what I feel don't coincide anymore. It used to be so simple."

"What changed all that?"

"You," she said softly.

"Me?"

"That's right. What I hear, what I see, what we do, what I know in my heart—it's all different now. You changed that."

"What do you know in your heart, Kenya?"

"I'm not the woman I was a week ago. Strange, huh? When I met you I had purpose and focus. I knew exactly what I was doing and why I was doing it. Now I feel so different. What used to be all business isn't anymore. All I want to do is be with you. What about you, what do you know in your heart?"

"I know that it's hard not to think about you when you're not around. This, you and I, we went too far, too fast."

She nodded. "Yeah, it makes me wonder, this thing we have, is it real or is it just something we made up to make the game more interesting? Is it just about the physical? 'Cause if it is then I think we've—"

"Is that what it is for you, just physical?" he asked.

"No, and that scares me. But the last three days in New York got me thinking. I have so much to tell you, but when we're together none of that seems to matter. I just want to be with you for however long I can."

"Actually, I think we know each other pretty well, and maybe that's just it. We're alike, you and I, the flip side of the same coin. We played this game for business but somewhere along the line it got personal," he said.

"I lost control."

"We both did. But it seems that our precarious situation is about to implode."

"You think so?" she asked, suddenly feeling the foreboding in the air.

"I know so." He reached into his pocket and pulled out the cell phone.

Kenya gasped slightly. "Is that my—"

"Cell phone, yes, you left it here that first night." He opened it. "At first I thought that it was Regina's. She's left hers here a few times. So I thought I would do her a favor and charge it. Imagine my surprise when I opened it. You forgot to save the last photo. So I saved it for you."

"Trey—" she began.

"What?" he asked, handing her the phone. She immediately opened it and saw that she'd saved one of the documents she copied that first night as wallpaper. The entire back screen was a copy of his document.

"You have to listen to me."

"No, I don't. You did what you said you'd do. Congratulations." He reached over and grabbed his red folder from the coffee table. "Here, take it."

She looked at it as if it would bite her. "What is it?"

"The hard-copy files you came for."

"I don't want your files, Trey. I know what I did was wrong. I came here to apologize," she said slowly. "I was wrong. I misjudged you and I'm sorry. I spoke to my mother this evening. She told me everything."

"I had no intention of hurting you, Kenya. You know that better than anyone." She nodded. "I asked you to trust me. I told that I'd never lie to you."

"Trey, what happened between us wasn't supposed to happen. I don't think either of us intended for it to go in that direction, but it did."

"Yes."

"It's not about who wins and who loses anymore. It's about what we felt, what we feel. Yes, I took the pictures. But that was before."

"Before we slept together that first night?"

"No, after. You were still asleep. I didn't exactly plan to do it. The briefcase was there and I opened it and saw letters regarding my father. It said that you intended to sell his business. I thought the worst."

"We're backtracking. This all happened almost six months ago."

"But my father didn't say anything until two days before we met. You have to know he didn't understand your game."

"Then he shouldn't have played."

"How is that fair?"

"It's not. The lure of easy money is seductive, particularly when you've already had a taste. But I don't make anyone sign on the dotted line. There's always an out. He could have just walked away. He didn't. Instead your father tried to take advantage of me. He knew exactly what he was doing. It just backfired."

"How can you be so cruel?" she said, turning to him.

"Me? You got the wrong person, sweetheart. Your father came after me, just like you did."

The sting of his words hit hard. "Why can't you listen to reason? He made a mistake. I made a mistake. It happens. It wasn't personal."

"No, sweetheart, it was very much personal. He didn't go after TE Acquisitions & Associates. He went after me. That's as personal as it gets."

"Fine, he was wrong. I was wrong. Is that what you want to hear? You were right. The lure of easy money has always been hard for my dad. He's played the lottery as far back as I can remember. When he won, we all said that it was just payback for all the money he'd squandered. So tell me, what if they can't stop themselves? They're victims, too."

"Then they shouldn't play the game."

"What about ethics?"

"What about them?"

"It's all a game to you, isn't it? Business, life, love. King of the castle, push everybody off 'cause the last man standing wins."

"It's a difficult position, yes. But I don't put anyone in it. Risk works both ways. It happens. We're done here. You can find your way out, unless you'd like to look through my brief-case again."

"I deserved that."

They glared at each other for a moment. "And what about us?" she asked. Trey looked away. "Trey, what about us?" she repeated. "Yes, I know it was a game we played. We both knew what we were doing. But I think we both took a hit."

"I don't want to play anymore." She paused. "I love you," she whispered softly. "I never thought I could say that again, but I can." She half chuckled as a tear slowly fell. "And you know, the funny thing is that it was supposed to be you. I was going to break your heart like you broke my father's. But I forgot, the Iceman doesn't have a heart." He didn't respond. She walked to the front door then turned back to him. He hadn't moved. "I guess you won. Congratulations." She left.

"No, you won," he said after the door had already closed.

Kenya drove home, parked her car and then just sat there in the darkness. How do you stop loving someone? She needed Trey to understand how much this company meant to her father. It was his chance. Something he'd been searching for all his life. But more important, she needed Trey to know how much he meant to her. How much she loved him.

Chapter 19

The meeting had been long and arduous, and was now hopefully about to end. Seven corporate types, a select gathering, had assembled at the conference table. They had been sequestered for two hours. After a head-to-head discussion, Trey finally made the final statement.

"Okay," Cal said, still obviously delighted to be included at the table. "Caine Enterprises basically needs new leadership. It's a sixty-five-year-old dinosaur that needs vision and direction. Our resources can do that." Trey nodded. Cal beamed.

"We can give them that from one of the divisions," Joshua added, giving his point of view. Trey read over the latest prospectus as he listened to the general discussion. It was nothing he hadn't already heard.

"Buying the company would increase our standing and open a new avenue in that market. We'll lose revenue from the initial merger, but long-term, we'll generate a stable base and add additional revenue," Cal added.

"They have a base in a market we've been unsuccessful in thus far, plus they have a good reputation," Trey said.

"Bottom line, they're top-heavy. They've been drowning in executive compensation for the past twenty years. The management staff is near zero productivity," Joshua said.

"Again, nothing we can't handle. Their reputation speaks for itself," Cal remarked.

"Granted, but so do a hundred and fifty other companies'," Regina said. "I say we pass."

"Actually, I'm inclined to disagree with Regina at this point," Cal said boldly.

"Actually, I'm inclined to agree with Regina," Joshua said. "Pass."

"We've already expanded our search and drafted the final paperwork. We'd lose five months' research and countless man hours," Cal said.

"Ten million in annual revenue isn't something you just walk away from. We could definitely use that in the push forward. Growth and expansion is imperative," Trey said.

"It's now or never." Cal sat smiling. He'd done what no one else even came close to doing. He'd successfully impressed Trey, although apparently Joshua and Regina still needed some convincing. But they didn't really matter in the larger scope of things. He had his eye on the seat beside Trey, and he intended to get there.

"I don't see what the problem is," Cal began while comfortably leaning back in his chair. "The paperwork is in, and everything is a go. We need to make a move before someone else gets wind of it." His confidence brimmed.

"Since you have not been here long, Calvin, we'll excuse

the fact that you don't know that much about this company," Joshua said accommodatingly.

"Having been called into this meeting, I presume my expertise and input is needed." He was obviously challenging Joshua. He turned his attention directly to Trey. "Caine is ripe for a takeover. He wants this and I think was should listen to him."

"We don't make investments based on a prospectus alone. You'll learn and understand that in time," Joshua said condescendingly. The not-so-subtle reminder of the pecking order sent a ripple of raised brows and sideways glances around the table.

"Maybe we should, at least on this occasion," Cal shot back.

Joshua smiled. "Calvin, there's more to this than jumping when someone says jump, unless of course that someone is your boss. We make the decision that's best for this company, not Caine."

"But the man knows his business."

"That might be so, but this is our business, not his. Unless, of course, you know something we don't." The no-nonsense tone in Joshua's voice caused those at the table to look around nervously. Calvin had been quite handily put in his place, again.

Cal visibly bristled. The possibility that he'd gone too far was very real. He intended to stand up to Joshua in front of Trey, but maybe that wasn't such a good plan. "Of course, Joshua, I didn't mean to imply that we should just invest because Caine wants us to. I was just saying we might not want to lose this opportunity."

"They've been losing revenue steadily for the past five years. Do we want that additional drain on cash flow? They may have hit their peak," Regina said, interrupting the testosterone buildup in the room.

"Maybe the company has plateaued," Joshua suggested.

"No, I don't think so. There's still money to be made," Trey said. "What are the projected numbers for the next five and ten years?"

"They didn't do that kind of analysis," Cal said.

"What do you mean they didn't do the projections?" Regina asked. No one answered. "Why not?" Regina asked. The room went silent as everyone looked around the table. It was obvious no one knew the answer. "How is it that a company like Caine didn't forecast its revenue projection? Trey, we need to hold off," Regina said. "The outside review and independent audits are still pending."

"What outside reviews and audits?" Cal questioned, beginning to flip through his file for more information. "I wasn't told we were doing any of that."

Eyes shifted again, but no one bothered to respond.

"Okay, let's close it down," Trey said. Notebooks and folders were closed as the rest of the staff at the conference table stood to leave. Regina, Joshua and Cal remained seated. The room cleared. Trey looked puzzled. "Cal, if you'll excuse us."

"Oh, me, sure…of course, I just presumed that maybe you might want to discuss this matter with me some more. I mean, I did bring it to the table and I am spearheading the research. So maybe we can—"

"No," Trey said plainly. Cal nodded then got up and left. Joshua and Regina looked at each other, shook their heads and smiled. He didn't have a clue. When the door shut behind him, Trey stood and walked over to his desk. He dropped the files then waited.

It was blatantly obvious that he was back. But instead of his generous smile, good nature and steadfast focus, a fierce determination darkened his usual pleasant demeanor.

Dressed in a dark tailored business suit and crisp white shirt, Trey stood at his desk with a scowl on his face that would terrify Attila the Hun. Joshua and Regina glanced at each other then focused their attention on Trey as he spoke. "All right, let's hear it," he said.

"Why is Cedric so anxious to sell?" Regina asked.

"You think he's holding back?" Trey asked.

"I don't know. But I do think that there's something up."

"He signed the waivers of intent, and the full disclosure release. Legally he's obligated to disclose all documents related to this merger. But we all know that doesn't always happen," Joshua said.

"We've looked at every aspect of the company. There don't seem to be any red flags," Trey said.

"That may be, but something's up," Regina insisted.

"Just saying something's up doesn't cut it, Regina. I need something concrete." There was a knock on the door. "Come in," Trey called out. It was Regina's assistant to tell her that she had an important call. Regina excused herself. Trey sat back down behind his desk. Joshua noted his pensive expression.

"You're going through the motions, but your heart isn't in it. It looks like the kill just isn't as sweet as it once was."

"Meaning?" Trey asked.

"Whatever happened, let it go," Joshua said.

"What are you talking about?" Trey asked.

"Kenya Whitaker," Joshua stated.

"What about her?" Trey asked

"You realize you're hooked, right?"

"I'll get unhooked, no problem," Trey said.

"The evidence says otherwise."

"You're obviously mistaken," Trey said.

"The head rules business, not the heart, Trey—your words."

"That's deep but irrelevant."

"Not in this case," Joshua said. "She's got you, man, you got emotional from the start. She just finished where her father left off."

"I don't think so."

"I didn't think I'd ever see it, but here it is in living color. You're in love with her."

"Love has nothing to do with this."

"Love has everything to do with this. Trey, look at you, you're vacillating over a deal. There was a time when you focused your anger. But with James Whitaker you let it get the best of you. I don't know if it was his fatherly image or what. But you saw something in him that touched you. Then when he betrayed you, you got pissed, understandably. Granted, you were provoked, he played you. The normal reaction would be to retaliate, which you did. Not cool. That's not how we play. This company has never been about that."

Trey looked at Joshua. They'd been friends and business associates for too long. He knew Joshua was right.

Joshua shook his head. "It seems only poetic that Ms. Whitaker continued where her father left off. She got you, man. You might as well surrender."

He looked at his friend and asked, "Me?"

"Yeah, you—you wanted revenge. You got it. You were pissed at Whitaker. He was the first man to ever test you and actually make a dent. It stung more because you really liked him. He was your father all over again."

"No."

"Come on, man, business is business. You never looked away from the truth before."

Trey finally nodded. "Yeah, fine, he pissed me off so I took his company."

"That's why you haven't done anything with it. It's not the trophy you thought it would be. It's more like an albatross."

"Are you finished?" Trey asked.

"Not yet, and now it seems that his daughter has taken up

where her father left off. But this time she hit you in a more damaging spot, your Achilles', your heart."

"Albatross, Achilles', you sound like a PBS special," Trey joked. Joshua looked at him seriously. "Yeah, yeah, I know," he conceded. "It's hard to accept what you've fought against all your life. You had to step up at an early age. You've been stepping ever since."

Trey shook his head. "I don't know what happened. In a week's time, she got to me. And after everything, I still can't stop thinking about her."

Joshua smiled. "The instant you mentioned her name, you were heading in one direction. A week, three days, an hour, sometimes that's all it takes."

"Somebody else told me that just recently. He said that once he looked across the room and fell in love. Bam, just like that."

"Happily ever after?" Joshua asked.

"No, he walked away. His freedom was too important."

"Looks like history repeating itself."

"One week."

"I guess anything's possible. I once heard this a long time ago. Most captured animals don't consider themselves caged. But they are."

Trey remembered it well. It was one of his theories. He had a lot of them, most about avoiding love. Unfortunately none of them applied. Colonel Wheeler was right. Love isn't about time, it's about the heart.

Trey remained pensive. He'd gotten too close, too quickly, and he wasn't sure how to get out or if he wanted to get out. The last realization hit him hard. Only once had he considered giving his heart to a woman and that ended, too. But that was nothing like this feeling. He'd easily walked away, but this time he knew he couldn't.

"Just like her father, she played me."

"Life is a cautionary tale, a lesson learned," Joshua said. "Get over it, you played each other."

"What, do you write these things down or something?"

Joshua laughed. Trey laughed. The mood in the room lightened as they went on to talk about Tony and Madison's return and the twins' leaving.

Kenya sat in the reception area, waiting. If Trey was avoiding her, he was doing a good job. She'd been waiting over an hour already. But it didn't matter, she'd wait all day if need be. Trey was going to listen to her and that's all there was to it.

"Kenya," Regina said, walking over. "I thought that was you sitting there. What are you doing here?"

"I came to see Trey. Is he available?"

"Actually, he's in a meeting right now. Is he expecting you?"

"No." The sadness in her voice was unmistakable.

Regina smiled. "Okay, come on, I'll take you to him."

"If he's busy, I don't want to disturb him."

"Don't worry about it. I'm sure he'll have time for you—this way." Regina and Kenya walked down the hall toward a bank of executive offices. Regina knocked, then peeked in. Trey and Joshua were just as she left them. Trey was perched on the side of his desk and Joshua was sitting on the chair in front of the desk. "Hey, you have a visitor." She stepped aside and opened the door wider. Kenya stood beside her.

Trey stood as Regina escorted Kenya into the office then closed the door. Joshua stood up and smiled. Now he understood Trey's distraction. Kenya Whitaker was beautiful and just Trey's type. Regina introduced Kenya to Joshua.

Trey and Kenya stared at each other, neither saying a word. Joshua and Regina smiled at one another. "Joshua, why don't we finish this up in my office?"

"Good idea," he said. They made a quick exit. When the

door closed Kenya walked over to Trey, who was still standing at his desk.

"Hello, Trey."

"Hello, Kenya," he said coolly. "What can I do for you?"

"Actually, it's what I can do for you," she said.

He smiled. "And what might that be? No, let me guess."

"Don't judge me before you know the facts. I think you told me that once," she said.

"Did I? Well, in this case I believe I already know the facts."

"I don't think so," she said.

"Kenya, what are you doing here? You have what you wanted." He walked around his desk and pressed a button. The glass wall and door instantly tinted. Their privacy was assured.

"You once told me that you'd never lie to me. But you lied."

He looked up at her, feeling the sting. "I didn't lie to you, Kenya, I think you have that turned around. You lied to me."

"Yes, I did. I lied and cheated and even stole. And you have no reason to believe anything I say now, but you lied, too."

"About what?" he asked.

"You were working with my mother to help my father. Why didn't you tell me?"

"Two reasons. One, it was confidential, between a client and myself. And two, you didn't ask. You asked about your father. Either way, it wasn't up to me to tell you."

"Mom told me last night. That's what I came to talk to you about before the cell-phone thing. I understand what happened now. I'm sorry. But the folder showed—"

"I presume you've already sent in your complaint to the SEC and you want to give me one last chance to reconsider."

"No," she said, reaching into her large purse and pulling out a large manila envelope. She placed it on his desk.

"What is that?" he asked.

She smiled. "You found my cell phone. You know exactly

what this is." He nodded. "Although it's not what you think. I'm not sending anything anywhere. I need you to know that. Not that it really matters, but I'd like to know what happened with my father and his company."

He smiled. "I thought you knew everything."

"I know what he told me and what my mom told me, but—"

"It's irrelevant now. You know what, all in all, I really liked your dad. He was the lottery winner who constantly drove me crazy with his moneymaking ideas and schemes. To his credit I was impressed. Your father accomplished something few do. To tell you the truth I still can't believe he had the nerve to make a play like that. He didn't even tell his partner."

"Cal knew."

"What do you mean?"

"Dad may not be a brilliant businessman, but he keeps great records. And when he does research, he leaves no stone untouched. Cal, Dad's partner—he knew everything."

"How do you know that?"

"In his papers, Dad notes that he found a vulnerable spot in your company. He called it your sweet spot. A while later he realized that it was possible to access and exploit it. There are e-mails between my dad and Cal. One even details how to get your stock legally using this sweet spot. Cal wanted to know what it was, but Dad didn't tell him."

"Really."

"Cal suggested in an e-mail that Dad should take advantage of it. Apparently Dad was still angry about your giving him an allowance with his own money. Cal gave him whatever information he needed and coached him on what to do. So, if anything, Cal knew and even shares equal blame. My dad may have found your sweet spot, but it was Cal who wanted to rip it open."

"Interesting, and you say your father has papers documenting this information?"

"Yes, why?" she asked.

"I'd like to see them."

"They're in the envelope."

"Thank you," he said.

A long silence opened between them. She wanted to say more but she didn't know what. "Trey, why are you being like this?" she asked.

"Like what?"

"Cold and unfeeling," she said. "This isn't you."

"Maybe you don't know me as well as you think you do."

She smiled. "Actually I do. I could never fall in love with you otherwise." He looked at her, his eyes burning into her, seeming to search for some inkling of deceit. "I guess that's it. I see the Iceman is back."

"He never left."

"No, you're wrong about that," she said. He didn't respond. "Goodbye, Trey." She hurried out of his office, hoping to get as far away as possible. She stood at the bank of elevators waiting. Damn, the elevator was taking too long. How do you make a clean getaway when the elevator takes forever? "Forget this," she muttered. She turned to take the stairs. Walking twenty-some floors down ought to calm her nerves a bit. As soon as she got to the door to the stairs she heard the elevator bell ring. It didn't matter.

Chapter 20

"Kenya?"

Kenya stopped then turned to see her sister holding the elevator doors open. "Sidney," she said, surprised to see her sister standing there. "What are you doing here?"

"What do you mean, what am I doing here?" Sidney smiled happily. "I work here. This is my job. I'm a temp, remember?"

"Here—you work here?" Kenya questioned. Sidney nodded. "Okay, you need to get yourself another job," she ordered.

Sidney looked at her sister. The expression on her face was telling. She should know, it was directed at her often enough. Kenya was pissed. "No way," Sidney said.

"Sidney, I'm not playing."

"Neither am I. I'm keeping it. It has great perks."

"Forget the perks, you need to quit, Sidney," Kenya insisted.

"Why should I? This job is perfect. I get paid, I get college credit and I get back at the man who ripped Dad off."

"What?"

Sidney smirked. "You know Asia can't keep a secret."

"She told you about Dad?" Kenya asked.

"Duh, yeah, she told me the highlights. She assumed I didn't already know."

"Wait a minute, you knew about Dad already?"

Sidney smiled. "You know, I am constantly amazed by the lack of faith this family has in me. I've known about it for the last five, almost six months. That's when I got this job."

"Sidney," Kenya said, stunned by the news.

"I overheard Dad and Mom talking. Figuring out the rest wasn't that hard. Dad's records are perfect. So when this position came up, I took it. Now we'll see who gets the last laugh." The elevator began beeping.

"Exactly what are you doing?" Kenya asked as she grabbed her sister's arm and pulled her away from the elevator. The doors closed.

"Nothing much," she said, smiling. "Just a bit of inside information sharing."

"Sidney, if you're talking about insider trading—"

Sidney laughed. "No, I wouldn't do something so corny. I'm simply playing chess, just like you taught me."

"What do you mean, playing chess?"

"I'm just making moves, putting players in place, a bit of advanced strategy."

"What does all that mean?" Kenya asked, getting more agitated by the minute.

Sidney looked around as a couple of employees walked by talking. They spoke to Sidney and she smiled and greeted them. Sidney walked over to the stairs; Kenya followed. "Dad has been after Trey Evans for months. He's never been able to get at him. So I found a way."

"What way?"

"There's a deal on the table. TE Acquisitions is merging with a company called Caine Enterprises. The announcement will be made next month. They're in final negotiations. Now here's the funny part. You know how I've had, like, a million temp jobs over the years?" she said. Kenya nodded. "Well, before getting a job here I had a job at Caine. You'd be surprised how much information you pick up when you're a temp. They act like you're invisible."

"What did you find out?"

"Caine has a silent partner who's not on the books. Actually Caine is more like a front man."

"So who's the silent partner?"

Sidney smiled and chuckled. "Phillip Garfield."

"Who?"

"Phillip Garfield, Trey's father."

Kenya went stone-cold. "What?"

"I overheard him talking about TE Acquisitions and how he wanted to get Trey back for taking his company. Just like he took Dad's company. So I started putting things in place."

"You're working for Caine Enterprises, too…both companies?"

"No, of course not," she said. "At least not anymore. I couldn't keep it up with my class schedule. It got too tricky after a while."

"So you worked at both companies, planting information at both."

"And neither one knew. I carefully placed pertinent information in their paths. They actually think the whole thing was their idea."

"Wait a minute, you can't just plant information without suspicion. I know Trey, he's too smart just to pick up information and use it."

"That's why I'm using a middleman," she said, then chuckled. "And he doesn't even know it."

"A middleman—who?" she asked.

"So by next month Trey's father will own a nice chunk of this company. I'll tell Dad about it just before the news is released. Dad will have his money back. Payback. Nice, huh?"

"Sidney, you can't do this," Kenya said.

"Why not?"

"Because it's wrong," Kenya said.

"How can it be wrong when you're doing the exact same thing?" Sidney said. Kenya opened her mouth to protest. "Actually your distracting him worked out well for me."

"I am not and besides, you don't know the whole story."

"And you do?"

"I didn't say that. It's just that there's more to this than I first thought. You need to let Mom take care of this."

"So why are you here now?" Sidney asked.

"I came to stop all this," Kenya said.

"Don't worry, sis, I got this." The elevator beeped. "He'll never know what hit him. Listen, I gotta go, busy working. Hold the elevator," she called out. She smiled mischievously and waved as the doors began to close.

Kenya shuddered. She stood like stone because she knew that smile. It meant that her little sister was about to get herself into major trouble. But this time she might not be able to get herself out. "Sidney, Sidney," she called out, but the elevator doors closed.

Now what? Trey was good, too good. He played this game for a living. He had to know that there was more going on. So why would he continue with this unless he didn't know? And if that was the case, he was just about to hand over his company to his father.

Kenya turned and went back to his office. His receptionist told her that he was in a meeting. Kenya asked about Regina.

She was in a meeting, too. Kenya nodded and left. She waited for an elevator in hopes of seeing her sister again, but didn't.

She called Sidney on her cell. It rang several times then went to voice mail. She left a message, then an urgent text message. She called Trey next. His answering system picked up. She left him a message that she needed to see him as soon as possible. By the time the elevator arrived to the main lobby she was panicked.

"Everything all settled?" Regina asked as she went back into her brother's office. "When's the wedding?"

"Wedding?" Trey frowned. "What are you talking about—what wedding?"

"Yours and Kenya's. See, I knew I was right about the two of you. The moment I saw her I could see it in her eyes. Then when you came down, I saw the exact same thing in your eyes. I knew you guys were meant to be together."

"Then you were wrong. There's no wedding."

"What?"

"You heard me, no wedding, and no relationship."

"Trey—"

"I don't want to talk about this, Regina."

"Good, 'cause all you need to do is shut up and listen. This is so ridiculous. It's always business with you, never any time for anything or anyone else. Does that sound familiar?"

"I don't know what you're talking about," he said, refusing to see the implied comparison between him and his father.

"Of course not. Ever since that court case with you and Dad when they called you the Iceman, you've turned into exactly what you hated."

"If you're referring to me being anything like Dad, then—"

"I'm not finished. You used to be the coolest big brother. I could come to you with anything, for anything."

"You still can," he said, feeling the sting of her words hitting him hard.

"No, it's all business with you. All you care about is this company. Trey, you never let anyone into your life anymore. You became just what they said, an Iceman. But then Kenya showed up and you actually let down your guard. Now you're gonna back off."

"There's more to this, Regina."

"What, that she's James Whitaker's daughter? So what."

"Joshua told you?" he asked.

"He didn't need to. I read the file months ago. The connection was obvious. So what if she wanted revenge and that brought you together."

"And that was okay with you? The fact that she wanted me in jail for something I was accused of doing?" he asked.

"Is that what she wants from you now?" she asked.

"No."

"Then what's the problem? Stop being so stubborn and let it go. You obviously can't focus on business or anything else until you do. Two weeks ago you were all gung-ho about the Caine deal. Now, you're vacillating."

"I'm not vacillating, I'm being careful."

"Trey, don't you see, that's why this Caine deal is all over the place. You can't lock it down because a part of you knows there's something wrong, but you're too pigheaded to really see the problem. I've watched you for years going from romance to romance. You never seemed to find the woman for you. Cool, I get that, you want to be sure. In Kenya, I think you found her. You just can't admit it. Don't mess this up, Trey. Listen to your younger sister for once. I don't want you regretting what could have been in another fifty years."

Trey didn't speak for a while. He just looked at the manila folder Kenya had laid on his desk. But instead of thinking about Kenya or about what Regina had just said, he was thinking about Colonel Wheeler.

There was a knock on the door. "Come in," he said. Mrs. Thatcher opened the door and the twins ran in. They saw Regina and ran right to her.

"Hey, you guys." She knelt down and hugged them.

"I thought it best for the twins to be here when their parents came for them this afternoon."

"Good idea," Trey said, giving Jonathan a high five.

A few moments later Joshua came in and a rousing game of toss the ball began. The twins reached as Trey and Joshua tossed the ball around the room. The room was so noisy that they barely heard the knock. Tony and Madison walked in.

"Hey," Madison said, falling to her knees. The twins rushed to her. She was in tears. Tony knelt beside her and hugged each child. After nearly ten minutes of embracing her children and catching up, Madison hugged Regina and Trey and Joshua. Joshua and Tony shook hands and Tony and Trey hugged. Madison hugged Mrs. Thatcher.

"Thank you, Mrs. Thatcher, I don't know what we would have done without you. You're a lifesaver."

"Hey, what about me?" Trey exclaimed, feeling left out.

"Oh, please," Madison said to her cousin.

"Come on, I was a huge help," he protested.

"Indeed he was," Mrs. Thatcher said.

"See," Trey said.

They all laughed as Trey described his first few hours with the twins. He confessed to losing them while on the phone because he'd fallen asleep. Madison was totally upset. "You did what?"

"I know, I know, I got yelled at enough by Kenya about that. Don't worry, it'll never happen again."

"It better not," she said, playfully hitting him on the arm.

"So who's Kenya?" she asked. Trey looked at Regina. "What?" Madison looked to Tony, who looked at Trey and Joshua. "Okay, somebody needs to say something."

"She's a friend," Trey said.

"Oh," Madison said. "A friend-friend or a *friend*-friend?"

"What does that even mean?" Tony asked, chuckling.

"He knows what I mean," Madison said.

"A friend, just a friend," Trey assured her.

She nodded but wasn't at all convinced. There was something different about him. She couldn't put her finger on it but in a week's time something had changed.

They discussed Kennedy, Juwan and Taylor, then went on to talk about the museum opening. Tony gave Trey a message from J.T., who went directly home to his pregnant wife. They all decided to get together that weekend, allowing Madison and Tony time to get resettled. As they prepared to leave, Madison talked Mrs. Thatcher into staying on with them for a few more days. She readily agreed.

Chapter 21

Kenya left another few messages on Sidney's cell, and then headed to the boutique. It seemed like days since she'd actually sat down and worked. As soon as she walked in Shelly looked up, half smiling with hope. "Did everything work out?" she asked, knowing that Kenya had gone to see Trey that morning. Kenya shook her head. "That bad, huh?" she asked.

"Worse," Kenya said.

"I'm so sorry. Is there anything I can do?"

"No."

"Are you sure?" Shelly asked.

Kenya nodded as she sat down at her desk. "Yes, positive. I'll be fine, I promise."

"Listen, why don't you just go home? Take the day off. There's nothing really pressing happening today anyway. Your client already picked up the christening gown, and I'll do the fitting at the theater this afternoon."

"No, it's my turn to do that."

"Actually, I really want to. I don't want to be here this afternoon."

"Why not?" Kenya asked.

"You'll be doing me a favor. I'm still working on the mother-of-the-bride dress. She has more changes. I don't want to be here when she drops it off. I swear if I see that woman one more time, I'll strangle her."

Kenya smiled. "Okay, just to save the woman's life, I'll trade you assignments. Besides, you'd look horrible in an orange prison jumpsuit."

"Thanks," Shelly said.

"No, thank you. Now before she gets here, I think I need to get some work done. Maybe it'll take my mind off things." Just as she pulled out her sketch pad someone knocked on the front door.

Shelly looked at her watch. "That can't be her already." She walked over and peeked out the door. "It's her." She looked at Kenya.

"I got it."

Kenya went to the front area and opened the door. She greeted Shelly's client, took down her changes and then promised to have Shelly give her as call as soon as she could. Ten minutes later she went back to the workroom.

"Thank you," Shelly said.

"No problem, although if I'm not mistaken, I think she wants it the same way you had it the first time."

"Figures. Oh, Asia just called. She wants you to call her back. She's at your parents' house."

"My parents' house? Why?"

"I'm sure I don't know. We chatted a bit but she never said."

"Funny," Kenya said, half smiling.

"I still say you should take the day off."

Kenya looked around her space. Shelly was right. There was no way she'd be able to focus on work anyway. She helped Shelly gather the supplies for the theater and put everything in her car. "I'm headed over to my parents' house."

"Good idea," Shelly said. "See you tomorrow."

Forty-five minutes later, through early rush-hour traffic, Kenya finally pulled up to her parents' home. She let herself in then called out, hoping Sidney was home. "Hello."

"In here," Asia answered.

"What are you doing here?"

"I got a call from Sidney suggesting that I come down this evening. Since I was already in Philly, I just headed farther south. What's going on?"

"Everything," Kenya said.

"What does everything mean?"

"It means that I messed up and Sidney's about to make it worse."

"Sidney's about to what?" Sidney said as she walked into the kitchen and saw her sisters at the counter.

"There you are—didn't you get my messages?"

"Hello, I was busy, I have a life. Believe it or not I have classes and assignments to take care of. This is my final semester."

"Fine. We need to talk about Trey."

"Trey Evans?" Asia asked. "The guy you're seeing."

"Not the guy I'm seeing, at least not anymore."

"Kenya wants me to back off but I'm not."

"Sidney, who are you feeding information to at TE?"

"Cal," Asia said. Sidney nodded.

Kenya turned to Asia. "Cal, Dad's old partner—how did you know, Asia?"

"Sidney told me."

"How did you find him? They told me that he quit the company."

"Tell her, Sidney," Asia prompted.

"He sold his shares in Dad's company to go to work for TE. That's where he works now."

"How do you know that?"

"Remember when I had a job as a bike messenger?"

"What? No. You had a job as a bike messenger? When? Never mind. You know, I don't even know you anymore."

"That's 'cause you're always so wrapped up in your own drama, first with Craig and now with the boutique. Wake up, Kenya."

"Would y'all stick to one thing, please," Asia said.

"Never mind," Sidney said. "Anyway, I worked as a bike messenger for about three weeks a while back. That's what gave me the idea. After I found out about what Trey did to Dad I wanted to get back at him. Coincidentally, I delivered this package to Calvin Potter at TE Acquisitions. It was from Caine Enterprises. I was still working at Caine at the time."

"Didn't Cal recognize you when you delivered the package? If I remember correctly you had a crush on him."

"Remember when I said that temps are invisible? Well, bike messengers are even more invisible."

"You made the connection," Kenya said.

"I delivered my own packages to Cal after that."

Kenya shook her head. "I don't know if you're a genius or just plain nuts."

"Both, if that helps any," Asia said. Sidney rolled her eyes.

"Okay, all this aside, we need to stop this now."

"It's no secret that you're seeing Trey. The question is, where are your loyalties these days, Kenya?" Sidney asked.

"They're exactly where they always are—in doing the

right thing. But in this case, this isn't it. Trey didn't do anything wrong."

"How can you say that?" Sidney asked.

"Are you saying that Dad lied?" Asia asked.

"I'm saying that there's more to this than we know." Both sisters looked skeptical. "It's the truth, Mom told me. She has the money. Trey took it and put it in an account for her."

"He's got you brainwashed, just like Craig did."

"No, he's nothing like Craig. I made that mistake, too. I was wrong. I was wrong about a lot of things. But I'm not wrong about this."

"Uh-uh, I'm not stopping anything," Sidney said.

"No, Sidney, we have to fix this," Asia said, switching sides. "If Trey isn't to blame, then we can't do him harm. That would be wrong."

"And if Dad gambled on the market and lost, then that's it. It's as simple as that. Blaming others is wrong."

"But what about his company?" Sidney asked.

"It'll be fine."

"Trey still owns it."

"Not all of it. He has the same percent he always had."

"So who owns the other part?"

"Mom," Kenya said.

"What?" Asia and Sidney said.

"I'll tell you about it later. Come on, get all your stuff. We're going back to Trey's office."

It was late and mostly everyone in the office had gone home. The three sisters stopped at the front desk and asked the guard to speak with Trey. He wasn't available. Kenya asked if Regina was in. She was. The guard put Kenya on the phone with her.

"Hi, Regina, this is Kenya Whitaker, Trey's friend. Trey's

not available and I have some important information for him. It's about the Caine merger."

"Come on up. I'll meet you at his office."

The sisters got visitor passes and took the elevator up. They looked at each other silently. It was time to come clean.

"I hope you know what you're doing," Sidney said.

"I don't have a clue," Kenya told her honestly.

As soon as the elevator doors opened Regina was standing waiting there with Joshua. Introductions were made. They went into Joshua's office. "Okay, you got my attention. Tell me about Caine," Regina said. Thirty minutes later, the Whitaker sisters laid out Sidney's plan and her part in Cal's unwitting cooperation.

Regina shook her head. "I knew there was something not right about this deal. It was just too perfect. Now to find out that our dad was pulling strings makes all the sense in the world."

"What are you going to do?" Asia asked.

"We'll back out."

"I mean about your dad."

"Nothing," Regina said. "But I guess I could ask you the same question."

The sisters looked at each other. "Nothing."

"It seems we all have father issues."

"What about your brother?" Sidney asked, knowing that Kenya wanted to ask, but she wouldn't.

"We'll show him all this tonight. We'll cut ties with Caine Enterprises first thing tomorrow morning."

"How legal is this?" Kenya asked.

"Perfectly legal," Joshua said.

"Thank you, I know this was hard for all of you, given the delicate situation. But we're really grateful. This could have been serious," Regina said.

"Well, maybe you could show your gratitude by—"

"Sidney," Kenya said. "We need to go now."

Kenya stood, as did the others. Asia, Sidney and Joshua walked to the elevator together. Kenya and Regina followed. "And what are you going to do about my brother?"

"Nothing," Kenya answered.

"You know he loves you and I suspect you love him."

"I do. But we have a lot of drama between us."

"Water under the bridge."

"No, not this particular bridge," she said. "I gave Trey a folder of copied documents I took when I stayed at his house. I stole them and I lied to him."

"I saw it."

"Then you know what I intended to do to him." Regina nodded. "And I know there's no way he can forgive me for what I did, and now for what my sister almost did. I can't forgive myself. I—we—had every intention of ruining him."

"But you didn't and given the sensitive nature of the documents, you certainly could have. So as I say, water under the bridge."

By the time they joined the others at the elevators, Asia was telling Joshua about her role on the soap opera.

"I thought you looked familiar," Joshua said.

"You watch soaps?" Sidney asked.

"Let's just say I'm well-rounded," he confessed.

"Now I know why I thought I recognized you," Regina said to Kenya. "Your sister."

Sidney nodded. "I work here. I'm a temp."

"She's a professional temp," Asia joked.

"No, I know you from GWU. Wasn't I your student advisor about four years ago?"

Sidney opened her mouth. "That was you?" she asked.

"I knew you looked familiar."

"Well, we'd better get going. Thanks again for seeing us so late."

"No, thank you," Joshua said. Regina nodded.

The sisters took the elevator down to the lobby. "Now what?" Sidney asked.

"Dinner's on me," Kenya said.

"Count me out," Asia said. "I have to catch a train back to New York tonight."

"Count me out, too," Sidney said. "I have a few hundred pages to read tonight. Finals are in a few weeks."

"Okay, change of plans. How about we grab a pizza and take it back to the house."

"That'll work," Sidney said. Asia nodded in agreement. "We can go to either the pizza place I waitressed at, or the pizza place I made deliveries for, or the pizza place I—"

"I can't believe I missed so much," Kenya said sadly.

Asia and Sidney looked at each other, then at her. "Missed so much? What do you mean?" they asked.

"With you two. I was so busy with school. Then being hung up on Craig. Then after that I dove headfirst into my work. I never took the time to just chill with my sisters. I'm sorry. I missed everything you were doing. Great things you were doing. Asia, you have one foot in superstardom and Sidney, you have had the most incredible college temp career ever. You've temped and done just about everything under the sun. Some kind of big sister I am."

Sidney hugged her. Asia hugged them both. "You're a great big sister," Asia said. "You stepped up, found out the truth and then helped us to do the right thing. You took responsibility for everything and even got Regina to keep Sidney on. She even promised Sidney a position after graduation. You did that. Can you imagine what might have happened if you decided not to step up? We'd all probably be in jail by next week."

"Wow, you make me sound like some kind of saint," Kenya said, then looked at Sidney, who rolled her eyes.

"You a'ight, I guess," she said.

"Yeah, you a'ight, too." She hugged her. They laughed.

After much debate over the menu, they picked up a pizza and took it to their parents' home. The lights were all on as they drove up. "Did you leave all the lights on like that again, Sidney?" Kenya asked, exasperated.

"No," she said firmly, hoping she hadn't.

"Well, somebody did," Asia said. Sidney glared at her. "I'm just saying."

"Come on," Kenya said as she turned off the ignition and got out of the car.

They all walked up the path as the front door opened. They screamed. "Mom!" Bumping elbows, the three sisters rushed to her. They all talked at once, then walked into the house. A smiling James stood inside, his arms wide and welcoming. "Dad!" they screamed again. The conversation was endlessly confusing.

"Okay, okay, I can't understand a word anyone's saying," Lynette said.

"I don't get it, what are you doing home so early?" Kenya asked.

"Yeah, you're supposed to be in Africa another three weeks," Asia added.

"Are you okay?" Sidney said.

"We're fine. South Africa is wonderful, incredible. But I missed home too much. I guess I'm not the world traveler I always dreamed I was. Having my three favorites—Kenya, Asia and Sidney—right here is good enough for me," Lynette said.

"How's everything here?" James asked.

The three looked at each other guiltily.

"What is it? What happened?" Lynette asked. "Sidney?"

"Me? Why are you looking at me? Well, I guess maybe..."

"Maybe you'd better go in and have a seat," Asia said. They all went into the living room, sat down and Kenya began telling the story. Asia added her part then Sidney added her part. Neither parent interrupted until close to the very end.

"I can't believe this," James said, standing and pacing. "No, no, no, please tell me you didn't. None of this was supposed to happen. You weren't supposed to get involved. This is all my fault."

"But we took care of it," Asia said.

"I exaggerated," James blurted out. "Trey wasn't solely responsible. I had my part, as well. I got mad, I went after him. I started it, everything. But we have to stop this now. It's already gone too far."

"Dad, we know. That's what we're saying—we did stop it," Kenya said.

"Yes, just now, we went to see Regina and Joshua."

James sat down, still holding his head.

"We talked to them and they're gonna take care of it."

"I think this family has a lot of communicating to do in the very near future," Lynette said. She went to stand beside her dejected husband. "We've all done some questionable things. Keeping secrets from the ones you love is not the family way. Whatever happens, love will always be here. We're a family, that means we celebrate the good, the bad and the in-between.

"I'm glad you made it right. The three of you worked together and I'm proud of you. We're proud of you. And we'll definitely talk about this some more, but right now—" she paused and looked at her watch "—it's late and I think we need to call it a night." Everyone nodded.

"I need to read and study," Sidney said.

"Kenya, can I get a ride to Union Station?"

Ten minutes later the family stood in the large foyer saying goodbye and making plans to get together that weekend.

Kenya dropped her sister at the train station then headed home. It was an impossible day that had ended as it started.

Regina, Trey and Joshua sat in Trey's home office going over the paperwork from James and Sidney Whitaker. "I can't believe they did all this."

"We should seriously think about giving James a position in our research division. He dug up dad's name in connection with Caine Enterprises almost eight months ago. That's where Sidney got the idea."

Trey shook his head. "It was pretty ingenious. I was too preoccupied with Kenya to see what her other sister was doing."

"Kenya and Sidney acted independently," Regina said.

Trey frowned. "You mean they were each plotting to bring me down."

"Apparently so," Joshua said, smiling.

Trey looked at Regina and Joshua and shook his head. "I guess I'm losing my charm with the ladies."

"You know if they hadn't decided to come to us, you would have signed the merger papers and that would have been the end of TE Acquisitions," Regina added.

"True," Joshua said.

"What do you want to do about Cal?"

"Sidney played him totally. I'm sure he still has no clue that she was pulling his strings. He never considered that he was being set up. He just accepted the information he was given and went with it."

"It shows a serious lack of character and business sense."

"I agree."

Regina stood. "Well, I need to go. I have a date."

"Again," Trey and Joshua said in unison.

Regina looked at them hard. "Yes, again. And before either one of you says anything, good night."

Trey and Joshua looked at each other and shook their heads. "Well, that's it for me, too," Joshua said. "I'll see you tomorrow."

"Take care," Trey said.

"Listen, don't concern yourself with Cal and Caine Enterprises. I'll take care of all that. It will be my pleasure."

Trey saw the gleam of excitement in his eyes. "Maybe I'd better take care of them. You look a bit too eager."

"I am, and with good reason." He smiled. Trey chuckled.

"They're all yours, enjoy."

Joshua nodded. "I will, thanks. Now you need to go to her. Talk, get this straightened out."

"What?"

"You know what—Kenya. Trey, you can't do this to yourself. You deserve more. She is that more. Besides, imagine the stories you'll be able to tell your children and grandchildren about fifty years from now. Good night."

Trey half smiled. Joshua had a way of doing that. "Night," Trey said as his friend walked out. He heard the front door close as he sat quietly in his office. The twins were gone, Mrs. Thatcher was gone and Kenya was gone. He was free now. By all accounts he should have been elated. And eight days ago, he would have been exactly that, but now…

He reached across his desk and picked up the phone. He called J.T. "Hey," he began, "I need a favor. I need to find somebody." They talked a while, then after hanging up, Trey got into his car and drove off. He drove to the boutique. It was locked. He got out anyway, knowing that even if it seemed closed there was always a light on in the back area. Tonight there wasn't. He looked down the street toward the alcove leading to the condo apartments above.

Without thinking, he went to her. He rang the bell but didn't get an answer. He stood waiting, thinking, knowing he should have said something. But he didn't and now she was gone from his life. He once promised to catch her when she fell—he hadn't. The emptiness sank deeply into his soul as his heart broke for the first time.

Chapter 22

"Hey, good morning. Are you ready for today? Man, I have a feeling it's going to be one of those days," Shelly said, rushing in carrying a large garment bag. "Girl, you would not believe the night I had last night. Talk about crazy. The costume fitting and the dress rehearsal were insane. I swear the only thing missing was Elvis, a couple of aliens and Mr. T on a unicycle."

"Morning," Kenya said, shaking her head. As miserable as she felt, Shelly was always a ray of sunshine.

"Hey, you okay?" She walked over as Kenya turned to her. "Man, girl, you look like the pits," Shelly said. "What happened?" Kenya told Shelly the gist of what happened the night before. "Kenya, I'm so sorry. But you saved the day. Actually you all did."

"It's my own fault, all of it. I should have listened to you, to Dad, to Mom. I should have just let it alone. He hates me. I could see it in his face yesterday. He hates me."

"He doesn't hate you, Kenya. How could he? The man is in love with you. Don't you see that? And besides, you just pulled his butt out of the fire. Believe me, he still loves you."

Kenya shook her head. "No, not anymore."

"Kenya, I'll tell you what I told you a while back. Love always finds a way. And when it's meant to be it will be. That thing before with Craig was nothing. This is meant to be—you and Trey together forever. Girl, I already have the wedding gown design picked out."

Kenya smiled and laughed at Shelly's optimism. She was the perfect friend in good times and in bad times. But this time she was totally wrong. There was no way Trey could ever forgive her. She couldn't even forgive herself.

"Are you gonna be okay?"

Kenya nodded. "Yeah, one of these days I'm gonna be just fine," she lied, knowing that she'd never get over Trey. "In the meantime, come on. We have work to do."

As soon as they began discussing changes to a design, the office phone rang. Shelly grabbed it while Kenya made more tea, absorbed in her thoughts. It wasn't until a pillow whizzed by her head that she realized Shelly was trying to get her attention. "Yes, yes, we can do that," Shelly said excitedly, smiling and motioning for her to come over.

Kenya listened in on the end of the conversation. It was a representative from Youngin's retail chain. They were definitely interested in purchasing clothing for all of their nationwide stores. Seconds after Shelly hung up, they squealed, hugged and danced around. "Can you believe it, they want us."

"Of course they want us. We are incredible designers."

The impromptu celebration lasted the next fifteen minutes until they realized what working with a nationwide chain might entail. "We have a massive amount of work to do."

"I know, where do we begin?"

"We need to call the manufacturer. Maybe one of us should fly out there."

"Good thinking."

"Marketing. We have to do a ton of public relations."

"Wouldn't it be fantastic if the boutique opened at the same time?"

"Brilliant. We need to write all this down." They both grabbed a sketch pad and began taking notes as they talked. They outlined a plan and decided who would handle each assignment. They agreed on everything. They planned the next few days and decided that Kenya would head to New York and meet with the company and Shelly would go to California.

"What about today?" Kenya asked. "What do you have planned?"

"I have the wedding from hell, again. The bride's mother changed her mind again last night. She left a message at the apartment." They both laughed. "I have to head back over there right now as a matter of fact. She wants her dress sexier now. Can you believe her?"

Kenya laughed and actually enjoyed the lighthearted moment. Shelly was the best. "Okay, you go. I'll get things started here."

Louise Gates was never one to stand on ceremony. She had a calling that she took very seriously. When she was asked to help, she did everything within her power to assist. But this time when she was asked for help from an unlikely source, she outdid herself.

Standing at the gated door, she knocked several times. There was no answer. She peeked through the smoked glass, seeing only her reflection and the empty shadow beyond. She knocked several more times before she saw someone coming. The door opened.

"Mrs. Gates?"

"Hello, dear. Shelly, right?" she asked.

"Yes, ma'am."

"Oh, please, call me Mamma Lou, everyone does."

"Of course, Mamma Lou. Uh, Kenya's in the back and I'm on my way out. Come on in, I'll walk you back to her."

"Thank you, dear."

"No problem, Mamma Lou."

Louise waited until Shelly locked the front door again, then she escorted her to the back. "Hey, guess what. We have company."

Kenya looked up and smiled. "Hi, Mamma Lou, how are you?"

"Fine, fine, dear."

"Can I get you something to drink—tea, coffee or water?" Shelly asked.

"No, dear, I'm fine. You go on, do what you need to do."

Shelly smiled and glanced at Kenya. "Okay, then I'll see you later. Wish me luck."

"Shelly, before you leave I'm curious. How did you ladies get on at Youngin's?"

Both Kenya's and Shelly's mouths dropped open. "It was you? You did that?" Kenya said.

"You got them to call us?" Shelly added.

"It really wasn't much. I wish I could have done more. You see, the owner is a dear friend of mine and is always looking for new talent. When I saw your designs, I just knew it would be a perfect match."

"Thank you so much, Mamma Lou," Kenya said.

"Yes, thank you, it was a wonderful interview. I think they were really impressed with our work. As a matter of fact they just called."

"They want to work with us," Kenya said happily.

"I should say so," Louise said. "My friend raved about your designs. She was very impressed," she reported enthusiastically."

"I don't know what to say. You're the best."

"Thank you so much."

"It was my pleasure, ladies. Seeing women standing up and living out their dreams is my greatest joy. I'm always happy to be of assistance."

"I wish I could stay longer, but I really have to go," Shelly said. "Thanks again, Mamma Lou," she said, hugging her warmly. "See you later."

As Shelly left, Louise turned her attention to Kenya. "And how are you this morning?"

"Good. Busy. This new project with Youngin's is going to change a lot around here. As a matter of fact we decided to open the boutique a bit earlier to coincide with the Youngin's launch."

"That's a great idea," Louise said. "I have a publicist friend who would be perfect for the announcement and opening."

"Mamma Lou, you've done so much already. I don't know what to say. How do we ever begin to thank you?"

"No, don't thank me. I haven't done anything. Actually Otis is the one."

"Otis?" Kenya questioned.

"Colonel Wheeler, he's quite a man." Kenya nodded. "He got a call last night from Trey."

Kenya went still. "He told you what happened."

"Only that you and your sisters saved his company, countless jobs and also how much he really loves you. I needn't ask if you love him. I see it in your eyes."

Kenya nodded. "I do love him so much. We've only known each other a short while, but my heart knows."

"Time has no bearing on love. You need to talk to him."

"How can I? After everything that happened. No, he was

right before. We can't change what was. The past will always be there."

"True, we can't change the past, but we can learn from it and hope for the future. Kenya, believe me, love has a way of making a way. It's never too late."

"But I hurt him. I can still see it in his eyes."

"Dear, you need to risk pain in order to find love."

"Kenya," a voice said. She turned. Trey stood behind them.

"He's offering you his heart. Accept it and forgive yourself."

"Trey, what are you doing here?" Her eyes were filled with remorse but her heart still longed for him.

"Surrendering," he said soulfully. "I don't want to spend another second without you. I can't."

"But, Trey, everything that happened, what I did, what we almost did. How can you even stand there and—"

"How can I not? I love you, Kenya Whitaker, daughter of James Whitaker. You changed my life, my world, my heart." She started crying. "Don't cry," he said, walking over to her and wiping the tears from her face. "I don't ever want to see you cry for me."

She laughed. "I can't believe you're here."

"I'm here, exactly where I belong and exactly where I intend to be for the rest of our life together, if you'll have me."

"What are you saying?"

He knelt down and took her hand. "Marry me, be my wife."

Tears flowed again as she grabbed him, nearly knocking him over. He stood and held her as she laughed, cried and kissed him. "Is that a yes?" he asked.

"Yes, yes, yes," she said repeatedly, kissing him each time. "Yes, Trey Evans, I will be honored to be your wife." They kissed.

Louise, who was nearly in tears herself, discreetly left. Colonel Wheeler and Shelly were standing in the front of the boutique, waiting. Louise nodded and gave a thumbs-up signal. Shelly cheered silently. Colonel Wheeler nodded and motioned for them to leave. Outside the three stood in front congratulating themselves and delighting in Trey and Kenya's joy. "Thank you for waiting to lock up, Shelly," Louise said.

"Oh, it's my pleasure. You know, I knew they were gonna make it. I could see it from the instant I saw them together. They had a kind of spark—crazy, huh?"

Louise and Otis glanced at each other and smiled. "Not at all. As a matter of fact, it makes perfect sense to me," Louise said. "So, Shelly, what does your boyfriend do?"

"Actually, I don't have one at the moment."

"Is that right," Louise said interestedly.

"And if I don't leave right now I won't have a mother-of-the-bride dress, either. I'm so glad to see you again, Mamma Lou, Colonel Wheeler. Thanks again for the Youngin's account. I gotta go. See you at the wedding."

Shelly rushed off down the street to her car, leaving Louise and Otis to chuckle. Louise linked her arm with Otis and the two strolled down the street, enjoying the day.

"You realize, of course, I'm still furious with you," she began. Otis chuckled. "Imagine, you getting a call from Trey asking for matchmaker assistance. I'm appalled. How in the world will I ever live this down? You, of all people, playing matchmaker." Otis laughed. He leaned in and kissed her forehead. She was his perfect match.

Epilogue

Like their courtship, their wedding had been just as quick and exciting. In the span of two months, they were married. A small but beautiful ceremony, it was a union of two hearts and two families. The reception was a mass of delight with Trey and Kenya's love as the centerpiece.

Guests mingled and adored the sumptuous food and flowers. But it was Louise who truly savored the beauty of the moment. She looked around the reception area, feeling the joy of her accomplishments.

Kennedy and Juwan were stateside, showing off her new tummy bump. J.T. stood by Juliet as she held their infant son in her arms. Madison and Tony gathered the excited ring bearer, Jonathan, and flower girl, Johanna. Senator Randolph Kingsley, his wife, Alyssa, and doctors Raymond and Hope laughed and talked about their pregnancies.

"It's a sweet day, isn't it?" Trey whispered to his bride.

Kenya smiled. "It certainly is. Thank you."

"For what?" he asked.

"For being so wonderful."

"You did that."

"You said you'd never change for anyone."

"I also said that I'd never wear one of these," he said, holding his left hand out. The simple platinum band wrapped comfortably around his finger. Kenya held her hand up beside his. The matching bands—with diamonds for hers—were a true reflection of their never-ending love.

"You know this is only the beginning."

"I'm looking forward to every second with you."

They kissed and the guests applauded.

"She is so lucky," Sidney said.

"Your time will come," Lynette promised.

James and Trey had long since buried the hatchet and James was back working at his company now under the direct control of Lynette and Regina. She held the purse strings and everyone was glad of it, including James. He still had his brilliant ideas, only now he funneled them to Joshua, who actually implemented a few.

As the end of the reception drew near the announcement was made for all singles to come to the dance floor. The women gathered first as the bouquet was tossed. Afterward the single men stood ready to receive the garter.

Louise pulled out her pen and paper and began taking notes. She delighted in this part. "What are you doing?" Colonel Wheeler asked as he moved to her side.

"Oh, nothing," she said as she continued to jot down names.

"Doesn't look like nothing to me," he said.

"Well, if you must know I'm taking a few notes, reminders really."

"Louise," he said.

"Otis," she replied. He chuckled and shook his head. "So, Mrs. Gates, you gonna marry me or what?"

"Oh, I guess I might as well," Louise answered.

Everyone in the room stopped.